"Do I amuse you?"

Rae thought she could detect a slight annoyance in the dark voice, and found she couldn't resist goading him. "You really shouldn't have gone to all this trouble—the wine and the music. I've heard of trying to impress a girl, but you've got a 'captive' audience. The James Bond routine really isn't necessary."

His startled laugh was genuine. Her own lips lifted again, in involuntary response to accept that she was laughing at *him* for a change.

"James Bond?" he repeated finally, unbelievingly. "I suppose that puts me in my place. A prick for any man's ego."

"No pun intended?" She questioned innocently, and was again rewarded by his smile.

Stop it, her rational mind scolded. *Who do you think this is? Dudley Doright? He holds your life in his hands...and you're flirting with him like a freshman at her first prom.*

Kyle + Ryan
3 C Batteries

ABOUT THE AUTHOR

Gayle Wilson, who has a masters degree in education, is a former teacher of English and history to gifted high school students. Her love of both subjects led her to first write historical novels before turning to romantic suspense. Gayle and her husband, whom she met on a blind date, live in Alabama where they both grew up. She has been blessed with a wonderful son, a warm and loving extended Southern family, and a growing menagerie of cats and dogs.

Books by Gayle Wilson

HARLEQUIN INTRIGUE
344—ECHOES IN THE DARK

HARLEQUIN HISTORICALS
211—THE HEART'S DESIRE
263—THE HEART'S WAGER
299—THE GAMBLER'S HEART

Only a Whisper

Gayle Wilson

Harlequin Books

TORONTO • NEW YORK • LONDON
AMSTERDAM • PARIS • SYDNEY • HAMBURG
STOCKHOLM • ATHENS • TOKYO • MILAN
MADRID • WARSAW • BUDAPEST • AUCKLAND

To my mother
for unconditional love

ISBN 0-373-22376-5

ONLY A WHISPER

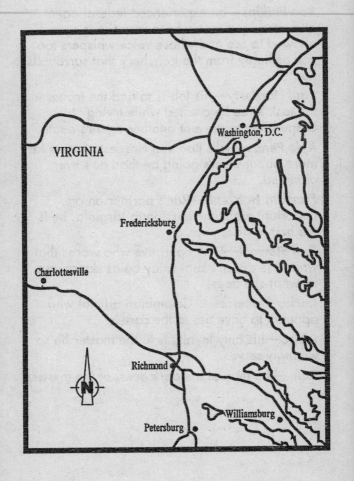

CAST OF CHARACTERS

Rae Phillips—an experienced federal agent abducted by a man whose face she is never allowed to see and whose voice whispers too compellingly from the treachery that surrounds her.

Paul Hardesty—his job is to find the traitor in the task force he created while trying desperately to prevent another agent's death.

Kyle Peters—tells Rae that Hardesty knows far more about what's going on than he's ever admitted.

Franklin Holcomb—Rae's partner on an important nighttime mission to Virginia, he is the first to disappear.

Dell Stewart—DEA operative who warns that what Rae doesn't know may be as dangerous as what she does.

Carlos Rameriz—a Colombian official who appears to have ties to the cartels.

Diego—his only loyalty is to the master he so willingly serves.

Rafe—the man at the dark heart of the mystery.

Prologue

December 1993

Freezing rain glazed the pavement under the headlights of the black Mercedes. Their glow cut through the glittering darkness like twin swords, the hiss of the wipers and the click of ice against the windshield the only sound in the private light show.

The chauffeur threaded the car through the narrowing streets, the buildings on either side dark, their workers having long ago deserted the area and headed to the lighted safety of their own neighborhoods.

The two men in the back had not spoken since leaving the huge underground garage, but in spite of their individual tensions, the silence was not uncomfortable. With the soundproof glass barrier before them, they were virtually alone, each lost in his own thoughts.

The driver finally brought the Mercedes to a halt before one of the run-down warehouses that lined the street. He had doused the lights before he made the final turn into this block, and the powerful car glided silently as a ghost to the curb. The engine continued to purr.

"You don't have to do this," said a voice, breaking the silence. The speaker sensed rather than saw the amusement in response to his anxiety.

"Someone does. And I *am*, you must agree, the one who is better equipped." The answering voice was gently ironic.

"There are other ways. Safer ways."

"We've been through this. You said Hardesty was trust-worthy."

"As far as we can tell from the information that's available. But who can know what men will to do for this kind of money? We're gambling with your life." The voice was strained, trying to make long-discarded arguments convincing, trying to give them new life.

He could hear the patient resignation in his brother's answer. "It is, after all, *my* life, and only one against so many others. The information I'll provide to Hardesty tonight will bring down the cartel, which is why we began, and we didn't embark on this without sufficient reasons."

"I remember the reasons—all of them. And I believed, until now, that I could let you go, knowing that the outcome outweighed the risks."

"Nothing will go wrong. All the arrangements have been made. There is no way to turn back now. It's too important. You don't mean what you're saying. That's your heart and not your head talking. Too many years of playing big brother."

"And you outgrew the need for big brother long ago."

"No," the other countered, laughing. "No one ever outgrows the need to be loved."

The speaker turned his head, pretending to look out the window at the darkened warehouses. They were men uncomfortable expressing their deep affection for each other, but that didn't mean they weren't aware of it. It provided a guarantee of their instant rapport even when they had been separated by years or distance. The speaker turned back, having mastered the pull on his emotions. His eyes had adjusted to the darkness enough to allow him to see the outline of his brother's head and shoulders against the lesser blackness of the night.

"It's time," the younger said finally, reaching to touch his arm.

His brother took the outstretched fingers and brought them to his lips to kiss. "Go with God." He whispered the traditional farewell, releasing the strong hand.

The familiar laughter almost broke his faltering control, and he heard the softly mocking voice in the stillness. "Or to the devil."

The man who had spoken opened the door and, moving with an athletic grace, was quickly swallowed up by the waiting darkness.

Remembering his instructions, the brother he had left behind tapped softly on the glass. The chauffeur put the big car in gear, and it rolled silently along the deserted street, turning the corner to disappear.

Chapter One

"Get your coat." Franklin Holcomb's voice broke through Rae Phillips's concentration on the information displayed on her computer screen. "The old man wants you. He asked specifically for you. It seems we need your *particular* expertise."

Rae understood the slight sarcasm. They were both aware that she had no particular skill that was not shared by each member of the task force for which they worked. They were all law-enforcement officers who had been selected based on their records and their well-documented abilities. Rae sometimes wondered if the fact she was Austin Phillips's daughter hadn't tipped the scales in her favor, but at more rational moments she put those doubts down to latent feminist suspicions. She was the only woman in the twelve-man group and, unless femininity counted as an area of expertise, she was as stumped by Paul Hardesty's request as Holcomb.

"Do you have a clue?" she asked as she cleaned up the file she was working on and saved her material.

"Nope, just meet him at the pad and he'll explain later. It's colder than a witch's ... Sorry, but that's sleet you hear against the windows. That chopper's going to be like a deep freeze. I don't think the old man even notices, but my shoulders'll be stiff into next week. I'm getting old, kid. Time to move on and leave it to you young ones."

He helped Rae into her navy wool coat, and she was grateful for the lined boots she had worn under the forest-green sweater dress. She wasn't looking forward to the helicopter ride any more than Frank was.

They were silent as they left the office, making their way to the elevator that would take them to the stairs at the top of the building, each imagining what might lie at the end of this late-night journey.

Rae could feel the thrump of the Huey's rotor vibrating through the metal stairway before Holcomb opened the door. The icy wind took her breath, and her eyes watered even though she lowered her head as soon as she stepped out on the roof. She followed Frank's scuffed wing tips to the chopper, never looking up, in an attempt to protect her eyes, cheeks and sinuses from the biting cold. She had grown up in El Paso and, like all desert creatures, she was most comfortable basking in the sun. She'd never made the adjustment to the D.C. climate.

The interior of the chopper was not noticeably warmer, but at least they were shielded from the wind. The fact that Hardesty himself was along on whatever mission they had undertaken was significant. He hadn't been an in-field agent in years. The knowledge that this wasn't going to be the kind of assignment that ended in the possibility of danger was, as always, comforting, so Rae began to relax for the first time since she'd been summoned.

She heard Hardesty shouting instructions to the pilot. Although she didn't catch the words, she knew by Frank's raised eyebrows that he had and that they'd surprised him. She put her hand on his knee, expressing her question with her own brows. He leaned against her ear, speaking in an almost-normal voice, but still she had to strain to hear the words over the engine's noise.

"Hardesty's worried about a tail. He told the pilot to watch and evade. Who the hell does he think he's kidding? We're the only ones crazy enough to be up in weather like this."

Apparently Holcomb's assessment of their ownership of the air was correct, for after only the most cursory search for trailers, the Huey dipped nose and headed into the night sky to the south.

The flight lasted less than half an hour, and they landed on the back lawn of what appeared to be a 1920s mansion. Rae again signed her question to Frank, but he only shook his head, shrugging his shoulders. They all ran under the blades to the "patio"—a term too casual for the expanse of tile and the stone banisters that stretched across the back of the huge house.

The interior was almost as dark as the lawn had been, but Hardesty led the way through the dim rooms with unerring familiarity. Rae heard the chopper shut down, and the silence was broken only by the click of their steps on the dimly visible black-and-white squares of the hall. Hardesty led them into the library, finally turning on some lights. Rae realized then why he had chosen this room, lined from floor to ceiling with books, with no windows to betray their presence.

"Sit down," Hardesty invited, but as always, there was no doubting the unconscious assertion of command. He was a man used to being in charge. He even looked the part, with his white hair and still-erect military bearing. Rae knew that he was only in his early fifties, but his decisive nature and premature graying had given him an advantage of looking "in charge" that he had parlayed into position years ago.

"There's liquor in the decanters. I know Frank's wanting something. Do you drink, Rae?"

"Occasionally, but I'm fine."

"Good, because we need you clearheaded. This is your show, and I'm afraid it's going to be difficult and prolonged."

Paul Hardesty paused, allowing himself a moment to study the lovely ivory oval of Rae's face. It was amazing that Austin and Elizabeth Phillips, the most ordinary-looking couple he'd ever known, had produced this woman.

Strands of dark auburn hair, helped by the wind outside, had escaped the low chignon to curl around her cheeks and temples. Rae waited for his explanation, her aquamarine eyes calmly resting on his face in spite of what he had just told her. She looked like a model or an actress—anything other than the steel-trap mind and finely coordinated body he knew Rae Phillips to be.

"We screwed up, and someone else paid the price," he said finally. She watched the tightening of his lips, and knew that he hated to be fallible. Any blunder of the force instantly became Paul's burden.

Rae simply waited, knowing that he would have to tell this in his own way, work around to what was obviously a painful situation. He took a long drink of the brandy Frank handed him, the light from the low chandelier reflecting off the crystal of his glass.

"A man contacted us through diplomatic channels at the highest level indicating that he had information that would enable us to damage the financial operations of the Medellin cartel, to identify the distributors, the middlemen. He even offered us a blueprint of their money-laundering procedures, the banks and companies involved, the ownership structures. You can imagine our reaction. Mine was disbelief, but we checked through those same diplomatic circles from our end and found the source to be...exactly what he'd said."

Rae wondered what the almost-indiscernible pause signified. That was something she had learned from her father. Use every clue, every facial twitch, every vocal nuance. Listen with your brain, not your ears.

"We made contact and arranged for transport of the merchandise, set up the meeting, but somehow—" again the pain intruded into the careful control "—*somehow* he was betrayed. The cartel got there before we did. They took some rather classic revenge before we arrived. They were brutal, but not very efficient. He was alive when we got to the pickup point. Barely alive, and obviously..." Paul paused again and shook his head.

Rae was grateful for the lack of details. She could only guess what the courier had suffered. She knew that even with her experience she was probably incapable of imagining the full extent of the damage the cartels committed without a moment's thought.

"And the information?" she asked, as Paul seemed disinclined to continue. He looked up in surprise.

"I thought you understood. He has the information in his head. Some kind of freak memory. He's committed it all to memory. He *is* the information. The doctor is trying right now to do what he can to help him hang on until you can take it down. He'll let us know when we can go up."

"'The medium is the message,'" Frank quoted softly, speaking for the first time since their arrival.

"Do you mean he's here?" Rae asked, incredulous.

"Of course. He was transported here while we were on the way. Why did you think *we're* here?"

"My God, Paul, you're playing with a man's life. He should be in the finest trauma center this country has. If we lose this man, we lose the possibility of finishing off one of the major cocaine suppliers in this country."

"We're going to lose him. He's going to die. Accept that because I assure you it's true. He wants to make that dying worthwhile. He came to give us information, and he's holding on by sheer force of will until he can. Your job is to help him."

"Why me?"

"Spanish is his native language. It's easier for him to give the information as he memorized it. You're the only one of us who is really fluent enough to do this under what will be, I'm afraid, very difficult circumstances."

The door to the library opened and a heavyset man walked in. He met Hardesty's eyes, shaking his head.

"Damned if I know how he's managing," he said, and shook his head again. "He's as ready as I can make him. I've given him what locals I can, not that they're going to make a lot of difference. Get her up there and let's get this over. It's against every principle I ever thought I had. I hope this is worth it, Paul. I hope you know what you're doing."

"Rae." Hardesty spoke the one-word command. As she stood, she could feel her knees tremble. She dreaded what she would witness as a dying man struggled to convict his torturers, but like Paul, she knew the necessity. He handed her the laptop he'd carried on the chopper, and she followed the doctor out of the warmth and light of the library up the dark, winding grand staircase that graced the front hall.

She thought about the scenes such a setting always accompanied in movies and on television. Floating ball gowns and romantic encounters. Rhett and Scarlett. Not death and pain. Not torture and murder and drugs. When they reached the top, the doctor hesitated, speaking to her directly for the first time.

"There's some trauma to the throat. I'm afraid a whisper is all he can manage."

"I understand," Rae said, her sense of dread growing.

"And he's asked that there be no light. When he found out you're a woman... Maybe he's protecting you. Whatever his reasons, given what he's willing to do for us, I thought..."

"Of course," Rae said, but an involuntary shiver not caused by the cold darkness touched her. "The screen will be lighted. It's all right. Will you stay?"

"Paul thinks it's better if I don't. Maybe the information's too sensitive for my clearance." His slight laugh was ironic. "I'll be outside if you need me." He pulled a hall chair next to the unopened door to reaffirm his intent. "Just call. I'll come. Are you going to be all right?" he asked, his long years of caring for those in distress telling him how much she dreaded what she would do, must do.

Rationally, Rae wanted the information as much as Paul. Through the eight years she'd worked in law enforcement she, too, had seen the trail of suffering left by the ghouls they were finally, with the help of the man inside this room, going to put an end to. She would be willing to die to bring about the final collapse of their empire, but it was going to be much more difficult to watch someone else make that sacrifice. This would take a different kind of courage, a cold-blooded courage that considered the end and ignored the means. She thought briefly of her father, and that gave her strength. She would do what she could to ease the way for this man to die, and before he did, she would help him repeat the names and numbers that would justify his death.

At her nod the doctor opened the door. She stood for a moment, waiting for her eyes to adjust to the blackness within. Gradually the light from the hall enabled her to see the small table close to the bed, whose occupant was simply a shape, a slight mound in the deep shadow. She closed her mind to the reality that this was a fellow human being, suffering agonies she could not afford to think about.

She walked to the table and, without looking at the bed, sat down and spent the few necessary minutes preparing her equipment. The routine tasks calmed her mind as she locked everything else away.

A voice, she thought. *A voice in the darkness. That's all he is.*

"I'm ready," she said in Spanish, speaking into the silent glow of the computer. She didn't turn her head to send her words in his direction.

The voice that answered out of the blackness was low, above a whisper only by the sheerest determination. His accent was classic, like a language tape, and she was surprised. The grammar and syntax of the short instructions he gave her marked him immediately as educated. She remembered Hardesty's remark that he had used the highest levels of diplomatic circles to transmit the original offer. She wondered briefly how he had gotten involved in the struggle against the men who had made their country's name an obscenity to law-enforcement agencies all over the world.

She blocked further speculation as the soft voice began to reel off names and companies, accounts and codes. The lists seemed endless. As she struggled to keep up with the flow of information through the long minutes, she wondered how he knew to dictate at the exact speed she was capable of handling.

Because he's used to dealing with good secretaries, she thought suddenly. That momentary flash of insight about this man she had been determined to consider only a voice gave her instead the image of a dark-haired executive seated behind a desk, quickly dictating some business communiqué. The picture was so clear that she strained to see the face in her vision and realized that she had lost whatever he was saying.

"I'm sorry," she whispered, and knew that he hadn't heard her when the low voice continued. She repeated the apology, speaking more loudly over his words. His voice faded, and she heard a soft movement. She knew somehow that his eyes were now on her face. She forced herself to stay focused on the screen that would clearly illuminate her own features for the man in the bed.

"I lost you. Let me read back the last I have and start from there."

"Wait," he said, the voice truly only a whisper now. "May I have some water. Since we've stopped..."

"Of course." She rose and then thought better of it. "I'll have to check with the doctor. I don't want to do anything that might..." Her voice faded at the very definite, if pained, laugh that interrupted her words.

"Of course," he said softly, and she could still hear the amusement threaded in that racked voice.

The doctor agreed with his patient's assessment. "What the hell difference do you think that could make?" he asked irritably, moving to minister to the dying courier and leaving Rae feeling foolish for her question. Since her self-esteem wasn't fragile, she mentally shrugged away his annoyance with her concern for the man she had listened to for the last half hour.

The worst consequence of the entire episode was that his amusement had now made him real to her—someone who could laugh in spite of all he had been through. He was no longer only a voice from the darkness, and she knew that she would never again be able to fit him back into the mental box she had tried to create.

"He can have water whenever he wants. Call me if he asks again," the doctor instructed before he returned to his vigil in the hallway where she'd been waiting. He added the afterthought, "He was distressed that you're worried about him. He says you're too beautiful for this filth."

"Is he—?"

"He'll last," the doctor interrupted almost abruptly. "He'll do what he has to do, if only from sheer hatred. Go in and help him."

When they began again the careful dictation of information, she knew that he now watched her face as he talked. She could not have told why she was so sure of that fact. Perhaps a difference in the timbre of the softly spoken words. Perhaps a slight improvement in clarity since he had turned toward her. Whatever had given it away, she had no doubt that he was as focused on her face as she was on the screen.

She fought an almost-irresistible urge to turn her head to catch a glimpse of him in the darkness, but she knew he was already too real to her. No longer a phantom, but a man. A man who had walked and talked and laughed. Who had loved and made love. A man who did not deserve to die like this. Away from his country, his family, among strangers.

She coldly blocked those thoughts and typed. *How much longer?* she wondered, but she knew that the more information she put down, the wider would be the devastation they wrought.

His voice faded, and she heard the shuddering breath he took before he spoke again. "A moment," he asked. "A moment and then we will go on."

She swallowed against the sudden tightness in her throat at his linking of her into this effort. They would go on together. She was making it possible for him to do what she now had no doubt he wanted. She lifted her fingers from the keys, becoming aware of the stiffness, the dull pain across her shoulders from the too-long day. She flexed them, lowering and then raising her chin to ease the soreness in her neck. She rotated her head and finally interlaced her fingers and pushed them to stretch the cold joints. The noise was too loud in the quiet room, a desecration of what was happening here.

"You're tired," he said in his beautiful Spanish. "We can rest. Ask them to bring you coffee." The hoarseness of the whisper attested to his own exhaustion, and she felt emotion again tighten her throat and prickle behind her eyelids. He was concerned for her. It broke her resolve so that finally she turned toward him in the darkness. Perhaps her eyes had stared at the screen too long, but in the dimness she could see nothing of the man on the bed.

"No." The denial was harsh, and then, more softly, pleading with her, he whispered, "Please."

She turned back to the screen, feeling tears threaten again. Rae Phillips never cried. She lived in a world of men who expected the same level of control from her that they themselves exercised and, right or wrong, it was what she expected of herself. She swallowed the lump that had been building and lowered her head. If she could not control the burning tears, she would not let him see them fall. She would not weaken him by exposing her pain for him.

"Don't," he said, revealing that he knew the struggle she was undergoing. "It's all right."

She swallowed again and lifted her head, putting her fingers back on the keys. She had unconsciously straightened her back, raising her chin at his command. The broken lips of the man in the bed lifted slightly.

"Whenever you're ready," she said, unaware how clearly her every emotion was revealed in the light from the terminal.

"Will you tell me your name?" he asked softly.

It was against every instinct, every tenet of training she had been given, but like the water, she thought, *What can it possibly hurt? What can it matter?*

"Rae." She breathed the single syllable into the light from the screen.

"I thought..." he began, and she could hear the puzzlement.

Her slight smile was a reaction not to his confusion but to the number of times she had answered the question through the years.

"Not the man's name. *R-a-e,*" she spelled. "I was named for my grandmother," she explained, the smile growing with the memory. "A good Biblical name. Rachel. But my father had wanted a boy, and Rae was what I ended up. You can't imagine the confusion it's caused through the years."

He said nothing else, although she waited, and finally when he spoke, it was not a response to that personal revelation. "Read back to me the last."

"Of course," she whispered. Together they picked up the thread of the detailed lists he had memorized. *A freak memory,* Hardesty had said. She had heard of such things, but she had never imagined that anyone could be capable of committing all this to memory and then spitting it out as if reading from the source. The sheer volume of what he was giving them was incredible.

After a long time the information came in shuddering gasps and broken inhalations. She wanted to get the doctor—perhaps there was something he could do. But then she thought—they had come so far together. She wanted him to finish, to complete this self-imposed task that was his revenge upon those who had done whatever had been done to him. She was torn between her concern for his agony and her desire to help him succeed.

It was not until the voice faded completely that she moved. She opened the hall door, and the doctor rose immediately, hurrying to the bed. She raised her left arm, propping it against the hard wood of the door frame and resting her forehead against it. Her tiredness was emotional, she knew, caused by her tension. She wondered if she were capable of returning to the room, to the screen, to that broken voice. She wondered if she would have to. Was he dying, even now, as she stood, trying to block the thought of that possibility from her mind?

"He'd fainted. I gave him what I could. Hardesty said not to give him anything that might interfere with his mental abilities, so I'm limited.... God, I hate this." The doctor brushed past her to resume his seat. When he leaned his head back against the wall and closed his eyes, she could see his tension as clearly as she had felt her own.

She steeled herself to approach the computer that glowed in the darkness like a candle in some isolated window.

"I'm sorry," he said, and in reaction to that soft apology, she felt the tears burn again. "We're almost through. Only a little more," he said to reassure her, to comfort *her*.

She couldn't answer, but she knew he expected none. She seated herself, putting her fingers on the keys as that implacable, indomitable whisper penetrated the darkness between them. She didn't know how long it went on. Time had become meaningless in the blackness of the room, in the night of what they were doing together. She typed until he stopped again. The resultant silence became painful, as painful as the hoarse, suffering voice had been only minutes before.

"Thank you," he said finally. There was nothing she could say, even if she could have spoken past the hard knot that blocked her throat. She competently began to complete her job and to pack up the equipment. She never looked at the bed, and with the loss of the glow from the screen, she knew that he could no longer see her face. Using the thread of light under the door as a guide, she moved across the room.

She wondered what she could say to him. She wanted to give him some message, but there seemed no words appropriate for a dying man who had just spent his last hours in agony rather than in the peaceful oblivion of drugs. He had chosen to spend them that way, and finally he could rest. He could loosen his determined hold on life and slip into the release that even she sought for him now.

She stopped by the closed door, turning to speak into the darkness. The phrase had come unbidden to her mind, but it was right, and so she whispered it to the man she felt joined to by some invisible linkage, by the hold he had taken on her emotions, as if his fingers were tangled into her heartstrings.

"Rest in peace," she said softly and then opened the door, stepping back into the light.

The doctor pushed by her as she moved out into the hall. She never looked back, but continued down the dim staircase. Her grotesquely exaggerated shadow, created by the light from the upper landing and perhaps now from the lights in the upstairs room as well, mocked her from the wall. Frank waited at the bottom of the staircase, and at the look on her face, he put his arm around her shoulders, squeezing gently. He released her to hurry—for a man of his age and bulk—up the stairs she had just descended.

Paul Hardesty was waiting in the library, his half-filled glass on the marquetry table beside him. He rose at her entrance, and after a brief glance at her pinched features, he poured a stiff two fingers into one of the old-fashioned glasses that rested on the tarnished silver tray beside the decanters.

She sipped it gratefully, welcoming the burn that at least represented life. She was suddenly so cold she shivered, although the house's heating system was operating efficiently, in view of the conditions outside. Shock, she supposed, as she drank another healthy swallow of the brandy.

"Did you get it all?"

Hardesty's harsh question broke through her self-absorption. Of course, his concern would be for the information now residing safely in the hard drive. Somehow she wished his first question had been about the condition of the man upstairs, but he would know the answer to that. He had told her that before she'd left this room.

"It's all here."

"What do you think? Is it as valuable as we hoped?"

She realized that she had never once thought about the value of the information, had never analyzed its possible use, in spite of the fact that she was certainly in a position to make that evaluation. Her whole concern, almost from the first, had been the medium and *not* the message, to paraphrase Holcomb's caustic remark.

"I don't know," she answered honestly. "It's extensive enough. If it's accurate, it's invaluable. Well worth what it cost."

"Worth more than that," Paul affirmed, "and you know it. I'm sorry to have put you through this, Rae. I know it was difficult. Women are much more sensitive to the suffering of others. The maternal instinct, I suppose. I know what this has done to you."

Rae's smile was bitter, mocking his easy assurance that he understood what she was feeling. "Maybe you do," she answered too sharply, "but I would defy anyone not to have been affected by what he accomplished."

Frank came into the library, saving his boss the necessity of a reply to what was, they both had recognized, a criticism and a rejection of his words of comfort. Holcomb held a small recorder in his hand, and he set it down on the table by Hardesty's chair, pushing buttons until the thready whisper Rae had listened to upstairs filled the room.

The pain belonged in the darkness, hidden, shielded from the ears of these listeners. It was almost a sacrilege to play it here in the light; to have recorded it at all struck her as the worst sort of depravity, an obscenity like a snuff film. She turned away as the two men listened. Perhaps they had heard all they needed or they had finally noticed her reaction, but the electronically triggered stop cut off the voice as effectively as his pain had sometimes done in the dark room. Even the cessation of the sound was an agonizing reminder.

"Why did you need me if you were going to tape it?" she asked bitterly into the silence.

"This is backup. In case you made a mistake. Yours is in a form we can send immediately to the computers. We'll have a translation to work with by morning. In spite of the excellence of the equipment, the sound quality of the tape is very bad."

"That poor bastard," Holcomb said softly. "I suppose the hoarseness is caused by his screaming when they—"

"My God, Frank," Hardesty's voice overrode Rae's gasp. She closed her eyes to stop the light-headedness that made her senses swim, then felt Paul's hand on the back of her neck, forcing her to sit, to lower her head down between her knees. Eventually he put her glass into her hand, and she was able to drink the remainder of the brandy and finally to look up into his concerned blue eyes.

"I'm all right," she said. "I can't get him out of my mind."

"I know. Let's get out of here. There's nothing else we can do. Let's go get this information home and plan the best way to use what he's given us. It's the most fitting tribute we can make. Do you understand, Rae?"

"I know. But Paul, I don't ever want to hear that tape again. Don't ever let anyone play it in my presence. *No one* should hear it. It diminishes what he was. I can't explain it any better, but that shouldn't be the only thing that remains of who that man was."

He nodded, but she doubted that he really understood. It was enough that he had agreed. Paul Hardesty would keep his word. That was one thing she was certain of.

They heard the chopper, and Rae began putting on her coat. Paul took the computer, leading the way down the hall to the French doors that would open onto the patio. She turned back to look into the interior. The stairs she had climbed were hidden by the intervening rooms. Finally she shook her head and followed the men out into the cold night.

Frank helped her into the Huey, leaning close to speak against her ear, "I'm sorry, Rae. I didn't think how that would come out. He was a brave man. He wanted this. Don't grieve that he succeeded."

She nodded once as she settled into the cold vinyl seat. She pressed Frank's fingers to let him know she had accepted his apology. She looked out on the Virginia countryside, watching the passing lights below. She knew that most of the people in the houses still slept, but here and there the early risers were beginning to stir and make ready for the day—the farmers, the delivery people, those who worked the early shifts at hospitals and factories.

The tears moved down her cheeks and her nose ran, but she didn't sniff in case they might hear above the din of the engine. She finally wiped her face with her gloves, her back resolutely to the two men.

To hell with it, she thought suddenly. *A man died tonight. A brave man, and I'm sorry. There's nothing wrong with crying for him.*

In spite of that conviction, she wept alone and before returning to the lighted office, she repaired all traces of the effects of her tears. She used her cosmetics like a warrior painting for battle, and when she joined the others, to be handed a steaming cup of coffee by Frank Holcomb, she was once again coldly, unemotionally in control.

Chapter Two

News of the raid by the Colombian authorities that resulted in the death of Pablo Escobar led to a small celebration, and in the midst of their elation, Paul told them the plans for using the information their informant in Virginia had supplied to mop up the remains of the Medellin cartel. The material had been cross-checked against everything they knew and, based on the most careful analysis, it appeared to be not only genuine, but every bit as extensive as Paul had hoped.

"Do we know how the guy got this stuff? Or even where?" Kyle Peters voiced the questions they all had.

Hardesty shook his head. "I know nothing more about the man than I told you," he denied. And that had been virtually nothing. He hadn't even mentioned to the group the diplomatic link. "This is obviously from something like the central records of the cartel. I can't even imagine why this information would be stored in one location."

"It may not have been. He could have assimilated it from a variety of sources and then mentally organized it into what we're looking at," Rae suggested quietly.

She didn't explain how she knew he would have been capable of that kind of intellectual activity. She was the only one of the force who had spent any time with their source, but they didn't know that. Paul had told her and Holcomb not to talk about their role in the exchange of information, so, of course, she hadn't.

"Perhaps what we have *is* the finished product of his efforts. It seems the cartel would be foolish to keep this kind of information in one place," Paul agreed.

She privately wondered if the cartel were that organized, but she didn't dare say that. Paul had warned them again and again about their tendency to underestimate the resourcefulness of their opponents. Just because they were criminals with the barbarity of savages in their methods of reprisal didn't negate their intelligence. She didn't want to hear that particular lecture again.

The meeting broke up shortly before lunch and although Rae was invited to join several of the small groups they separated into, she refused. She had her own question for Paul, so she waited patiently, still sitting at the conference table until the room had cleared.

She could see by his eyes that he had been expecting this, and she watched him come over to the chair next to hers and sit down. Like the good interrogator he was reputed to be, he waited for her to speak.

"Tell me about him," she finally said.

"I don't know anything more than I've already told you. I swear that's the truth, Rae."

"I don't mean who he was," she said and then hesitated. "I mean . . . at the end."

He took a deep breath and looked at the windows across the room. The shades were partially drawn, but the winter sunlight allowed her to see his features clearly. His lips tightened almost imperceptibly.

"He died shortly after we left the house. The doctor was able to give him enough morphine that he wasn't in pain at the last. I swear that, Rae."

She had watched the muscles tighten around his eyes and knew something was wrong with what he had just said. He was good, but no one could achieve perfect control. That slight, involuntary movement had some significance, only she wasn't sure exactly what. She filed that information away for later consideration and listened to the rest.

"He just slipped away. He didn't speak again after you left. The doctor said it was as if he had nothing else to say. There was no message."

She smiled briefly, shaking her head. "I wasn't looking for messages. He was kind to me. I wanted to know that he..."

Paul finally spoke into the silence. "The doctor did everything he could, but the damage was too great. And, Rae, if it's any consolation...I don't think he would have wanted to survive, given his condition."

She looked down at her hands, knowing that was probably the truth. However, she was aware that something in the recital of events Paul had just given her was a lie. Perhaps the doctor had administered too much morphine. Would it not have been a kindness in that situation? Finally she sighed over the unanswerable and got up.

"Thanks for telling me."

"I've been expecting you to ask. I wondered why you waited." They both knew his comment was a question.

"Maybe I didn't want to know. As long as it wasn't put into words, I could pretend."

"He's dead, Rae, and that's the reality. Stop pretending."

She nodded and went back to her office. There was too much work to do to waste time on the past. She controlled her mind and finished early. She treated herself to Chinese and a paperback romance on the way home, determinedly closing the door on the events that had taken place in Virginia.

April 1995

"HAVE YOU HEARD about Holcomb?" Kyle asked as he propped his hip against her desk, a habit she hated because he always managed to brush against her leg as he did it. He was their resident ladies' man, and since Rae was the only resident lady except Paul's sixtyish secretary, she had come in for her share of Kyle's carefully orchestrated hits. So far she had ignored them, but she moved her knee away from his calf.

"What?" she snapped, not looking up from the report she needed to complete before this day turned into another late nighter.

"Franklin's disappeared." He leaned conspiratorially toward her ear, but Rae knew she was probably the only one in the office who hadn't heard whatever gossip Kyle was about to share. She had been tied up at her desk all day.

"What's the joke? I don't have time for this, Kyle. In case you haven't noticed, I'm working."

"No joke. He didn't show up the last two days, and finally Hardesty got off his butt and sent somebody to his apartment. Forced entry, blood, the works. Washington's finest were conspicuously not called. An in-house investigation is ongoing. Stay tuned for further bulletins." Kyle gave the whole story sotto voce and then sauntered away before her shocked mind could formulate the questions she wanted to ask.

"God," she breathed, staring unseeingly at the figures on her screen. She had worked directly with Frank only that one time in Virginia, more than a year ago, but the force was small enough that they were always in close proximity. She sat stunned for a few moments and then went to Hardesty's office.

She knocked, entering at his invitation. He looked like he hadn't slept, and she wondered how much he knew that Kyle hadn't told her.

"I guess you've heard by now," he said, seeing the shock of that knowledge in her face.

"Is it true?"

"I don't know what details you've been given, but he seems to have disappeared. The apartment showed signs of violence. There was no disarray and the blood had been cleaned up, but the struggle he'd put up was obvious enough with the right equipment. His car was still in the lot."

"What was he working on?"

"Nothing particular. Some background checks on Jamaican immigrants. Small potatoes. I guess he stepped on somebody's toes." Paul shook his head slowly, unbelievingly. "It compromises the force—but to what extent, we won't know for some time. We were so careful to maintain anonymity. I don't know what he did, but the rest of you may suffer."

"You don't think it could be connected with the cartel?" The question seemed logical to Rae. It was certainly the biggest thing they had worked on, their greatest success.

"Not after all this time. The Medellin organization is nonexistent, so I don't think..." Paul said musingly, but she could tell, in spite of his immediate denial, that the wheels put in motion by that idea were all turning.

"Get everyone who's still here together for me, would you, Rae," he commanded, apparently rejecting what she'd just asked. "I've been postponing the inevitable. If you all know, we might as well discuss the implications."

The group was subdued, but the conversation centered around the Jamaican Posses, known for their violence, and Rae didn't again make the suggestion she had voiced to Paul.

The shock of Holcomb's disappearance faded as the days passed. It was a dangerous profession, and no one had been in it long without losing a colleague. The assumption that Frank had been careless was one they all made, and so his death became in their minds simply the unfortunate result of his own mistakes. They shut it away and worked more carefully.

It was not until Jeff Reynolds's body was found, totally by accident, that the real fear began to permeate. Rae hadn't even noticed Reynolds's absence. He was the youngest of them all, with a reputation he'd brought over from Justice, but she'd never worked with him. His specialty had been the Russian gangs who operated out of New York. Had she noticed he was missing, she would have assumed he was there.

Paul didn't wait before calling them together this time. The tension in the room was palpable. Rae thought she could almost smell the fear. A coincidence of this magnitude in a group as small as theirs? It was difficult to believe, but Paul put that interpretation on it. She supposed there was nothing else he could do.

She returned to her desk and soon found Kyle at her elbow. For once, she was grateful for his company.

"Did you believe that crap?" he asked, drinking the cold coffee in the bottom of her cup. She had noticed the greasy film before and decided somebody had better wash the coffeepot, but it didn't seem to bother Kyle.

"No," she answered truthfully. "But I didn't believe the Jamaicans were behind Frank's disappearance. They would have just left him there. They wouldn't drag his body away. A warning's more effective with visual evidence."

"You think this is a warning?"

"I don't know what I think now. I just didn't think Frank's disappearance made any sense. It was sheer luck Jeff's body was found. I don't believe that was intentional."

"A definite screwup on the part of whoever killed him. And his injuries? You *did* recognize the style? Classic." Kyle said only what she had been thinking.

"Colombian. The cartels," she agreed.

"Yeah. Now that scares me. If it's the cartels and not individual mistakes..."

"If we're right and Paul's wrong, then they probably have all our names. Two out of twelve. And the money-laundering operation is the biggest thing we've worked on."

"Let's get out of here. I've had about all of this phony reassurance I can take. I don't trust Hardesty any further than I can throw him," Kyle said bitterly.

Although she didn't distrust Paul, she sympathized with Kyle's feelings because she felt their boss definitely knew more than he was telling. She was tempted to take Kyle up on his offer. She wanted to talk over what had happened with someone who understood all the implications, someone with whom she didn't have to guard her tongue. But she had to finish this report. It was due to another agency, and Paul had trusted her to get it out.

"I've got to get this done."

"So how much do you lack?" he asked easily.

"Maybe an hour. More if there are interruptions."

His laugh was understanding. "Okay. I get the message. If I remove myself from your desk and let you work in peace, could you meet me in, say, an hour and a half?"

She wondered if this might be as big a mistake as she thought, but what the hell. She didn't want to eat alone, and Kyle was a co-worker. If she kept that interpretation on it, he would be forced to, too.

"Okay. That sounds good. Where do you want me to meet you? I'm not dressed for anything fancy."

"You look great. Nobody would mind your gracing the best restaurant in town just like you are, but what about the Golden Door," he suggested, smiling at her.

She mentally groaned at the awkward flattery, but since the Door was her favorite Chinese restaurant, she managed to keep her answering smile in place as they made the final arrangements.

With Kyle and almost everyone else out of the way, she worked quickly, finishing long before her estimate. The building was practically deserted, but as she was preparing for the transmission of the report, she noticed a light in Hardesty's office. She completed her last jobs, and then found herself standing before his door. She hesitated and finally knocked softly.

"Come in," he said, so she opened the door and found him leaning back in his chair, hands crossed behind his white head.

"Rae," he acknowledged. "I've been thinking about what you said."

"What I said? About what?" she asked, but she knew.

"If Frank's death and now Jeff's could be connected with the cartel."

"That wasn't the song and dance you gave us today."

"Yeah, but you all looked at me like you recognized the tune. Look, I've gone back over it all. I don't know who this could be. We picked up all our targets here, and the Colombians had already gotten Escobar."

"Oh, come on, Paul. We're not that stupid. The big ones are always covered. Why are you trying to paint this as coincidence? It won't wash."

"Well, when you figure out what the hell it really is, you let me know." She could hear the anger in his voice at her disbelief that there was no one left in the Medellin cartel to be a danger to them.

She shook her head, starting to leave.

"Rae," he said softly. The anger was gone, so she turned to hear him. "Be careful. I may not have an explanation, but I don't like what's happening. You be extra careful."

She watched his eyes for a long, silent moment, but there was nothing she could read in their clear blue depths. They looked, as always, guileless as a baby's. Finally she simply nodded and let herself out, closing the door behind her.

WITH TRAFFIC and the difficulties of getting a cab, her arrival at the restaurant was not many minutes off her original estimate. Kyle had already ordered appetizers. They talked about the food and the previous meals they had had here, never together. They shared backgrounds and family information and other innocuous first-date kinds of chatter. It was not until they had chosen the main courses that they got down to what they both wanted to talk about, down to the only motive that could bring two people who were so different together: self-preservation.

Rae asked the first question and then wished she hadn't.

"What went wrong with the arrangements to meet the courier who provided the information on the money laundering?"

"What do you mean, 'What went wrong'? I didn't know anything went wrong. We got the stuff." Kyle wiped plum sauce off his chin and looked at her with what appeared to be genuine puzzlement.

"Forget it. Maybe I was wrong."

"Come on, Rae. You can't just throw something like that out and then back off. What makes you think something went wrong?"

She hesitated and finally decided to share enough of what she knew to let Kyle understand her thinking. "Paul told me that we'd screwed up—his exact words—and that the courier had paid for it. I assumed the pickup team was late, and the cartel got to him first."

"How would the cartel know where the pickup was to be?"

She hesitated again and finally put the thought that had been festering in the back of her mind for months into words. "Someone told them."

"*Someone* being?"

"I don't know. I don't know who would be in a position to do that other than the pickup team. Or Hardesty."

"God, do you realize what you're suggesting? That one of us—"

"Yes." She took a deep breath. "I've thought about it since..." She hesitated, for some reason reluctant to reveal her involvement that night, and finished, "Since Paul let that slip. I waited for him to act and he hasn't. So I decided I was being ridiculous. No one's been—"

"Holcomb and Reynolds," Kyle interrupted, obviously thinking out loud. And obviously no longer listening to her doubts about her theory. She couldn't decide whether or not she was pleased by his ready acceptance of what she'd suspected for so long. "Were they the team?"

"Frank was at headquarters. He couldn't have been. I don't know about Reynolds, although that wasn't his usual job."

"Damn," Kyle said softly, apparently seeing all the implications. "Can you see Hardesty bumping off his own people?"

"For selling information to the cartel? For almost losing the biggest break we've had against the drug lords in years?

Yeah, I could see Hardesty doing that," she affirmed quietly.

"But why so long? Why wait so long before he acted?"

"To be sure who was responsible?" She threw out the possibilities she'd considered. "To make us believe it had nothing to do with the operation? Paul would do whatever he thought was necessary without a second thought."

"That's almost as scary as thinking the cartel's out for revenge, except . . . if it is Hardesty taking out the pickup team, it should be over. That may be why he's working so hard on this coincidence fairy tale. If it's an internal housecleaning, no one else should disappear."

"Do you honestly believe two people would be involved in a sellout? I told you Frank was at headquarters."

"Then maybe his death wasn't related, and Hardesty used it as cover to bump off Reynolds. Two-for-one day."

"Or we're being picked off *one by one* by some revenge-minded Colombian. Somehow I can't see Paul doing those things to Jeff."

"He's cold-blooded enough to mutilate the body after he killed him. If he thought we'd buy it. No one saw the coroner's report but Hardesty."

He studied her face for a moment before he continued, "So what do we do?"

"We're careful. We take precautions. We're aware. And we wait. If we're right . . ." She didn't finish the thought because if Kyle was correct about Hardesty taking his own revenge on Jeff for betraying the operation, there should be no more deaths. Another death would almost certainly mean the cartel.

When Kyle brought her home, she invited him in for a drink. It wasn't late because they both had to work the next day. She expected his usual flattery and at least a play for more than a good-night kiss, but she was pleased to be wrong. He treated her like a colleague and after a few minutes, he got up to leave. She walked him to the door.

"I'll see you tomorrow," he said. When he gently looped her hair behind her ears, she smiled at the gesture. It was something she did at work to keep it out of her eyes, and she knew now that he had watched her and was unconsciously copying her habit.

He lowered his mouth to hers, and his kiss was more pleasant than she had anticipated. His lips were firm, and he knew exactly what he was doing. She wondered why she had always considered him nothing more than the office flirt. He was handsome and well-built, on halfback lines, slightly thick for her tastes. Physically, not mentally thick, she amended. She enjoyed the kiss, but when his hand touched her breast through the cotton dress, she knew she didn't want that intimacy. It didn't feel right. She broke the contact, moving away from his body.

He raised his head and studied her face with blue eyes that suddenly reminded her of Paul's. Clear and honest.

"Sleep well," he said, and turned back to her as he opened the door. "Lock up. Every lock you've got. Do you understand?"

"I will. Don't worry. I enjoyed tonight," she offered the back of his head.

He didn't turn around again, but he said before closing the door behind him, "Yeah. Me, too. Maybe too much."

She looked at the door for a long time after Kyle left. Then she secured all the locks and turned off the living-room lights and went to bed, but it was several hours before she slept.

TWO WEEKS went by before anything else unusual happened. Unless Kyle taking her to a couple of pleasant lunches was unusual. There were no more accidental bodily contacts at her desk. He behaved like a perfect gentleman, to use her mother's term. He asked her out once, and she really had another commitment. He didn't seem to resent the refusal, saying something about a rain check.

Then there was another disappearance—Drew Gates. No signs this time of forced entry. No blood. Just gone. Vanished off the face of the earth.

The strain was beginning to show on them all. She wondered how many of the task force changed their locations. She didn't sleep at her apartment after she heard Gates was missing. She took a room at one of the motels near Dulles. She didn't tell anyone, and it was not the only precaution she took. She didn't stay at work past five anymore. She left with the crowd from the other offices. She walked off in a different direction each afternoon and changed taxis several times, usually moving through stores or crowded restaurants from the front entrance to the back and then out onto a different street, blending with the crowd. She even wore a hat or a scarf to hide her hair, obeying all the instructions she had thought so ridiculous when she heard them in training.

She followed every stricture religiously, but as the days slipped into weeks, everyone relaxed. Nothing else had happened, and by now she needed things from her apartment. She was tired of living out of a suitcase, tired of the same dresses, tired of the spy stuff. One evening, after her careful hopscotch routine through the stores and a quiet dinner at a small neighborhood café across town, she went back to her apartment. There was an empty suitcase in the top of her closet. She would fill it up and then again avoid the place like the plague.

THE PHONE SHRILLED harshly into the quiet dimness of the elegant room. The dark, long-fingered hand that reached to stop its invasive noise prevented a second ring.

He lifted the receiver, and Diego's voice spoke into his patient stillness.

"She's here."

"Bring her," he said calmly and replaced the phone in its cradle. He had waited a long time for the message he'd just received. He took a deep breath against the churning anticipation, fighting for his usual control against the emotions the call had evoked.

Business, he reminded himself with a certain cold bitterness. *Only business.* Even as he said it, he knew it for the lie it was.

His fingers lifted unconsciously, but when he realized what he was doing, he forced his hand to drop, to lie clenched in his lap. And then, again, he simply waited.

HER APARTMENT WAS comfortably familiar. Nothing out of place. Nothing that was not as it should be. She checked it out carefully, even carrying the gun she had never fired except at a target. There was no one in the rooms she'd decorated so lovingly when she'd moved to the city. Her plants looked past help, all but a mother-in-law's tongue that appeared not to have noticed the several-weeks-long lack of water. She set it in the sink and filled the soil to overflowing twice, watching the water swirl down the drain.

She checked the refrigerator, but since she didn't cook, there was nothing too disgusting in it. The oranges in the drawer were dried and hard, and she poured the soured milk down the drain. Everything seemed to have survived her absence. She wondered if she were being foolish. She hated the way the motel was eating into her savings, but, she thought with a certain irony, she would probably hate being dead even more.

She struggled to get the big suitcase off the shelf of the bedroom closet and found it was full of clothing she had intended to take to one of the shelters. She dumped it on the bed, then, disgusted with the way that looked, threw it onto the floor of the hall closet.

She systematically filled the suitcase with lingerie and the rest of her summer wardrobe. She tossed in a few pairs of shoes and the remainder of her makeup. That should get her through the next few weeks before anyone noticed that she had been wearing the same four or five dresses over and over. She even had some leisure clothes packed this time. She hadn't thought about how long she might want to hide out the first time she'd done this.

She wished she could talk to someone at work, but she didn't want to feel like a fool if they were all calmly going about their normal routines. And she still hesitated to reveal her new address, even to her colleagues. That instinctive distrust bothered her more than the fear of their ridicule, however.

She took a final look around, deciding to leave the plant in the sink. She put in the plug and filled it halfway with water. The clay pot would absorb enough to keep the plant alive. She put a couple of the others in, thinking that if there was any life left, they might revive. She cut out the lights and looked through the peephole of the front door. There was no activity in the hall, but she slipped her gun out and, slinging her purse strap over her left shoulder, picked up the suitcase with her left hand.

She stepped out into the hallway and looked up and down. Nothing. She checked the door, and the knob turned under her fingers.

"Damn," she said under her breath. She decided it was quicker to put on the inside latch than to dig for her keys. She set down the suitcase and then her purse, whose strap had slid down her arm. She opened the door, reset the lock, closed the door and tried it again. The lock turned once more under her fingers. She was reaching back inside, puzzled by the antics of a lock that had, up to now, never given any trouble.

The hand gripping her elbow literally stopped her heart. She turned in automatic reaction, bringing the gun around, but she never completed that move. The fist that connected with her chin effectively put an end to whatever intention she'd had. Her head slammed back into the frame of the door, and the gun slipped from her suddenly nerveless fingers. As she slid down the wall, she watched it bounce in slow motion against the gray commercial carpet. She felt her knees give way, and her eyelids dropped, but not before she had glimpsed the dark complexion of the man who stood before her.

Like an amateur, was the last bitter thought that flashed through her mind before she hit the floor, already deeply unconscious.

Chapter Three

She came to on the back seat of a car. A big, comfortable back seat. Unless you were suffering from a massive headache and nausea. Unless your hands were taped together at the wrists and your vision blocked by some kind of blindfold. She stayed awake long enough to make those disheartening discoveries, and then the blackness closed in again, stealing around the edges of her consciousness despite her best efforts.

SHE WASN'T DEAD. Your head didn't hurt if you were dead. She must have been aware of the voices at some level for a while. Spanish, softly spoken, too quiet to allow her to make sense of the words, or perhaps her brain still wasn't working. She didn't think they spoke Spanish in heaven. Or in hell. She wondered briefly why she had always assumed they spoke English in the afterlife. Maybe it was like tongues in the New Testament; everybody heard whatever was said in his own language.

She must have faded out again after that last less-than-coherent line of thought. There were no voices now, but she definitely heard something that was familiar—the faintest trace of sound, tickling her consciousness like a song you knew you'd heard before, but couldn't quite remember.

Rejecting the impossibility of trying to identify the noise, given the crescendo of pain in her head, she tried instead to get enough saliva together to swallow, to ease the dryness of her throat. The blindfold was still in place, but at least her hands were free.

"Ms. Phillips?" The slightly accented baritone spoke quite near her, to her left—from behind the back of the couch she was lying on, its upholstered rise against her left shoulder. The deep tones were far more polite than they should have been, given the situation. Far too pleasant.

"Look," she said, fighting to control her own voice, to make it as calm as his had been. "I don't know who you are or why you brought me here, but you've got the wrong person. You've made some kind of mistake." Even talking hurt her head. The words beat against the back of her skull like a hammer. *Think,* she demanded against the pain's distraction.

"Rachel Phillips," he said, and it was not a question.

"I'm not Rachel Phillips. I told you—"

"Rachel now only to your family. To your mother. Rae to your friends."

"I told you—" she began again.

"Please, don't pretend you believe we are stupid enough to approach the wrong person. Diego had been waiting a long time for you to show up and finally his patience was rewarded. I assure you he made no mistake about your identity."

"Diego?" she questioned. There was more than one, of course. The silken voice certainly didn't match the image burned into her consciousness of the coarse face she had seen briefly in the dim hallway.

"Diego brought you here."

"I don't know any Diego. I don't know Rachel Phillips. I don't know why you would hit me and tie me up and—"

"I'd like to ask you some questions," he interrupted again, softly reasoning against her manufactured anger.

There was nothing threatening in the quiet suggestion. Nothing to produce the creeping horror that began in her bowels and iced its way upward until it froze the breath in her lungs. She fought for control while the rumors about what had been done to Jeff Reynolds and the memory of the courier's agonized whispers beat beside the pain in her head, joined with it and tried to overcome her control. She wondered how quickly she would give in. Everyone did. There were thresholds of suffering beyond which not even the strongest of will or body could hold out.

"What are you going to do?" she asked, suddenly panicked. Despite her effort at control, she could hear the child's terror in the question. Nightmares. Monsters. She knew with chilling certainty that the monster under the bed this time was real—terrifyingly real—and there was nothing she could do about it.

"I'd simply like to ask you some questions. Despite Diego's—" he began.

"Work for it," she interrupted softly, bitterly, willing her defiance. She was so scared. She could feel the fear coiling in her guts.

"I beg your pardon?" he asked, the silken voice devastatingly polite.

If she didn't get her act together, they would begin, and she knew she would tell them whatever they wanted. She would eventually, of course, but there was something at the core of who she was that made her determined to resist as long as she was able.

"I don't know anything to tell you. So whatever you're planning, I suggest you get the show on the road."

"Whatever I'm planning?" he repeated, sounding genuinely puzzled. "I don't think—" He stopped suddenly. "You believe I intend to hurt you."

"Silly me," she said scathingly. This time, when the beautiful voice came to her out of the darkness, she clearly identified the nuance of tone—amusement.

"Too many movies, Ms. Phillips. No one uses torture anymore. Drugs are so much more efficient. With the right drug, you'd tell me anything I wanted to know in five minutes."

Either way, she admitted, he was right. Maybe quicker than five minutes if it was torture, but somehow she was infinitely relieved because she believed him. It was possible he was just playing with her, but there was something in the quiet amusement that she latched onto. She believed him. Despite her training. Despite her situation. *Because you want to. Because you're so damned afraid.*

"I don't *know* anything to tell you," she said again. She thought she could hear the regret in her own avowal.

"Then I'll tell *you,*" he replied, still amused, patient with her puny defiance. "You have only to listen."

The slightly awkward phrasing was not unpleasant. Like the faint accent, it added richness to the deep timbre. She wondered briefly what she found so reassuring about this Colombian bastard's voice. So…appealing, for God's sake.

She thought of what she knew about hostage psychology, about the Stockholm Syndrome. She wondered if she could already be trying to build bridges to her captor. She was at his mercy. Did she subconsciously want to please him so much, in order to protect herself, that she was giving him attributes that she knew he couldn't possibly possess?

You have only to listen, he'd told her. Better than what she'd been anticipating. She had time to wonder briefly what he knew before he told her—in excruciating detail.

"Your people carried out a series of raids and arrests early last year aimed at the operation of the Medellin cartel. The information that was used to shut down the money-laundering operation here was supplied by a man who contacted your agency through diplomatic channels. Paul Hardesty, your immediate superior, set up a meeting to receive the information the source offered. Instead, the informant was betrayed by someone in your task force."

The silence stretched out between them as she assimilated this. He had put into words the suspicion she had lived with so long, the suspicion she had voiced only to Kyle. Apparently that supposition had been correct, confirmed by someone who certainly was in a position to know.

"Do you remember the operation?" he asked finally.

"I don't know what you're talking about."

"You were a member of the 'cleanup crew.' Damage control. You and Paul Hardesty and Franklin Holcomb flew to Virginia. Once there, you listened to the information this man had for your agency, and you personally typed what he told you into a computer.''

As he talked, she was again in that cold, dark room, with the glow of the screen and the voice of a dying man whispering out of the blackness. Dying to put an end to the same scum who was sitting here beside her now, safe and taunting. Probing. Seeking other victims.

''Do you remember that night, Ms. Phillips?''

I remember, Rae thought. *I'll never forget.* But caught in her memories, she didn't answer him.

So he asked again, ''Ms. Phillips, do you remember that man?''

''I don't know what you're talking about,'' she said.

''I'd like you to tell me his name.''

She couldn't fit that into the script she'd been writing. Why the hell would he want the name of the source? He was dead. He'd been dead a long time, and this man must certainly know that.

''Ms. Phillips.''

''It's your nickel,'' she said, stalling, trying to buy time. It was a phrase her father had used. In late-night phone calls from snitches, informers, always trying to work a deal. Her father's stock answer had been that they talk and *then,* based on the information, he would offer. *Your nickel.*

''I beg your pardon?'' The amusement was back, the idiom too old, probably, to make much sense to this man.

''It means . . . I mean that *you* want to talk, so talk. I told you. I don't have anything to say. I don't know what you're talking about.''

''All I want is a name.''

''I don't have it. I don't know what you're—''

''Please. This is becoming tiresome. You used the information this man supplied to shut down most of the Stateside operations of the Medellin cartel. With the assassination of Escobar by the Colombian authorities—''

"Assassination?" she gathered her courage to jeer. "Like a politician? Did you think that Escobar had been elected to run Colombia?"

"He ran the cartel—one of them—until his death."

"And in Colombia, he who runs the cartel, runs the country?" she asked mockingly.

"Who runs Colombia now?" he asked softly.

It stopped her. The government of Colombia had stepped up its efforts to loosen the control of that country by the drug syndicates, making important arrests this summer at the top of the Cali organization, but the violence was still pervasive and the flow of drugs had not diminished. And there were persistent whispers of official corruption at the highest levels.

"You?" she suggested, injecting sarcasm. "Is that where all this is leading? You want my vote? Sorry, I'm not a citizen."

There was silence for a moment, and she heard his small sigh and the noises of his body shifting position. The betraying rustle of clothing. The slight creaking leather of the chair. She could even smell the faint, pleasant aroma of his cologne.

"Three people are dead." The dark voice spoke again, pitched more softly than before, and the amusement was definitely gone. "Three men you worked with. Three agents who were involved in that particular operation."

She said nothing, but she swallowed the sickness and then remembered that he could see her mouth and throat clearly. In her blind isolation she had forgotten that although his expression was hidden from her, everything but her eyes was exposed to his examination.

"Franklin Holcomb, Jeff Reynolds, and Drew Gates."

"I don't know—" she began, but the voice continued over her denial.

"One fourth of your task force."

"You questioned all those men, and you still don't have your answer?" she taunted aloud, suddenly knowing that must be true or she wouldn't be here. *Don't play with him.*

Don't play his games, her mind warned, but she knew now that none of them had told him what he wanted to know. No matter what he had done to them, none of those men had talked, and they were her team. She felt a deep sense of pride in that realization.

"They didn't know his name," he said simply.

She realized with despair that that was probably the truth. She had been the closest to him—the man who had died in that cold Virginia bedroom—and she hadn't known his name. She had never asked Paul.

"Perhaps only Hardesty knows." The dark voice echoed her thought.

"Who's Hardesty?" she asked. "I don't know what you're talking about," she said again.

"Someone knows his name, and I want to know who."

"Why?" she asked, giving up the pretense. He knew too much. He was far too well-informed, and it was obvious he hadn't bought her denials. She had wondered about the operation so long. Here, at last, was the source to answer her questions. "He's dead. He died that night, but not before he told it all—every name, every crooked company, every account number. Despite what you'd done to him, he told it all."

Irrationally, she thought it was important to tell them that. They'd killed him, destroyed who and what he was, but he'd defeated them in the end. And so, defiantly, she reminded them.

"Hardesty told you he died," he said, his voice betraying no emotion. Uncaring that she'd pointed out to him his defeat. Uncaring that he had killed a brave man.

"Yes," she whispered.

"And you believed him?" The amusement was back.

"What's that supposed to mean? He died. He was dying as we talked."

"You believed Hardesty?"

"He died," she said. "If you knew—" She stopped, realizing that the man she was talking to, sharing information with, the man with the pleasantly seductive voice, knew very well what had been done to the courier. He might even have done it himself.

"I know," he said, and there was an echo of emotion in the richness of his tone.

Amusement? she wondered. Anger? Before she could decide, given the agony in her head, he continued, again controlled.

"He lived long enough give you the information. Perhaps he lived longer."

"Paul told me he died."

"Paul Hardesty has lied to more people in his lifetime than you've met in yours," he said, again amused. "Proficiency in lying is probably in his job description."

Unwillingly, she remembered her own conviction that day that Paul was not telling the complete truth about the courier's death. She must never reveal her feeling that Paul had lied about the way the courier had died. Given that encouragement, this man would *never* give up his pursuit of the person who had brought down the cartel, and more of the task force would face the situation she now found herself in. They wouldn't know the name he sought, and they would die because of it. When he had the name, she knew it would be used to track down the family members of the man who had died that night, to hunt them down to make examples of them: *This is what happens to those who betray the cartels.*

"Someone in your group knew his name, and I want to know who."

"I don't know his name," she said. It was the truth, but he wouldn't believe her, of course. He hadn't believed Holcomb or Reynolds or Gates, so they had died. She shivered again. She didn't want to die. She didn't want to be hurt or drugged, and she didn't know. She had nothing to tell him. She'd never known the informant's name, and he was dead. She didn't want to die because of a man who had been dead for months. Dead and buried. The man she'd met that night in Virginia wouldn't want her to die because of him.

"Someone does. Someone knows his name."

"But..."

"Yes?" he said softly, inviting her to spill her guts.

It made no sense, and he knew everything anyway. He knew far too much. More than she had known, if he was right about Reynolds and Gates being involved, maybe as the pickup team, but if they were, and they were dead, and they hadn't known his identity, then who did?

"Why does it matter who he was? What can it possibly matter now?" she asked. She could no more have stopped the question than she could have stopped breathing. Her head hurt when she tried to think, and she wanted to understand what had happened that night. She'd wondered so long, and now so many people had died.

"Did you never wonder where he got the information he gave you? How he got it?"

"He'd memorized it."

"Where did it come from?"

"I don't know. We wondered. We thought..."

"Yes?" he prompted gently.

"You go to hell," she said fiercely, suddenly realizing that she had been discussing the operation with him. That damned seductive voice. Question-and-answer time. Tell him what he wants. Insidiously, his voice, calm and reasoned and beautiful, had made her talk to him. She hadn't meant to, but her head hurt, and he already knew so much. *Why shouldn't he?* she thought bitterly. *He was the cartel.*

"Think about it," he suggested quietly, but again the hair lifted on her arms. She was being given a chance to see things his way, to realize he held all the cards.

"We can talk tomorrow," he continued, almost kindly. "You need to rest. Diego will carry you to your room."

"You tell Diego to leave me the hell alone. Wherever you want me to go, you just tell me. But I don't want *that* bastard's hands on me, either."

"Either?" the silken voice questioned. "Wishful thinking, *querida?*" he asked, his amusement again obvious.

She struggled to sit up, furious with him. Furious because he was laughing at her. Furious because of his interpretation of her remark. She made it at least partway up, her feet on the floor, but suddenly the vertigo swam in her head.

She heard his voice from a long way off. From the darkness surrounding her. Commanding. In Spanish again. There was no doubt, of course, who was in charge here. There had been no doubt from the beginning.

She was lifted in massive arms, hard as tree trunks and about that size. Her head lolled against Diego's shoulder, and finally she relaxed and let him carry her because there was nothing else she could do. Not now, at least. *Soon,* she thought. *Soon I'll think what to do. But not now.* It was all too hard. It was far easier to let go into the darkness and away from the pain. Away from having to think. She wondered briefly what she had told him, and then she didn't wonder about anything.

"Ms. PHILLIPS."

She was dreaming. Of the whispering darkness. Lost in the cold black.

"Ms. Phillips."

Only it wasn't Virginia, and the voice calling her name...

She opened her eyes to total blackness, but she couldn't feel the blindfold against the movement of her lashes. She blinked slowly, still befogged by sleep and the pain in her head. The voice had been very real and very close.

"Do you know what day it is?"

Obedient to his demand, she tried to think. She had always wanted to please people, to follow the rules, to be a good little girl, so now she tried to think to please the dark voice. What day was it? She struggled to remember. She had gone to work. She'd gone back to the apartment after work, but that had been a Friday night, so, she supposed, it must be...

"Friday night," she whispered. "Saturday? I don't know what time it is."

"And your birthday?"

Birthday? What the hell? Maybe he wants to send me flowers, she thought, the grogginess beginning to clear, and despite the dull ache in the back of her neck, she smiled at the idea. *Right. And a diamond bracelet. And a Jag. A green Jag. British racing green.*

"August 18."

"The year?"

She knew the year—1963. But— *What's it to you?* she thought. *Screw you.*

"I don't remember," she whispered, and she heard him laugh, the rich, pleasing sound coming out of the darkness across the room. Her eyes had adjusted somewhat so that she thought she could see him there, only a darker shadow against the blackness of the shade-drawn night.

"'Vanity, thy name is woman,'" he quoted softly, still amused.

"When's *your* birthday?" she challenged.

"*I* don't have a concussion," he said.

"And I do?"

"I don't know. That's what I'm trying to find out."

"By making me talk to you?"

"It seemed wise to check on you."

"Because if I kick out, you won't get any answers?"

"I thought you didn't have any answers."

"Then go away and let me sleep," she said.

He was in her room, she realized suddenly. He had been watching her sleep, like some kind of voyeur. He shouldn't be here, and she didn't buy that crap about a concussion.

"Get out," she ordered, but the effort was very great. The pain was less, but the lethargy remained.

"Go back to sleep, *querida*," he ordered softly. There was no anger at her defiance, and that surprised her. She had an idea he was used to being obeyed, as Diego obeyed him. She wondered idly how high up he was. After Escobar's death had he stepped in to fill the vacuum at the top of Medellín? Was he now the top dog in this very dog-eat-wolf world? The head wolf, maybe?

"Who are you?" she demanded.

"Who was the man in Virginia?" he countered. "I'm very willing to exchange information."

"I told you. I don't know who he was, and he's dead. He's been dead a long time."

There was no answer from the dark corner across the room. No sound at all. She closed her eyes and took a breath of the air-conditioned coolness. She could hear the unit running smoothly somewhere in the night beyond the windows. Suddenly she was aware that she could again smell his cologne. She wondered what it was. The men she knew evidently couldn't afford the kind of cologne he wore. Too expensive for those who didn't sell death and destruction to schoolchildren.

She began to drift again, relaxed despite the dark, watching figure. Like his voice, the subtle scent was too agreeable. Too beguiling. She fought against the pleasure, but that was too much trouble also, and finally she gave up the pretense of resisting and allowed herself to be carried back into the enfolding peace of sleep. She was not aware when the watcher in the darkness gave up his vigil.

"YOU'RE OBSESSED with her," Diego accused.

Because he recognized the truth of the statement, he didn't answer.

"What if she didn't look like that? If she weren't so beautiful? You know—" Diego began again and was interrupted by the authority in the deep voice.

"I don't know. That's the problem. Three people are dead, and I'm no closer to the answer than I was before," he said softly.

"If she was involved with what happened that night..." Diego began, and then paused, unwilling to attempt that argument again. "Are you sure you really want to find *all* the answers? Perhaps you've forgotten—"

"God, Diego, how could I forget?" The virulent bitterness in the deep voice stopped the suggestion. "How do you think I could ever forget?" He paused to bank emotions he never allowed and then continued reasonably, "I have to be sure."

"What about the money? The money in her account? He told you about that and it was true."

"The money's not *proof* of anything. Evidence, perhaps, but not proof."

"I don't think you want to find the proof. I think—"

"I really don't give a damn what you think."

"You're *not* thinking. Not with your brain."

"That's enough," he commanded sharply, and then more gently, regretting his anger with Diego. "Do you honestly think that if I believed she *was* the one, I would hesitate? You know, better than anyone else, you know..." The deep voice fell to a whisper, and stopped. There was silence in the room for a long time.

He became aware that Diego's huge hand rested comfortingly on his shoulder, and he finally reached up with his own and touched the massive fingers.

"It's all right. We just don't have all the pieces of the puzzle. I don't owe them anything, and before I do what they've asked me to, I intend to understand it all. All of it. Everyone's role," he said with deadly softness, and finally Diego removed his hand.

RAE SLEPT OFF most of the effects of the door frame connecting with the back of her head and woke with a dull headache no worse than the ones she sometimes had in the afternoon if she didn't get her caffeine allotment. Her immediate need was for a bathroom, and she struggled to sit up on the edge of the bed, waiting for the room to stop spinning. She made her way carefully to the partially open bathroom door, holding on to any furniture that conveniently came to hand. She attended to the needs of nature and then wondered if she dared shower.

She stripped quickly, denying the fear that might make her change her mind, and stepped into the shower before the water had heated. The coldness had the desired effect as she ducked her head under the stream to help clear away the last of the cobwebs. She used the bath soap to wash her hair, not bothering to look for shampoo, hurrying before they could come in and find her naked.

She was not intruded upon. She was surprised to find the suitcase she had packed last night sitting just inside the bedroom door. After rummaging through the clothing it held, she knew without a doubt that it had been searched. There was something very disturbing about the thought of their handling the intimate apparel in her case. Diego, perhaps, pawing through her lingerie with his ham-size fists. Or the other one. The one with the silken voice and the expensive cologne. That thought was even more frightening somehow—too intimate a contact with the enemy.

She found that her hands were shaking as she pulled on her bra and panties, struggling a little because her body was not completely dry, the material catching against the remaining moisture. Somehow she knew she had to hurry, that this blessed privacy wouldn't last long.

She was dressed, however, in clean slacks and a sleeveless cotton top, towel-drying her hair when, without any warning, the door opened.

It was the man from her apartment hallway. Diego. The one who had carried her upstairs. He gestured for her to precede him through the open door, and she dropped the damp towel on top of the mahogany dresser and then gave it a push so it fell down onto the carpet. It had seemed a shame to ruin the finish of the antique with a wet towel.

The absurdity of her concern for their furniture amused her, and the humor gave her courage, so that she accompanied Diego down the stairs, finger-combing her damp hair away from her face. No wonder he'd had no trouble carrying her last night; the shoulders that moved beside her were massive, the arms bulging, the muscles clearly outlined under the silk shirt he wore.

"Where are you taking me?" she asked as they neared the bottom of the stairway.

"He wants to see you," Diego said.

Like a woman in love, she thought, *in Diego's world there is only one "he."* And now, she acknowledged bitterly, probably only one in hers, too. The same "he." The "he" of the seductive voice. The "he" who controls.

They stopped before a door, but she couldn't be sure it was the room she was in last night. Diego had stepped behind her and as she stood, willing herself to calmness in order to face the man who was waiting behind the closed door, he tried to slip the blindfold over her eyes.

This time, reacting without thought, she fought its darkness. She landed two good blows with her elbow and then, turning, with the edge of her hand, using all that she had been taught, and satisfyingly heard the grunts as she connected. He lifted her against his chest and, catching her hand, twisted it behind her back. She broke the hold by kicking back hard, hitting him sharply in the shin, just as she'd been instructed in training so long ago, pleased that it had worked as well as it had then. Diego pushed her away from him, but more confident now, she attacked again, trying to remember all the tricks you were supposed to use against an opponent who was so much larger.

Suddenly Diego gripped her wrist, turning her body around in one smooth motion. He twisted her arm high behind her back, her hand against the back of her own neck. Desperate, she tried to kick again, but he simply moved her farther away from him with upward pressure on the twisted arm. The resulting agony made her gasp, but determined, she kicked once more, connecting only with air, and was rewarded with increased leverage on her arm.

She cried out, unable to prevent the involuntary reaction. So much for the crap about using a larger opponent's own weight against him; she guessed they had to tell you something in all those endless classes.

"Stop it," Diego growled.

She found herself straining on tiptoe to relieve the torment in her shoulder.

"The blindfold is necessary," he said. "His orders."

"All right, damn it," she gasped, hating herself for giving in so easily, but her eyes were brimming with tears. And she had thought she might hold out if they tortured her, she remembered in disgust. They were rapidly destroying all her preconceived notions about how she would react in a situation like this.

The pressure eased, and she almost cried out again with relief. Submissive now, she allowed Diego to put the blindfold over her eyes, knowing she'd lost another round.

He led her into the room. She hated the dependence the blindfold forced, awkwardly trying to follow Diego's guidance, stumbling once over the edge of the thick carpeting. He took her to a chair, placing her hand against its upholstered arm. She eased down into the depths, the pain in her arm and shoulder finally beginning to subside. She cupped the elbow of the aching arm in the palm of the other hand.

She could hear their voices, whispering from across the room, and she strained to understand what they were saying. Then there was only one voice, speaking very rapidly and, she thought, angrily, still pitched too low to distinguish words. It was Diego, telling his grievances to his partner, she assumed. At least he had been bothered enough by what she had done to react with anger. She had thought their fight was pretty much like a fly attacking a buzz saw.

Knowing they were paying her no attention, she moved her hands to examine by feel as much of her surroundings as she could. She was sitting in a wing chair, she decided, her reaching fingers exploring. The voices had stopped, but it took her a moment to realize that.

A hand touched her cheek. She flinched, but he caught her chin, turning her head back.

"Don't touch me," she said aloud and jerked her chin from his hand. She knew it was not Diego, but the other, the one who had no name, only a voice. Of course, she didn't know how many of them there were. There might be a dozen in the room now, for all she knew, but the subtle aura of that expensive cologne was very close.

"You must realize the blindfold is there for your sake."

"For *my* sake?" Foolishly, she began to argue, hating the thought of having her eyes covered and doubting that it would make any difference now. They weren't going to let her go. They hadn't released the others. They were all dead, and she would be, too, so why the blindfold?

"You have already seen Diego," the voice responded calmly, "but no one else. That is, of course, to your advantage."

"Who are you?" she asked, cutting to the chase.

"I hardly think that's relevant."

"Relevant?" she echoed, suddenly losing her reasonableness. "You're damned straight it's relevant. It's the most relevant thing in this entire situation. You have your goon beat me up and bring me here. What do you think gives you that right? Who the hell are you, you slimy Colombian bastard? What do you want from me? I told you I don't know anything about the courier except he's dead. He's been dead a long time. Rotting in a grave somewhere. You can't do anything else to him. It's over. He won and you lost, and there's nothing you can do about that now."

The fury that had flooded her at his calm patronizing was destroying her control. She wanted to cry, but she would never give him the satisfaction. This bastard would *never* see her cry.

"Diego assures me he was only defending himself," the voice said softly, but the amusement was there again under the polite surface. He was laughing at her.

"You think it's funny that your trained gorilla can manhandle me? You think it's funny to hurt women? You make me sick."

"I don't think it's funny," he replied, and the voice had been wiped clean of any inflection she could read. "I meant what I said as a compliment. Diego is enormous, but he found it difficult to control you. He felt he had no other option than to overpower you. You continue to challenge him. First you try to shoot him and then here, this morning, to attack him. You have my apologies for both of those incidents. It was never my intent that you should be hurt. Perhaps if you promise to stop attacking Diego..."

The quiet suggestion trailed away, but underlying the politeness, she could again hear the undertone of amusement.

Mocking her puny efforts. They were *real* concerned about her resistance. *Real* bothered by her ineffectual attempts to exercise some control in her situation.

She didn't realize how bitter her small laugh sounded. She shook her head at his mockery. "Yeah, right. Diego needs protection from me."

"Diego reacts. He doesn't always think. Please, don't attack him again. For your *own* protection."

There was nothing threatening in the tone. The words themselves were clear enough. If anything, there was only regret in the warning.

"Go to hell," she said, turning her face away from where she knew he was sitting. Close enough to reach out and touch her chin. Close enough then, perhaps, for her to...

"Don't even think it," he said softly, his amusement again clearly revealed.

"You need protection from me?" she mocked. "Afraid? Maybe Diego's too big for me to tackle, but how about you, boss man? Or do you depend on the gorilla to fight your battles?" The thought was sudden, but she knew she was right. "He's your bodyguard. Your personal goon squad," she guessed.

"Diego has been with me a long time," he acknowledged. And then, "Diego?"

She felt the huge hands fasten over her shoulders. He had wanted her to know that the giant was standing behind her, ready to do just what she had taunted him about. Ready to leap to the defense of the other, should she be foolish enough to think of attacking him.

The one with the silken voice must have made some noiseless communication, for suddenly Diego's hands were removed, and they sat in silence for a moment.

"I'd like to ask you some more questions," he said finally.

Smiling, feigning an amusement she certainly didn't feel, she shook her head. She hated the darkness of the blindfold, the inability to see what was going to happen, to be able to prepare for it. She remembered what he had said about drugs and dreaded most of all the prick of a needle, dreaded the loss of control. That had always been so important to her, and it was the key to what she must do now, of course—control what she could and let the other go.

"Go to hell, you bastard," she said again. Like a broken record, she knew, but she had no other defense, only her determination not to betray the others. Like Gates and Reynolds and Holcomb. Her team. She only hoped that in what was coming she could be as strong as they had been.

Chapter Four

"What do you know about the courier?" he asked.

"That he's dead."

"Did Hardesty tell you how he approached your agency?"

"He didn't tell me anything."

"Other than it was done through diplomatic channels?"

She tried to think. He knew that. He had told her that. Was he fishing? Trying to trick her?

"He didn't tell me that. You did."

"Colombian, of course?" he said softly. Almost as an afterthought.

"What?" she asked. Paul had only said diplomatic channels. She had assumed Colombian, but she realized now that she didn't know that for certain. She hadn't been told his nationality.

"He approached Hardesty through a Colombian diplomat?" he patiently clarified.

"I don't know. Paul didn't tell me anything about the courier. Whatever information you're fishing for, I don't know."

"Perhaps," he suggested, "you aren't aware that you know."

"You have all the answers. I don't know why you're wasting your time questioning me," she said, immediately regretting the sarcasm. If he decided questioning her was a wasted effort, he would be free to dispose of her or to move on to less pleasant methods of interrogation than sitting in this imposed darkness listening to his beautiful voice.

"Did you never wonder where your source got the information he gave you?"

He had asked her that before, so it must be important— how the man in Virginia had gotten what he'd given them. They *had* wondered, had even discussed it, but she couldn't make any sense of his repeated questions inviting her speculation. He must know where the information had come from.

"No," she lied.

"You didn't wonder how he was able to assemble such a wealth of data?"

"I didn't think about him. I took down what he said and then he died and that was it. In this profession you don't think about the people who die. You can't afford to."

"This profession?" he repeated.

"I'm a cop," she said. "People die, and the rest of us who are still alive move on."

"I don't believe you are that cold-blooded, *querida*," he denied, amused.

"Believe it. I'm a cop, and those are the rules."

"You are also a very beautiful woman. Too beautiful, I think, to be involved in all this. You should be dressed by one of the Paris fashion houses, draped in diamonds, laughing on a lover's arm." His deep voice was strangely caressing, like the hands of that mythical lover, touching her in the darkness. Again she had to consciously fight its appeal.

"Yeah, well, I never meet any wealthy lovers. Just cops and crooks," she answered mockingly, resisting the allure of his voice, but she had no trouble denying the image he'd suggested. It was certainly foreign to who she was.

"Do you enjoy that life-style? Being a cop? Pinching pennies for luxuries? Saving to buy new clothes?" he questioned softly. His fingers touched the sleeveless top she wore, catching a fold of material between them. She knew what she was wearing was cheap, certainly by his standards. She could feel his fingers move against the thin cotton. She could even hear the sound the fabric made in the quietness.

His fingers brushed lightly down her arm, his thumb trailing over the softness inside her elbow, circling once against that sensitive skin and then moving slowly down her forearm, tracing the vein to stop at her inner wrist. She felt a small lurch in her stomach that she knew wasn't fear. His touch, like his voice, was very pleasant and very practiced. Its seductive quality was something she knew she had to resist.

"Get your hands off me and go to hell," she said, turning her face away. She pulled her wrist from his hold and crossed her arms protectively over her body. Away from those warm, mesmerizing fingers. He caught her chin again and, holding it tightly enough to control, turned her head.

"There is a great deal of money to be made in what you do," he suggested quietly, his tone subtly altered. She knew immediately what he meant. She had known of cops on the take through the years, but she would never admit that to him. She lifted her chin from his fingers, and he let her go.

"I'm sure you'd be very impressed with my paycheck. It might pay your manicurist for a couple of weeks. You're right. Big bucks," she agreed, forcing a laugh.

"I'm not talking about your salary. I'm talking about payments for information. You're in a sensitive position. You have access to information for which some people would pay a great deal of money. Have you never been tempted? Tell me, and make me believe, *querida*, that you've never profited from your position."

There was no condemnation in the gentle probing, but the idea was again so foreign to her values, it was itself an accusation, and she answered it.

"I'm not filth like you," she said, letting her contempt show.

"Filth," he repeated softly, but she couldn't read the undercurrent. Anger, she would have understood, but that wasn't the emotion that colored the richness of his voice.

"I don't sell out my friends, so if you're offering me money—"

"Someone made a great deal of money from betraying our *friend* in Virginia. Was it you?"

"I would *never* do that. I couldn't. Don't you understand?" she said, and then realized the futility of trying to explain. "You don't have a clue what people like me are all about. All you know—"

"I know someone on your task force sold information about the courier that night," he interrupted. "About the warehouse. Someone betrayed him."

"I had *nothing* to do with that setup. If it wasn't the pickup team—" she began, and then cut off the urge to argue her own innocence. She was playing into his hands.

"If it were not the pickup team?" he questioned softly, automatically correcting her grammar.

With a small laugh, she shook her head again. He really was very skillful, which, of course, was why he was here.

"Look, I'm not going to tell you anything. So..." she began, and then, at her foolishness, felt the cold fear again.

"Why don't you think about it some more," he said reasonably. "Diego will take you back upstairs. This time, I suggest you go without trying to overpower him. Spend some time thinking about what you have to gain by remaining stubborn. And," he added, "about what you have to lose."

She didn't answer him. There really was nothing else to say. He was right.

She felt Diego's fingers on her wrist, urging her up, so different from those of her questioner. She stood, letting the giant guide her out of the room and up the stairs. When he left her alone in the bedroom, she removed the blindfold she'd resisted. Think about it, he'd suggested, and she knew her time and his patience were running out.

THE BEDROOM offered little in the way of possibilities. She had heard the key turn in the lock as Diego left, but she checked the door anyway. Locked and very solid. The house was too well-built to have doors that offered someone her size a chance to batter them down. The furniture was all too massive to move. Apparently he'd brought a chair in from the hall last night for his vigil over her. She wished they weren't so damn clever. She could at least have given them a little trouble by wedging the back of the chair under the doorknob. They'd have gotten in eventually, of course, but the thought of their annoyance was briefly satisfying, until she remembered that it would probably be safer *not* to have them annoyed with her. For self-preservation she knew she must cooperate to the limits permitted by her own code of ethics.

She walked to the double windows and raised the heavy shade. She was looking down into a rose garden, with hundreds of hybrid teas and climbers rioting over scattered trellises. The massive blooms of the teas, heavy in the heat, drooped on their tall stalks. She knew if she could open the windows, she would be able to smell the fragrances released by the sun.

Her fingers trembling suddenly, she touched the metal lock and, holding her breath, felt it turn easily under her fingers. There was no grill over the outside. Could they have assumed because the bedroom was on the second floor that she wouldn't try to get out this way? They didn't know her very well, despite the obvious quality of his information. Rachel only to your mother, he'd said so smugly.

You leave my mother out of this, she thought. *Don't even say the word. You probably don't have a mother. Snakes are hatched.*

She knew she was only delaying, savoring the small flame of hope that the turning lock had provided. Putting her hands on the top of the lower half of the mullioned window, she lifted. Nothing. It didn't budge. She bent her knees, putting her thigh muscles into it. Still nothing. She stepped back slightly and examined the wood surrounding the panes.

The window had been nailed closed. She could see the heads angling to bite securely into the casement. Primitive, but highly effective, given that she had nothing to work with. She doubled up her fist and hit the top of the lower casement. The pain was astringent. Nothing was going to be easy. She wasn't dealing with idiots. She knew that. Why believe they would ignore the obvious escape route out the windows?

Breaking the glass wouldn't do any good. She couldn't break the wooden mullions and shatter the panes without making a lot of noise. They'd be up here before she'd destroyed enough of the window to get out. She looked around the bedroom for something she could use to pry the nails out and then moved into the bathroom. For thoroughness' sake, she looked in all the drawers and even through her suitcase, wondering briefly if she could take the case apart and use one of the metal ribs. *Yeah, right. With my bare hands. Superwoman rips up Samsonite.*

She sat on the bed and tried to think. The dangers of the two-story drop never even crossed her mind. A chance was all she'd asked for, and if she could only get the windows open—

The knock was unexpected. Apparently someone had suggested manners to the gorilla. Silken Voice, no doubt. The one with the charm and sophistication. A little accent. A little foreign intrigue. Cesar Romero. Or Ricardo Montalban, maybe.

When the knock came again, she responded. Her mother had taught her manners, too.

"Come in," she called, never moving from the bed.

She listened to Diego unlock the door and watched his caution in opening it. Only when he saw where she was did he turn to pick up the tray from the hall credenza.

A knife, she thought, the hope again like a sudden flame. *Or a fork. The handle of a spoon, even. As long as they weren't plastic.* She schooled her face and simply watched as he set the tray down on the mahogany dresser.

"*Gracias,*" she said.

"De nada," he responded automatically and then, seeing her lips quirk, he added, "You're welcome. He said to wish you enjoyment."

Diego turned and disappeared, dutifully locking the door behind him.

She was sprinting across the room before he'd completed the action. Fork, spoon *and* knife. A simple place knife, but maybe it would do. *Hallelujah. How long before he'd return?* she wondered. *Maybe thirty minutes. Thirty minutes to work. And to eat. They'll be suspicious if I don't eat,* she told herself.

She lifted the cover over the plate and found eggs Benedict and there was coffee in the silver pot. The mingled aromas made her mouth water. She couldn't resist a bite. The coffee she gulped to wash it down burned her mouth, and with tears in her eyes, she grabbed the knife and headed toward the windows.

When Diego returned for the tray, she was sitting on the bed, defeated, bitter, and feeling very stupid. The empty plate and coffeepot were on the dresser, along with all the utensils. So much for idiotic ideas, for visions of arranging her own rescue. She might as well have tried eating her way through the window as prying those nails out.

"He invites you to dinner," Diego said. "Tonight. Downstairs."

"Please convey my apologies," she said with sarcastic politeness, "but I'm *sure* I have other plans." She managed a small smile at the feebleness of her pull on the tiger's tail.

"At eight."

"He can go to hell."

"If you aren't ready by then, he said I'm to help you dress."

"You always do what he says?" she asked, feeling despair. This, too, was a battle she would lose, she knew.

"I'll come for you. He sent you this."

The garment bag had remained out of sight in the hall until the invitation had been properly delivered. It was opaque and zippered. Nothing of what it contained could be seen. When she didn't move in response to its appearance, Diego stepped to the closet and placed the crook of the hanger over the frame of the double doors. He never turned his back on her. He walked to the dresser and picked up the breakfast tray, carrying it out to the hall table where he carefully set it down to relock the door.

When she was alone, she was fully aware of the tension she'd been hiding. She took a couple of deep breaths, forcing her hands to unclench. She wasn't enjoying his game of cat and mouse—threats followed by seduction.

She got up and walked across the room to the garment bag. Curious, she unzipped the heavy plastic and slipped it off to reveal the dress it contained.

You should be dressed by one of the Paris fashion houses, draped in diamonds, laughing on a lover's arm, he had said. If she were, this was certainly what she would be wearing.

Against her will, her fingers caressed the material. She wasn't even sure what the fabric was, but it was heavy, expensive, and very beautiful. The black would be a perfect contrast against the ivory of her complexion, and with her hair.

You bastard, she thought, her lips lifting involuntarily into a smile. *Even I didn't know I'd be attracted to something like this, so how could you have known?*

She found the label, hand-stitched into a seam, and recognized the name. She couldn't pronounce it. She had never heard it pronounced, but she'd seen it a dozen times in the social pages, the gossip columns—things she would deny that she ever took time to read. Curled up in the big chair in her apartment, wearing outsize sweats and wool socks against the cold, she read about parties that might as well have taken place on the moon as across town on Embassy Row.

She wondered if it would fit. She knew then she was caught. There was no way she was going to let this hang here and not try it on. Not to wear it for him, but for herself. Just once to see how she would look...*dressed by one of the Paris fashion houses.*

She slipped out of her clothes and stood a moment in her utilitarian bra and panties. It seemed a sacrilege to put the dress on over them. Under its décolletage, her bra would certainly show. Even as she thought that, her eyes moved back to the bag. Of course, he'd taken care of that, too. The undergarment she found there was black and one-piece, silk and lace, designed to follow the cut of the dress. There were also off-black silk hose and high heels. Everything was her size. She wasn't sure whether to be angry or flattered. *Or amused,* she thought, smiling again. She imagined that dark seductive voice reeling off her sizes to some saleswoman.

She resisted for at least ten seconds and then peeled off everything she was wearing. She slipped into the teddy, fastening the strategically placed hooks and eyes, and found that it fitted perfectly. Ignoring the sheer stockings, she stepped into the high heels and walked to the mirror.

The woman reflected there was no one she knew. She shook her head, but as she had known she would from the beginning, she turned back to the dress. She slipped it off the hanger and dropped it over her head to settle like a second skin against her body. She reached behind to fasten the zipper. When she turned back to the mirror, it was to confront her own reflection with a sense of wonder.

Unconscious of the very feminine gesture, she watched the hands of the woman in the glass gather strands of long red hair and hold them on top of her head. Tendrils escaped to spill over her cheeks and neck.

It was so damned perfect. So right. It was nothing she would have chosen, even if she had been able to afford it. This was not the way she saw herself. Sophisticated and sexy. Soft and seductive. The reflection in the mirror was not the cop. Not Austin Phillips's daughter, who had won her first marksmanship medal at seven.

At the thought of her father, she released the curling strands, allowing them to fall in disorder around her face. She stood for a long time, looking at the stranger in the mirror. She had denied selling out the courier, had reacted with anger to his accusations, but she had been mesmerized by his bribe, his gift. She wondered how he could have known she would be tempted by this when she had not.

"No," she said aloud, denying its pull, and hurriedly her fingers found the zipper.

When the beautifully feminine garments were all safely hidden by the opaqueness of the bag, she dressed once more in the slacks and shirt she had worn earlier. She didn't have a choice in whether or not she went downstairs tonight—Diego had made that plain—but she certainly had a choice in what she wore.

She lifted her suitcase again onto the foot of the bed and began to sort through for something that would serve as appropriate dress for dinner with a drug lord.

LONG BEFORE EIGHT, she was sitting carefully on the edge of the bed. She felt the fine tremor in her fingers grow the longer she waited, and then the door opened and it was time.

Diego held the hated blindfold and, recognizing that in this also she had no choice, she stood patiently as he fastened it over her eyes and checked its tightness. He made no comment about the dark green cotton dress she had chosen to wear instead of what his boss had sent up.

Although she had dreaded the awkwardness of blindly stumbling with Diego down the long staircase, he guided her instead to an elevator. She tried to decide if the descent was one floor or two, but the ride was quick, and then they were on a surface that clicked under their heels.

Diego knocked and at the response, took her arm to guide her inside and seat her again in a wing chair. She could feel the softness of the covered arms under her fingers. She placed her hands in her lap, forcing them to relax, and then recognized the familiar fragrance touching her senses.

"Thank you for joining me," the deep, accented voice said, very close to her.

Definitely Cesar Romero, she thought, her lips lifting. Old movies. Black-and-white. The suave Latin lover. It was exactly what he sounded like.

"I wonder what *that* thought was," he said, amused, but she only shook her head.

"I'm sorry the dress didn't fit."

"It fit," she said, and then regretted letting him have the satisfaction of knowing she'd tried it on.

"But for some reason you chose not to wear it?" There seemed only polite interest in the question and apparently no anger.

"My mother warned me never to accept gifts from strangers."

"Most women your age have learned to ignore their mother's advice or at least to temper it with their own wishes. I was looking forward to seeing you dressed as a woman so beautiful as you *should* be dressed. I hope I haven't offended you."

"You don't give a damn whether I'm offended or not. You're just used to having your own way."

"You're probably right," he said, laughing, this time letting his amusement show. "And you, of course, are determined that I won't 'have my way' as far as you're concerned."

Have my way piqued a definite reaction in her mind. She wondered if he realized the sexual connotations of that old phrase. The Victorian villain trying to *have his way* with the trembling virginal heroine.

"I didn't like the dress."

"You're a very poor liar, Ms. Phillips," he said softly. "The dress was perfect and you know it."

Because she did know it, she was left momentarily with nothing to say. He, of course, didn't appear to have any problem handling her refusal of the garment he had chosen for her. The perfect host, he simply moved on to other things.

"Would you like wine?"

She felt her heartbeat accelerate. *Drugged?* she wondered briefly. *"The better to eat you with, my dear," said the Big Bad Wolf.* The analogy certainly fit. Would he prefer her that acquiescent? Drugged and dressed in that damned black teddy? Her mouth quirked again, refusing to picture herself in the role of helpless, subdued maiden.

"And I'm still wondering what amuses you," his silken voice questioned.

"I *would* like wine, please," she suggested instead. At least she would have something to do with her hands besides let them tremble.

She listened to the shifting of ice as the bottle lifted, the soft tumble of the liquid against the glass and then someone took her hand and, turning it, placed the glass into her fingers. *Diego or his boss?* she wondered, but somewhere inside she knew. Her stomach had again reacted to the simple touch of those long, lean fingers.

She raised the glass to her mouth and drank too much. *Like some wino,* she thought, wondering if he would be amused by her obvious lack of sophistication.

"Do you approve?"

"Are you asking my approval of the wine? What do people say when they don't know anything about art? 'I only know what I like,'" she mocked.

"Do you?"

"What?" She was thrown off by his calm response.

"Like the wine? It seems a simple question. I didn't ask for the vintage."

"God, you could probably do that," she acknowledged, laughing. "Roll it around on your tongue and reel off the year and vineyard. 'Grown on the south slope during a very dry summer.' I didn't go to that school. While you were raking in millions in the street trade, I was working my way through college and law school."

"You're a lawyer?" he said, the interest clear in his voice.

"I told you. I'm a cop. I never finished law school."

"Why?"

"Lack of ambition?" she lied, mockingly, remembering her father's death and the endless anger and depression that had sapped her concentration, driving her to more immediate goals.

"So you became a cop. Are you happy being a cop? Are you a good cop, Ms. Phillips?"

He was making fun of her, she supposed, but she wasn't ashamed of what she did, certainly not ashamed in front of this South American gangster.

"When we're successful, I'm happy. When one of you succeeds in escaping justice, I'm not. And I was good enough to put a major hurt on your little operation. That was a very happy moment."

"The money-laundering crackdown? You were *happy* despite the fact that important links in that chain escaped?" he asked, his tone quietly ridiculing her claim. "In spite of the fact that your own friends have paid the price for the ineptness of Hardesty's entire operation? In spite of the fact that you are here as a direct result of its failure? Is that your definition of success?"

She knew he was right—that his sarcasm was probably justified, based on recent events. And that angered her. "I have *very* few regrets about the success of that operation."

"And those include?"

"The fact that you're here is obviously one. The others are none of your business," she answered childishly, thinking of the man who had given them the information. She regretted his death, his suffering, but she believed that, like her colleagues, whose deaths she also regretted, the courier had been willing to sacrifice himself to bring these people down.

He laughed softly at her answer, but he didn't ask again. She sipped her wine and gradually became aware of the music that surrounded them as delicately as his expensive cologne. Classical, she supposed. That was something else an education in the school of hard knocks didn't include.

She thought of her father saying he loved "the classics," and of her eventual discovery that he meant the classics of rock and roll, of the late fifties and the glorious sixties. Those were her classics, too. She wondered if this sophisticated gangster beside her knew Buddy Holly or the Coasters. *Eat your heart out, Bach,* she thought, unconscious that she was smiling again.

"Perhaps it's I who amuse you?" he suggested.

She thought she could detect a slight annoyance in the dark voice and found she couldn't resist goading him.

"You really shouldn't have gone to all this trouble—the wine and the music. I've heard of trying to impress a girl, but *you've* got a captive audience. The James Bond routine really isn't necessary."

His startled laugh was genuine. Her own lips lifted again, in involuntarily response to his ability to accept that she was laughing at *him* for a change. She silently acknowledged the self-confidence that allowed him to recognize her ridicule and be amused rather than angered by it.

"James Bond?" he repeated finally, unbelievingly, and then he laughed again. It was, she was forced to admit, a very pleasant laugh. "I suppose that puts me in my place. A prick to any man's ego."

"No pun intended?" she questioned innocently and was again rewarded by his laughter.

Stop it, her rational mind scolded. *Who do you think this is? Dudley Doright? He kills people for a living, and you're flirting with him like a freshman at her first prom.*

She became aware that he was saying something to her, and she bent her mind to the task at hand, which, in spite of the way she had been reacting, was not repartee.

"So that I hesitate to tell you what's on the menu. I should have sent out for hamburgers, I suppose."

"Chinese," she said unthinkingly. "I'm a sucker for Chinese."

"I'll remember that," he replied softly.

"For my last meal?" she asked, the bitterness not feigned.

"Are you always so pessimistic?"

"No, nor am I stupid. Are you trying to convince me that you're going to let me go?"

"Even if I don't plan to release you, it doesn't necessarily follow that I'm going to need to have a last meal prepared for you." The gentle amusement at her expense was this time not upsetting, considering the topic.

"So you're not going to kill me and you're not going to let me go," she said, allowing her disbelief to show. "What does that leave? Selling me to the white slavers?" She mocked his attempted assurances, assurances she wanted very badly to believe. "Making me your personal—" She stopped suddenly because that idea, given the atmosphere tonight and the remembrance of the black silk teddy, was no longer so far-fetched nor the least bit humorous.

"Go on," he suggested softly, the dark voice flowing over her like warm honey.

She found she could no longer mock the idea of something happening between them. There were too many emotions trapped in those thoughts. She didn't want to die, and she was honest enough to admit that she had to keep reminding herself of who he was and of what he did. It was all so foreign to the man he seemed. There was nothing coarse about him. The sophistication she had tried to ridicule seemed as genuine as his attraction to her. Unconsciously, she had been aware of that attraction from the beginning, from the night she'd awakened to find him sitting in her room, concerned about whether she had a concussion.

She wondered how far she'd be willing to play to that attraction in order to stay alive. She should be disgusted by the very thought of catering to his feelings for her, of using them, but in all honesty, she wasn't. She had even flirted with him, and she began to try to rationalize why. He'd had her brought here, but he hadn't hurt her. Not really. His goon had, of course. The thought was sudden but, in remembering, somehow she was very sure: the angry voice in the conversation after this morning's incident had been his, furious over Diego's treatment of her.

The silence stretched between them. She was glad he couldn't see her eyes, grateful for the first time for the concealment of the blindfold. She knew how dangerous her attraction to him was, but she couldn't make him fit what she knew about the murdering scavengers who ran the cartels.

Her rational mind might issue all the reminders, but when he talked to her in that dark, seductive voice, she wanted to believe what he said. She had wanted to believe him from the beginning, when he'd been so comfortingly amused by her fear of torture. She'd blamed it then on her aching head, on her desire to know more about what had happened the night the courier was betrayed, but she admitted now that those were not the only reasons. Part of it was her fascination with him, with that damnably alluring voice and those caressing fingers, with the fact that he had sat up all night to watch over her because he'd been afraid she might have a concussion. Fascinated against her will with his perfect, beautifully accented English and his scent. With his wine and his choice of music. Nothing he had revealed indicated he was the kind of man she knew he had to be.

Somewhere a door opened, and she listened to heavy footsteps cross the floor toward them. *Diego,* she realized suddenly. *Damn it.* They had been alone and she hadn't even known it. She had assumed his bodyguard had been behind her chair as he had been before. Instead... *Damn it,* she thought again, bitter at the missed opportunity.

"What is it, Diego?" he asked, but she was unable to read the emotion hidden in the velvet voice. Annoyance at the interruption, perhaps? She wondered if she had thought that because it was an emotion fluttering somewhere in the back of her own mind.

There was a softly whispered message, delivered too discreetly for her to make any sense of the hissing sibilants that were all she heard. She waited, wondering about the implications of whatever was happening for her situation. Whatever was going on, he hadn't been expecting it. She had read that clearly enough in his voice when Diego entered the room.

"I'm sorry," he said finally. "It seems that we'll have to postpone our dinner. A rather urgent matter has come up. I hope you'll forgive the change in plans."

"Do I have an option?" she asked, smiling, still listening carefully to his tone, trying to understand whatever was contained in the calm apology. It was so frustrating to have to judge everything that was going on only by his voice. She had never before realized how much she depended on being able to read motivation in someone's face, in his eyes. In her present situation it was vital to know what he was thinking, and she knew nothing at all. Only that something unexpected had happened, and she didn't have a clue what.

"Diego will take you back to your room. He'll bring you a tray while I attend to this. Forgive me, *querida*. I had looked forward to tonight. Perhaps..."

She waited, but he didn't finish. Then she felt Diego's fingers on her arm. She rose and let him guide her again to the elevator, and on the short ride she deliberately forced her mind away from the man downstairs.

After Diego had left her alone at last, having first brought the promised tray and then returned to carry it below, she lay in the darkness, forcing herself to think about escape, about anything she'd learned during her captivity.

The most promising realization was that there must be someone in this vast house besides Diego and his master. Someone had cooked the elegant dinner Diego had brought up tonight and her breakfast this morning. Servants. If she could somehow make contact with whoever ran the place for them ... Why had the one with the silken voice changed his mind about dinner? What urgent business had interrupted his plans for her? In the midst of all those questions and possibilities, she found herself remembering that he had called her *querida* again, and that there had been, quite clearly revealed in the calm politeness of his dismissal, real regret.

Chapter Five

Finally she slept, exhausted by her failure to find a solution and by her despair over her initial stupidity of allowing herself to be taken. She had no idea how long she had been asleep when she was roughly shaken awake by Diego's hand on her shoulder.

"Wake up," he commanded. "He wants to see you."

"Let me go to the bathroom, brush my teeth," she said, stalling, and trying to guess what time it was. There was no light silvering the heavy shade. It must be the middle of the night. If so, why was he waking her up? Whatever his reasons, none of the explanations that flitted like shadows through her mind were pleasant, so she kept on stalling, trying to decide what to do. "Whatever his highness wants can wait five minutes."

Instead, Diego roughly grasped her elbow, gripping hard enough to bruise, and jerked her off the bed. Where he was concerned, the kid gloves had come off, and her building fear threatened to stop her breath.

He roughly tied the blindfold over her eyes, too tightly, and then almost dragged her, still protesting, down the hall to the elevator they had used earlier. Diego was angry, furious as he hadn't been even when she'd attacked him, but he wouldn't answer any of her questions. Because she knew he was only a reflection of his master, she felt fear twisting in her stomach like an animal caught in a trap.

Her captor had only been playing with her earlier, lulling her into a false sense of security, trying to make her believe what she *had* believed—that he was attracted to her and that his attraction offered protection.

She concentrated on stilling the tremor in her hands, but when she stood outside the door as Diego knocked, her knees, exposed below the hem of the long T-shirt she wore as a nightgown, were shaking so hard she wondered if she would be able to stand upright before him, much less defy him.

Diego opened the door and pushed her inside, no longer offering guidance. In her blindness, she stumbled forward, her foot catching on the edge of the Oriental carpet. She fell hard and lay stunned a moment against the roughness of the wool, her knees and the heels of her hands having taken the brunt of the fall.

"Get up," Diego's master said, and from the coldness in the dark voice she knew all her fears had been justified.

She used her hands to push up onto her knees. She knelt there for a moment, trying to find some fragment of self-control before she had to deal with him, but he spoke again, apparently mocking her pain and fear.

"I told you to get up. Do it now. I assure you I am entirely unsympathetic."

She climbed shakily to her feet and hoped that she was at least facing him. Diego pulled her down into a straight chair, and when he began to tie her hands behind her back, she was almost sick with terror. *He had promised,* she thought childishly, clinging to the idea that he was attracted to her. *He wouldn't do this to her. He wouldn't really hurt her.*

When Diego moved away, she could only wait for whatever came next, but what occurred was totally unexpected. Diego's master threaded long, hard fingers through her hair, moving them slowly upward from the back of her neck, caressing her scalp as a lover might after a night of passion, and then gently combing down through the tangles Diego had not given her time to brush out. The hypnotic pull of his fingers was relaxing, and finally she took a deep breath, feeling some of the fear ease. He still found her attractive. He still wanted . . .

The sudden clenching of those caressing fingers in her hair jerked her mind away from that pleasant fantasy.

"You bitch." The dark voice was soft and very close to her ear. "Damn you to hell for the lying, betraying bitch you are."

"I don't know what you—" she began, but his fingers tightened against the hair he held, and she gasped, feeling the pressure at the roots.

She tried to regather her pride, her determination. *He's only pulled your hair,* she thought desperately, willing herself to courage. *He's not pulling out your fingernails.* The image of dungeon and inquisitor standing over his victim was too real.

"Don't," he said, the silk dangerously back. "Don't lie to me or you'll be even sorrier than you are now. Just listen. Franklin Holcomb was with you at headquarters that night, is that right? He was *not* a member of the team who went to the warehouse? He *couldn't* have been because he was with you at headquarters and later in Virginia?"

She nodded carefully against the grip of his fingers. Either she had gotten used to the slight pain, or he had eased his hold. She took a deep breath and slowly released it, waiting for whatever he would ask next.

"I have tonight received confirmation that that information is incorrect. Holcomb was one of the two people Hardesty originally assigned to the warehouse that night, and that team *must* have known the name of the man they were to meet."

Trying to think where this might be heading, she swallowed to ease the tightness of her throat before she answered cautiously, "That can't be true. Besides, Frank's dead, so even if… Whatever information he had, died with him."

"Is he dead?"

"He disappeared. You killed him or someone controlled by you did."

"Then why am I questioning you so anxiously about his whereabouts that night?" he asked sardonically. "Perhaps Holcomb's not dead. You disappeared, and you are, unfortunately, still alive. Still lying and plotting. Why don't you convince me otherwise? Tell me why Holcomb couldn't have been a member of the pickup team."

"He was at headquarters," she began, trying desperately to think what she *could* tell him, what wouldn't endanger other members of the task force. She could feel his tension, clearly conveyed through those long fingers still entwined in her hair. "He came for me. Hardesty sent him to get me."

"Did you see him before that?"

She tried to remember if she had, and if so, what the implication of that information might be, but she *knew* Frank was dead. Paul had told her that. What could it matter what she said about Frank now? She settled for the truth.

"I saw him at the coffeemaker about an hour before he came to get me. We talked about the cold and the possibility of ice on the roads."

"Are you sure of the time and location of that fascinating discussion of the weather?" The soft question came against her ear, close enough that she could feel the warmth of his breath.

"Yes," she said, trying to decide if he were attempting to trick her. "About an hour. No longer than that. Maybe less."

"Then he couldn't have been, to your certain knowledge, at the warehouse?"

"No," she agreed, calculating. "Not given the time frame. We hurried to the house in Virginia. The courier was dying. Dying... very painfully," she whispered, again feeling the cold horror of that dark bedroom, seeing the ghostly light of the screen. "Hardesty wouldn't let the doctor give him anything but locals. Frank couldn't have—"

The reactive tightening against her hair seemed involuntary, an automatic response to what she had said, but the pain it produced was sudden and unexpected, so that against her will she voiced a small wordless whimper of protest.

"You lying bitch," his voice grated beside her ear. "I have his picture. *And* yours. Together that night outside the warehouse where the courier was tortured. You were Holcomb's partner at the house in Virginia. You were his partner at the warehouse. And earlier, it seems, when the two of you made arrangements for the cartel to be there first."

"No," she whispered, shocked he could believe she would have had anything to do with that. She didn't even think about the implications for her safety in what he had said. She only wanted to deny that she could be capable of that betrayal. "God, you can't think that I—"

"Did you enjoy the sounds he made?" he broke into her denial, and the sickness created by his suggestion climbed into her throat.

"Stop it. I wasn't there. I wouldn't—"

"Did you watch?" he continued softly, ignoring her plea.

"No," she said again, his words reviving the nightmares that had haunted her sleep so long ago. "No," she repeated, moving her head in negation and with that involuntary movement, painfully became aware once more of the hard fingers that were still threaded too tightly through her hair.

Perhaps he, too, became aware when she moved that his fingers were locked in the disordered strands. He loosened their hold suddenly, pushing her head away as if no longer able to stand being in contact with her. With his release her chin fell to rest against her heaving chest.

"God," he said softly, "how can you be so beautiful and so ugly, so damned ugly inside, where it matters what a woman is? So treacherous. You deserve whatever happens to you. I should have let—"

"No," she whispered in protest. A protest still as much against his accusation as against the threat. But she had heard that, too. *Whatever happens to you.* Despite his intimidation, she was determined not to beg and not to reveal how frightened she was.

There was a silence, her dread of whatever would come next growing, but she was not left in doubt for long. The heels of his hands were suddenly on either side of her temples, pressing, his fingertips on the top of her scalp. She knew he was sitting slightly to her left, almost directly behind her, from the position of his fingers as he forced her head up. Then Diego turned back the blindfold, and she was held so she could see only directly in front of her.

The grainy black-and-white photograph wavered before her eyes. It had been so greatly enlarged that the quality was awful. She automatically recognized one blur as herself, not from the indistinct features so much as from shape and intuition. She then tried to focus on the figure standing beside her, hidden in the shadows of a dark street lined with equally dark buildings. Warehouses, she knew, only because he'd told her.

It wasn't Franklin Holcomb, she was sure. The body was wrong. Not middle-aged enough. She had liked Frank, she thought irrelevantly, and she knew that the man in this photograph wasn't him.

"That's not Frank—" she began and felt the strong hands tighten against her temples. She closed her eyes against the increased pressure.

"Don't," he said softly, in warning. From the tension in his voice it was obvious that he was at the end of his own rigid control. "Don't lie to me again. Be very careful."

"I didn't lie. That's not Franklin Holcomb," she said carefully, trying to obey the harsh command and to convey her surety at the same time.

"My sources are very certain of the information they provide. *They* have learned I don't like liars."

"It can't be the warehouse. I wasn't there," she began, and then she knew. "Kyle Peters." She blurted the realization aloud, unthinkingly speaking the name as soon as the recognition flashed into her head, because the identification should prove that this couldn't be what he had said. "But this had nothing to do with the operation. That's Kyle and me the night—" She broke the thought. *Dear God, what had she just done?*

The hands eased their pressure, and then the blindfold was again pulled down securely over her eyes. Her head was released, and the quiet voice spoke very close against her ear.

"Thank you, Ms. Phillips," he said. "You've been very helpful."

She had given him a name he hadn't had. She had told him a name, the name of someone who hadn't even been involved that night.

"You bastard. You stinking Colombian slimeball—"

"Shut up," he ordered sharply. "I've heard all the ethnic insults from someone like you I can stomach. At least I don't betray to their enemies people who are trying to give me information. At least I don't arrange for the torture of—"

"I wasn't *at* the warehouse," she interrupted, furious again about what he was accusing her of. "If that *is* the warehouse, then the picture's been chopped, doctored, by someone trying to make you believe I was the one. I don't know who betrayed the courier, but it wasn't *me*." She stopped suddenly, wondering why she was attempting to justify herself to this... She couldn't think of a strong enough name to call him.

"Diego."

She heard his command and the heavy footsteps and then the closing of the door. They were alone, she realized suddenly, but a lot of good that did her with her hands tied behind her back.

"Tell me about your relationship to Kyle Peters," he suggested softly.

Don't talk to him, her mind commanded. *You've already given him a name he didn't have. A friend's name. Information he needed.* She tightened her lips and waited.

"Is he your lover? Does he touch you like this?" He slid callused palms over her upper arms, moving them slowly down to cup her elbows briefly, the tips of his fingers again touching the sensitive skin inside them. "So smooth," he whispered against her hair. "So soft. Like the finest silk under my hands. How can you be so beautiful and so damned treacherous?''

She felt her nipples tighten as his tongue teased around the outer edge of her ear and then slipped inside, his breath warm over the moisture it left. She shivered when his hands moved to span her waist and then lifted to rest briefly over her rib cage, one on each side. She began to breathe more deeply, in long, shuddering breaths.

Feeling that reaction, he allowed his hands to move until they rested in the hollows beneath her high breasts.

''So beautiful,'' he whispered again. ''Do you like his hands on your breasts, my beautiful traitor?''

She shook her head in denial and felt the swing of her hair brush his face. He was so close she was surrounded by the seductive, haunting fragrance of his body.

''Do they respond to him as they are responding now to me?'' he murmured.

She felt his thumbs brush over the hardened nipples that pushed under the thin cotton of her T-shirt, aching for him.

''Do your breasts peak for *him* like this, *querida?* Does he kiss you there?'' he asked, his mouth now caressing her neck. ''This eagerness makes me wonder how you would respond to my touching you in more intimate ways. I wanted you when I believed you are what you pretend to be—a good cop,'' he said mockingly, his tongue gliding over her skin just like the warm, smooth silk of his voice. His thumbs teased again over the pearled nipples. ''Now that I know you're not—that you are, instead, something else, something despicable, as deadly as a black widow—why shouldn't I let myself enjoy touching you, holding this beautiful, betraying body I've dreamed about? You called me filth, *querida*,'' he whispered. She could feel his lips, which were still touching her skin, lift and the small breath of his laughter against her throat at that memory, his amusement at her insults. ''As I touch you, I wonder that I can still feel this hunger for the filth I now know you are.''

''No,'' she denied again, but she waited, hypnotized like a cobra's victim, trembling; and finally his mouth moved through the strands of her hair to find the small hollow where her collarbone met the slim column of her neck. His lips were tender and his tongue moved so knowingly.

She shivered and felt, against all sanity, her body becoming aroused—the rush of moisture, the sweet ache of desire. What was happening to her? All she had been taught about hostage psychology didn't offer an explanation for the fact that she wanted what he was doing. She didn't want him angry, didn't want him to believe she could have betrayed the courier. In her fear and confusion, it was comforting to know that he still desired her. As he'd just confessed, in spite of what he thought she had done, he couldn't keep his hands off her.

When they closed over her breasts and he caught the engorged nipples to roll them between hard fingers, the pleasure of that gentle pressure after his anger and her fear made her moan deep in her throat. She leaned her cheek against his. She could feel the slight masculine roughness of his face, the texture of his hair and the scent of his body around her, so that she only wanted to rest there, safe, she knew, in his arms.

"Do you moan for him, *querida?*" he asked, breaking the spell he had woven. She wanted to cry out when he abruptly removed his hands and allowed his body to shift back, away from any contact with hers.

There was a long pause, and she heard quite clearly the breath he took before he asked again, the deep voice restrained and free of both anger and seduction, "Tell me about your relationship to Kyle Peters."

In control now that he was no longer touching her, as angered by her own inexplicable reaction as she was by his violation, she turned sharply in the direction of his voice and spat very deliberately in what she prayed was his face. She thought she might have been successful, given the harshness of his Spanish expletive.

She could only imagine what his reprisal might be. So far, she had not really been brutalized. Frightened, but not hurt, and she supposed she should be grateful. But now... God,

she was a fool to taunt him. This was not the way to survive. She had known that from the beginning.

"Diego!" he shouted. She was aware there was nothing
but fury in the command. She heard the click of the lock in
immediate response to his call, Diego with his ear against the
door probably, only too glad for a chance to obey his lord-
ship's orders. Especially if they involved manhandling her
again.

"Get her out of here," Diego's master grated, and behind the concealing blindfold, her eyes closed in relief. No
matter what he believed she had done, he wouldn't hurt her.

Diego untied her hands, all the while holding her right
wrist in a grip like a vise. She was waiting for him to pull her
up, for his guidance, and even when he turned her arm, she
didn't understand. It wasn't until she felt the jab of the
needle, its sting as unexpected as stepping barefoot on a
wasp, that she understood.

"Damn you," she said, desperately struggling to pull her
wrist out of Diego's bruising hold. She fought with her left
hand to interfere with what he was doing, but he had turned
so the bulk of his body was between the needle and her use-
lessly flailing fist. She could feel the effects of whatever he'd
injected beginning to soar through her veins. Behind the
blackness of the blindfold, her world began to shift and ro-
tate.

"I don't *know* what you want to know. I don't know
anything about the warehouse. I wasn't there. I didn't have
anything to do with that. Please, don't do this," she begged.

"Damn you, Diego. What the hell are you doing?"

She heard his question from a great distance, drifting into
the mists, and vaguely Diego's answer.

"You want to know what she knows? Ask her now and
she'll tell you. Ask her what happened that night. About the
twenty-five thousand dollars. Ask her, if you *really* want to
know."

She tried to deny the accusation again, but she couldn't
think how to form those words. She wanted him to rescue
her, and she wondered why he was letting Diego do this.

Those were the words that floated to the top of her consciousness. Only those.

"Help me," she whispered, already falling under the power of the drug because, with what Diego had given her, she had no choice.

By the time he was there, she wasn't aware that the arms she had wanted, had begged for, were holding her, or that she was once more surrounded by the sweet, invisible aura of his presence.

WHEN SHE AWOKE, there was no impression of light through the blindfold, and gradually she realized there was no blindfold. But she couldn't find the rectangle of lesser darkness where she knew the windows to be. The room was as black as the inside of a coffin.

Out of that blackness had come the voices. Hardesty's and poor Frank's. Kyle's. The agonized whisper of the dying courier. Diego's. And her captor's silken caress. She had talked to them all, but she couldn't remember what they had asked. Or her answers. Only that she'd done exactly what Diego had promised him she would. She knew with sick certainty that she had told them everything they wanted to know. Everything she knew.

Her throat ached rawly when she tried to swallow. She felt the tears of self-pity start, but she forced them back. Crying wouldn't help. She needed to think—something she hadn't been very successful at up to now. She jerked and cried out when his hand slipped under the back of her head and lifted.

"Be still," he ordered softly. "It's ice."

Amazingly she felt the blessed coldness against her lips. She let it melt down her throat as his hand held her with rock-steady sureness, her aching head resting against its strength.

"More," she whispered, and then, like a polite child, she added, "please."

He allowed her another mouthful, soothing over the drug-induced dryness, before she opened her lips to beg again.

"No," he said, "no more. You've been very sick. I don't want to set off the nausea again."

He carefully laid her head against the pillow, and she felt the weight of his elbows leave the mattress. She knew he was sitting beside her although she couldn't even make out his outline in the darkness.

A sudden fear touched her heart and in her weakness she spoke the thought aloud, "What have you done to my eyes?"

"Nothing's wrong with your eyes," he said quickly, and she was reassured by the genuine horror in his voice. "It's very late. There's no moon, and the shades and draperies are both drawn. There's nothing wrong with your eyes." His voice was calming now, soothing.

"How long have I been out?" she questioned. He was the only fellow human in her world, and she had to communicate her fear to someone, in spite of the fact that he was one of those who had done this to her. He was also a living, breathing creature, and he had given her the blessed ice.

"Too damn long," he replied, and she could hear the concern and anger in his voice. He took a deep breath and whispered, "I'm so sorry, *querida*. So sorry for everything."

"You have to believe me—"

"I know that you weren't at the warehouse. I know it all."

"I didn't...I could *never* have betrayed him. I couldn't do that."

"I know," he said, soothing the renewed agitation that he might not believe her.

"And the money. I don't know anything about money," she continued, trying to convince him of her innocence. No one must ever believe that she would betray a man to what the courier had suffered. He *must* understand that.

"Hush, my heart. I know everything. Close your eyes and rest."

There seemed nothing else she needed to say, and finally, obedient again, she closed her eyes against the pain in her head.

"God, you were so sick," he murmured.

She spoke past the agony, not thinking, simply reacting to the anguish in the beautiful dark voice, "It's all right. I know you didn't mean to hurt me."

She realized she was attempting, ridiculously, to comfort him, but her head hurt too much to formulate why she wasn't supposed to assuage the pain she could hear in his voice. She only knew that she wanted to.

They didn't speak for a long time until finally the dryness of her throat forced her to beg again, "Could I please have some more ice? I don't feel sick anymore, but my throat's so dry."

His fingers held the crushed ice to melt against her lips and onto her tongue.

"My head hurts," she complained softly when the cold had eased her throat.

"What?" he whispered, his thumb caressing the line of her jaw.

"My head," she murmured. She heard the indrawn breath and then his lips were moving against her temple, as tenderly as a dragonfly touching the water.

"Here?" he asked, as his tongue caressed the throb of pain.

"Yes," she breathed into the darkness.

He spoke, his mouth leaving soft kisses across her eyelid now, "I'm so sorry, *querida*. I'll never hurt you again. I swear to you. Never again."

"Let me go. I won't tell anyone. Please, just let me go." She waited for his answer, thinking that in his regret he might weaken enough to release her.

When he slowly sat up, moving away from her body, she knew what his response would be. "I can't. Not yet. There's too much I don't understand. Until I do, I *can't* let you go. It's too dangerous."

She strained, trying to see through the darkness, to steal even the smallest glimpse of his face, but although he was so close to her, she could see nothing.

She supposed that she should be grateful for his promise. She even believed him, but she wanted to go home. Back to her life and away from the pull of this dark stranger who controlled her emotions. She wanted the familiarity of her apartment, her furniture, her clothes. She wanted explanations from Paul Hardesty. She wanted harsh fluorescent office lights and gossip. Greasy coffee and sexist jokes. She'd had enough danger and adventure to last her a millennium.

"Please," she whispered and felt the tears she had denied so long begin. They rolled across her temple where his lips had rested, and she couldn't stop them. She sobbed once into the darkness, then bit her lips to block the sound. His fingers found her closed eyelids, brushing the moisture from her lashes.

At that tenderness, she tried to regain control, but now she had started, she was helpless to prevent the flood of all the pent-up fear. She sobbed again, turning her face against his palm. He caressed her there, as he whispered words of comfort and finally, after a long time, words of love. She cried as he held her face and talked to her above the sobbing. In the days that followed, she would never be sure what she had really heard and how much of that tenderness her drug-fogged brain had created.

Finally the sobs died away to small hiccuping breaths, and he used the corner of the sheet to wipe her face.

"You've made me cry more than I've ever cried in my life," she murmured, drained and exhausted by the release of the tears, embarrassed now.

"Women cry," he said gently, as if that explained and excused. "All women."

"I don't. Austin Phillips's daughter doesn't cry," she said fiercely, wanting the emotional armor she had always worn to be once more in place.

"Your father?"

"He wanted a boy. I was a poor substitute."

"So you became a cop. To please him?" His fingers eased the tear-dampened tendrils from her temples, but the feel of them moving in her hair evoked the scene earlier tonight, so that she turned her head away from their caress.

"Don't. Don't touch my hair."

He removed his hand, and she heard the sigh.

"I'm sorry I hurt you. I don't know what to do."

"Just don't touch my hair. I know that you're trying to help, but please, just don't touch me anymore."

"Go to sleep," he commanded softly.

"I don't think I can. I don't think I can sleep." She wondered if she would ever sleep again. "Talk to me," she begged. *Keep the darkness at bay.*

"About what?" For the first time, amusement drifted back into the richness of his voice.

"About anything. About your family? Your childhood?"

"I don't think I can do that, *querida.* Not even for you."

"Then about your country. Tell me about it. Where you lived. Where you grew up. Your favorite parts." It seemed little enough to ask after all he had done to her.

She was still surprised, however, when he agreed. "All right," he said, "but close your eyes. Relax. I'll stay here until morning. I promise I won't leave you. Close your eyes, my heart."

When she had obeyed him, the beautiful voice whispered out of the darkness and over her senses. She could never remember what he told her, but it had the desired effect. He talked a long time after she no longer had to will her eyelids to stay closed, long after she had ceased to be aware of him at all.

He kept his promise and dawn was breaking when he gently untangled her fingers from his. The fear was finally gone from the tear-stained face, relaxed now in sleep, exposed by the soft light that had begun to creep in around the shade. Then it was too dangerous, so he moved quietly to the door and out of her room.

WHEN DIEGO CAME to find him later, he was touching the photograph he had been given. It lay in the very center of the massive desk, and he was examining it as if his fingertips could tell him the secrets it contained.

"Is she all right?" Diego asked and watched as his master removed the dark, finely shaped hands from the picture.

"I think so. Damn it, Diego, you gave her too much. Why the hell—" He stopped, shaking his head, because they had been through this already. Diego had done what he had done out of loyalty—and love—however misguided his action had been. There was no use remonstrating with him again, especially when he remembered the depth of Diego's remorse, faced with his own fury and her innocence. He said instead, "I hope you're finally satisfied she's not hiding anything."

Diego had no answer for that rhetorically bitter comment.

"Why did he send the picture?" he asked instead.

"I don't know. Maybe he thought we wouldn't have access to the equipment to analyze it, but *she* knew who was in the picture, and he had to know she would," he answered, thinking out loud. "Or maybe he thought we wouldn't stop to question her. Just accept his proof and—" He stopped, wondering again, as he had throughout the night, how he would have lived with himself if, in his anger, he *had* hurt her.

"What do you know about Peters?" Diego asked.

"No more than the others. Not enough. One secret at a time," he said, his patience hard-earned. "Now, however, our friend has given us something to work with. The picture and the money. That was a very serious error in judgment, Diego. Money always leaves traces, no matter how skillfully you try to hide it. That's something I know a lot about," he added, the amusement back in the silken voice. "More than he can imagine."

Diego watched the long fingers move again over the face in the photograph. Finally he said aloud what he had thought about in the hours since the woman, under the effects of the drug he'd given her, had begun to talk, her memories of those long-ago events spilling over them in a flood.

"Now you know that she's obsessed, too," Diego said.

He watched without pleasure the slight smile that lifted only one corner of that hard mouth.

"Obsessed? Perhaps," his master said, the smile deepening slightly. The rich voice, when it eventually continued, was softly reflective, "Obsessed with a dead man. With a man who died one night, a long time ago, somewhere in Virginia."

Diego's eyes rested on the thumb that unerringly found and moved caressingly again across the blurred face of the woman in the photograph, and finally, unable to watch, Diego turned and left him alone.

Chapter Six

When Rae awoke the next day, it was very late. She felt exhausted, despite the hours she'd slept. It had not been a natural sleep, of course, and her head ached again, almost as badly as it had the first morning she'd awakened in this bed.

She still wore the T-shirt she had pulled last night from the jumbled items in her suitcase. She touched the thin, betraying cotton that must have revealed exactly how his touch affected her. She closed her eyes, remembering the texture of his hair, like silk next to her skin, when she had rested her face against his. Dark hair and eyes, she was certain of, but nothing else.

In the middle of those speculations, she realized she was daydreaming about the man who had kidnapped her. What the hell was wrong with her? She forced herself out of bed and under a hot shower.

She scrubbed every inch of her skin as if she could wash away last night. Then she scrubbed again, trying to remove from her body all traces, even the emotional ones, of his hands and lips, but somewhere inside she knew it was an exercise in futility.

She washed her hair and stepped out of the shower to dry off. She studied her face a long time in the mirror, wiping the glass periodically to remove the fog that formed and then re-formed. There were no outward signs of what had happened to her these past two days. It was there, however, in her eyes. She had always met life head-on, sure of her goals and her abilities. Only her father's death had thrown her, and now this.

She turned from the mirror to walk back into the bed-room. She lifted her suitcase onto the bed and dressed quickly in the most practical underwear she owned—no black silk—and then tan slacks and a peach cotton sweater.

She used her makeup to mask the evidence of last night's ordeal and finally surveyed the finished product in the bed-room mirror. At least she gave the appearance of being back to normal, calm and in control, outwardly unaffected by his interference in her life.

She straightened the room, closing the case and hanging the towels in the bath, finally sitting cross-legged on the bed to comb her damp hair. She forced her mind back to the events of last night. Someone had given him her picture to make him believe she was the one who had betrayed the courier, the one who was most likely, therefore, to know his name. Why was the courier's identity so important? Even given the cartel's reputation for swift and brutal retalia-tion, they seemed to be going to a lot of trouble for re-venge.

Logically, whoever had given her captor the photograph must be trying to detract attention from his own guilty knowledge, but whoever had betrayed the courier had al-ready dealt with the cartel. So why not deal with them again? Why try to feed her to this particular wolf? Her use-less conjectures were interrupted by a knock on the door.

"Come in," she called, and as Diego entered and depos-ited the tray he carried on the dresser, she wondered why he'd bothered to knock. He hadn't knocked last night.

"He would like to see you after you've eaten." Diego even managed to make it sound like a request.

"Here?" she asked.

"Downstairs."

"If I refuse?"

"It is your decision whether or not you'll see him."

That's certainly a change from last night, she thought bitterly. *Your decision.* Which implied no one was going to jerk her off the bed and drag her downstairs for more fun and games.

"Doesn't it bother you that I can identify you, Diego, and not him? He's been very careful not to reveal his face and yet he's sacrificed your anonymity happily enough?" The question was more than idle curiosity. Divide and conquer. If she could get Diego to question what he was getting out of this deal . . .

"He has his reasons."

"Whatever he does is fine with you?" she mocked, letting her amusement show, hoping to anger him enough that he would explain his devotion to the man who waited downstairs.

"Yes," he answered calmly. There was only an underlying pride in his voice.

"How long have you known him?" she asked, not really expecting a response. That was certain to be forbidden territory.

"We were children together."

Rae fought the urge to smile at the idea of someone like him and Diego as boyhood companions. Diego's small dark eyes watched the idea give her amusement.

"He was my friend," he said, denying her disbelief. "I was always the outsider, the one the others played tricks on, but he never tricked me. He was my friend. He was quick-silver."

He had slipped into Spanish for the last word, and she was fascinated by that strange description. She watched his eyes relive the past and knew without asking that he would die for the man downstairs. It was a loyalty money couldn't buy and the kind the cartels were built upon.

"Will you come?" Diego asked, reminding her of his invitation.

"Yes," Rae agreed. She had a few things she wanted to say to Diego's master.

She stopped him at the door with her question.

"What does he look like, Diego?"

He turned back to face her after a long pause, but she could read nothing in the look he gave her.

"Like a man," he answered simply. He waited for her mockery but, warned by something in his dark eyes, she didn't speak again.

LESS THAN AN HOUR later Rae was following Diego down the stairs, shivering involuntarily at the memory of last night's journey. He had not blindfolded her, and he made no attempt to do so before he knocked and waited for permission to enter. She found herself anticipating, hoping finally to see Diego's master face-to-face, wanting to know what the man looked like who had created the dark fascination she no longer bothered to deny.

It was not until the deep voice gave permission and they entered the room that she realized that wasn't going to happen. She allowed her eyes a moment to adjust, but even so, she could see nothing of the features of the man who was seated across the darkened room. The lamp resting on the surface of the massive desk he sat behind had been arranged in such a way that its brightness hid his face.

Diego directed her to a chair near the door, as far away from the desk as the dimensions of the room would allow. She took a deep breath, waiting. *His nickel,* she thought. He was the one who asked her to come downstairs, to meet with him. Let him make the first move.

"How do you feel?" The silken tone disturbed the quietness of the dim room.

"Like someone hit me in the back of the head with a shovel," she said, her own voice ringing too sharply, angrily, into the heavy atmosphere.

Again the silence grew between them.

"I'm sorry," he said, finally. "Although it's important that I understand the events of that night, I want you to know that I would never have condoned the use of drugs."

She laughed, its sound brittle, a contrast to the quiet sincerity he had managed to inject into his voice. God, he used that gift like a musician playing a priceless instrument. All the lies sounded better covered by the beauty of his voice.

"Do you honestly expect me to buy that holier-than-thou routine? When it comes to terrorizing people, you don't strike me as a novice. Is this how you get your kicks? You indulge yourself by tying up women and putting your hands on them when they're helpless to prevent it? Or is that the only way you can get close enough to a woman to touch her? Is that the real reason for the blindfold and hiding behind that light? You have to have your women tied up and drugged because you're so—"

"That's enough." At the sharpness of that command she swallowed the rest of the bitterness, turning her head away.

"You have a right to the anger you feel. I've done enough to you to cause it, but the drug was not part of my plan. Diego believed that you were lying and that I..." He paused, sounding uncertain for the first time, and when he spoke again, it was something different. "I thought you might be interested in learning why I brought you here and what happens next. However, if you're not..."

He waited, surely knowing that she would have to respond to that offer.

"Of course, I'm interested in whatever you've got planned for me. I can't tell you how reassuring it is to know that you *have* plans for my future. Could I have that in writing, please?"

She had steeled herself to hate him, to destroy whatever inexplicable attraction she had felt, but when she was with him those resolutions were meaningless. Even if it were the one trump in her hand, she couldn't chance what happened to her when he touched her, when he caressed her either physically or with words. She knew *that* danger was as real as if he decided to kill her. At least then she would die with her integrity intact. She realized he was speaking again, and she blocked the confusion he always caused to focus on his words.

"...the kind of person who would betray her co-workers. I apologize for that assumption, but I had been told you were involved in everything that went on that night. I needed to know exactly what your role was. I still need to know which of you holds the secret of the identity of the man who died that night.''

"So you had Diego drug me in order to find out?" she accused. She wasn't buying that business about it not being part of his plans. Diego didn't make a move unless his string was pulled by this dark puppet master.

''Diego acted on his own.''

"Right," she said, laughing, mocking him. "You don't *really* expect me to believe that, do you?''

This time the silence lasted even longer, as if he were weighing how to answer her, how to make her believe. Apparently he wasn't accustomed to people who openly expressed their disbelief of what he said. When he spoke again, it wasn't to her.

''Diego, I would like you to make the same offer to Ms. Phillips you made to me last night. She is, after all, the one who was injured by your actions.''

Rae didn't understand, not even when the giant took the gun from his shoulder holster. She fought down the small surge of panic, but Diego held the pistol loosely in his hand. He moved until he was standing directly in front of her, between the light that so effectively hid his master and her chair. He knelt on the Oriental rug, her eyes following his movements.

As graceful as a dancing bear, she thought cynically, *and just as well-trained.* It was not until he placed the gun in his mouth, the muzzle against its roof, that she understood what was happening. Sickened, she closed her eyes against the images that filled her mind.

''Yes or no, Ms. Phillips?'' the dark voice asked calmly. ''I assure you, whatever your choice, Diego will obey.'' And Rae believed him. Diego would obey. A willing sacrifice in whatever was going on here. Her choice.

With Diego out of the way, she might have a chance. Of course, since the master was offering her this opportunity, he must be prepared for that eventuality. Still, she knew she should shout yes and increase her chance of escape, however small that chance might be.

"*He was my friend,*" echoed instead. She remembered the memories in the black eyes of the man who was now kneeling before her and those in his voice. "*I was always the outsider. The one the others played tricks on, but he never tricked me. He was my friend.*"

Diego might not be very bright, but he understood loyalty. And it was possible it had happened as he'd said, Diego taking the initiative with no direction this time from his master.

You want to believe that, her mind mocked, *because you don't want to think he's capable of ordering what happened last night.* Her heart argued against that logic, *Then why did he sit with me, hold me while I was sick?* She was suddenly sure of that memory, surfacing out of the dark mists. Hard arms holding her. Strong, yet incredibly gentle hands helping her through the maelstrom of nausea caused by the effects of the drug.

"Ms. Phillips?" he asked again.

"No," she whispered past the sickness in her throat, knowing she was a fool.

"Diego," he said softly, releasing the man on the floor. Eyes lowered, Rae didn't watch the giant rise to his feet to take his accustomed place behind her chair.

"I would like your promise that you will remain in that chair until Diego comes back for you," said the voice that had whispered endearments to her last night. After the same voice had damned her soul to hell as a lying bitch. In spite of it all, she had to force her rebellious mind to remember who he was and what he had done.

"If I refuse?"

"Then Diego will take you back upstairs."

"And if I agree?"

"Then Diego will wait outside the door while we talk."

"In private?"

"Yes."

"So you can put your hands on my breasts again? So you can make love to someone who can't resist you?"

"I didn't bring you here for that. I swear I won't touch you. You have my word."

"Why should I believe you? You're such a trusting individual yourself. You drug me to make me betray my associates so you can kill them, and then you—" She cut off the description of what had happened last night. There was no use saying it again. "You go to hell," she suggested instead. "I won't make deals with you. Diego can leave or stay. I don't care. Aren't you afraid I'll overpower you? You might need Diego to protect yourself, remember? *Mucho hombre,*" she mocked him.

Again the silence echoed. A heartbeat. Then two.

"Yes," he agreed softly, and she wasn't sure if that was supposed to be an equally mocking answer to her question or an expression of his supreme self-confidence, his smug agreement with her last phrase. Before she could decide, he continued, as calmly as before. "Then Diego will take you back upstairs. You have my assurance you won't be hurt again during your stay. Thank you for seeing me."

Rae felt Diego's hand on her arm, but she didn't respond. Her lips betrayed her, giving him the promise he had asked for. "I won't move from the chair until Diego comes back. You have my word."

Diego released her arm, and she sensed the silent communication between the two. As always, the master's stronger will won, and the door finally clicked closed behind Diego.

She might as well take advantage of the situation. It was possible that he did feel a degree of regret for last night. If so, he might tell her something she could use.

"You promised you'd tell me what your plans for me are. Can I assume they don't involve my immediate release?"

"Yes."

"I thought so. How long do you plan to keep me here?"

"Until I know who dealt with the cartel. After that, I see no reason to hold you any longer."

"I don't understand. You must *know* who..." she began, and then stopped. This had troubled her from the beginning. He *was* the cartel. How could he not know who had betrayed the courier? When he spoke, it wasn't an answer to her question. It seemed to have nothing to do with the conversation they were having, but she listened anyway. She told herself that this was why she'd stayed downstairs, why she had given her promise—in hopes that he would give her something that would let her understand what was going on.

"After Pablo Escobar was killed, it was discovered that there was a billion and a half dollars unaccounted for, a billion and a half of his personal fortune that had simply vanished. Everyone knew the money should be there, but it wasn't, and no one could find it."

He paused, but she only waited. She had heard rumors about Escobar's lost treasure before, but she'd discounted them as fantasy.

"That money had been invested, almost certainly abroad, to take it out of the reach of the government, should Escobar be taken. It has never been located."

"I don't understand what all this has to do with—"

"I asked you before. Did you never wonder how the courier got the information he gave you that night?"

The realization of what he must mean was as abhorrent as the image of Diego with the gun against the roof of his mouth.

"His accountant?" she asked. "Is that what you're trying to suggest? That the courier was Escobar's accountant?"

There was the small but distinct hint of laughter, quickly suppressed, but that amusement was reflected in the dark voice when he spoke again. "Not exactly—" Whatever he had intended to tell her was deliberately broken off, followed by a long pause, and then he continued smoothly, "Not exactly, Ms. Phillips, the term I would have chosen. But I suppose," he finished softly, "that your assessment is accurate enough for our purposes."

"I don't believe you," she said.

Her mind went back to that night and the dying man—a man he was suggesting was a part of the evil that was Medellin, a very vital part.

"He wasn't..." she began, realizing belatedly that there was no argument she could make against his claim. She had spent only a few hours with the courier. She had no way of *proving* that the man she had listened to that night wasn't involved in the cartel. His courage and endurance, his willingness to die in the fight against the drug lords, his concern for her in the midst of his own agony—all had made too great an impression. Despite her captor's assertion, her conviction was just as strong now as then that the courier wasn't that kind of man.

"I don't believe you," she said simply. There was nothing else she *could* say.

"All right, *querida*," he suggested softly, amused again. "Offer another explanation. Why is everyone so interested in the courier? Why have so many people died? Think."

And as she did, she knew his explanation made it all fit. The courier had made his agreement with Paul to provide the money-laundering information in exchange for protection, for a promise to make him disappear. Once he was out of the reach of the cartel, and Paul had everyone believing he was dead, he would quietly start reeling in the money he'd hidden for Escobar. God, it all fit. It all *fit*. He had known Escobar was going down, and he'd timed it just right. He made the offer to Paul and got out before the takedown in Colombia. It even explained why the courier's name was so important to this man. He wasn't interested in revenge. He wanted something far more tangible—the billion and a half dollars, the location of Escobar's lost fortune that the courier could give him.

"He wasn't that kind of man," she said softly, remembering, still fighting the suggestion that the man in Virginia had not been what she had thought him to be.

"You're so certain of the character of a man whose name you never learned? A man you spent, at most, a few hours with, under circumstances..." The dark voice hesitated.

"He wasn't the kind of man who would work for the cartels. In any capacity. I know that. You're wrong," she said, the memory of that man and that night too important to her to allow him to destroy it. "And he's dead," she added, still denying her own scenario. "He died that night. Paul told me—"

"With a billion and a half dollars riding on it, would *you* be willing to take Paul Hardesty's word?" he interrupted quietly.

She suddenly remembered her own conviction that Paul hadn't been telling the truth about the courier's death. Something in what he'd told her that day had rung false. She had thought, then, that the lie involved the manner of death, but what if... What if Paul had instead been lying about the whole thing?

She closed her eyes against the bitterness of her growing disillusionment. "Why did he still give us the money-laundering information? We'd failed him, betrayed him. Why would he endure that agony to give us those names?"

She waited, but he didn't answer, and it didn't matter. She could guess. "Because *we* offered him the best shot at surviving, at getting out. If he kept his deal with us, Paul would get him away. Into witness protection or out of the country. When he recovered, he could start collecting the overseas investments Paul didn't know about, and no one would be the wiser. Everyone would think he was dead."

Finally it all made sense. Except his role. The role of the man with the beautiful voice.

"Were you the one sent to torture him?" she questioned. "Were you the one who failed?"

"I had nothing to do with torturing him. You have my word on that."

"The word of a drug lord? You must think I'm a fool."

"I had nothing to do with what happened to the courier," he repeated calmly and convincingly.

He really was very good, she thought again. *No wonder they had entrusted this mission to him.* She shook her head slightly, and, although he was hidden from her eyes by the carefully placed light, it was evident he could see her quite clearly.

"I represent other interests," he said.

Of course, she realized suddenly, *not only Escobar's people would be interested in recovering that money. Not given the amount.*

"But why kidnap me?"

"You were the closest to him. You had the most contact with him. You might have known something that you didn't even realize you knew. My... task was to find out what, if anything, you knew."

She filed away the memory of that small pause, to be examined later.

"And thanks to Diego's injection, you found out I know nothing. Why you?" she asked, really wondering.

"I am the one best equipped."

"Why?"

His hesitation was again brief, but she knew it also was significant. Her father had taught her that.

"Because I hold a position somewhat analogous to that held by the courier," he said finally.

"'Somewhat analogous'?" she repeated, questioning. *Who the hell used a phrase like "somewhat analogous" in everyday conversation?*

"I would be able to recognize the importance of any information concerning the investments and to pursue it. I would know what to look for."

"An accountant," she said.

She could again sense his amusement from his quiet agreement.

"If you will."

"For the other guys. The uptown boys. The cartel with all the class and polish," she said. "Yeah, you fit better with that crowd. I was having a little trouble picturing *you* playing footsie with Escobar. Those people had no manners. No charm."

"Those slimy Colombians?" he asked sardonically. He didn't bother to mask the bitterness in his tone. He waited for her reply, but when she said nothing, he moved on instead to what he had promised—information about her immediate future.

"You may have a radio, and Diego will bring you books from the library here. It's extensive and well cataloged. If you have preferences, write them down, and I'll find them before I leave."

"You're leaving? Leaving me here with Diego?"

"You're perfectly safe with Diego. I swear to you. As long as you don't attempt to overpower him. You're not *really* afraid of Diego, are you?"

She considered briefly and knew that, as he had suggested, she really wasn't. "No, I'm not afraid of Diego. How long will you be gone?"

"Does that matter to you?" The teasing note that had been absent this morning was back, and she admitted to herself that she had wanted it there. "Will you miss me, *querida?*"

"Like a toothache," she mocked.

"A toothache?" he echoed, his laughter as pleasant as she'd remembered. "You are definitely not good for my self-esteem. I'll be gone three days. Behave yourself and I'll bring you something."

"Someone's head in a sack? Or is that the Mafia? No, that was a horse. Gosh, I'm getting my movies all mixed up. You people aren't nearly that subtle."

"'You people'?" he repeated, and the teasing quality was gone, replaced again by soft bitterness. "I'm sorry to disappoint you, but I don't carry heads in sacks—horses or otherwise. I'll see you when I get back. It would be nice if you could work through some of that prejudice before then. I'd be eternally grateful not to have to listen to the character assassination of my countrymen."

"It's *your* character I'm assassinating, and I don't think prejudice plays a role here. I have firsthand experience with *your* charm and style. I just find I prefer someone a little less physically threatening."

"Someone like Kyle Peters."

It made her sick to remember that she had given him that name, so she tried to downplay any significance he could attach to Kyle's role in all this. "God," she accused, laughing, "you sound like you're jealous. You should hear yourself."

"You can do better than Peters."

"Well, I don't know about that, but I can certainly do better than you."

"I don't think I issued any invitations, *querida.*"

"I know. I'm just not your type. Too skinny and headstrong. You'd probably like 'em weak and willing. Barefoot and pregnant. Luckily I don't qualify. Have a safe trip. Diego and I will get on like a house afire, I'm sure. I'll even work on not thinking too harshly of you and your countrymen. I'll block all I know about 'you people' from my mind. *You've* been so charming. Enough to turn a girl's head from all those misconceptions. I can't imagine where people get the idea that you're brutal and dishonest."

"There are many decent and hardworking people in my country. They have all been tarred with the same brush of suspicion and hostility that you are now using. Not all Colombians are dealing drugs."

"Well, forgive me, but all the ones *I've* ever come into contact with are. Are you suggesting that my line of work is at fault in producing the misconceptions I have about you?"

"I don't really give a damn what you think about me. I simply feel that you have judged the citizens of an entire country by the actions of a few individuals."

"It comes with the territory. Either you're on the map with a less-than-noble reputation or nobody knows your name. Nobody asks you to the dance."

"Then perhaps I'd prefer being unknown."

"I think you can safely assume that while you may personally remain unknown, your country is another matter. Your actions certainly aren't helping her reputation, so forgive me if I don't buy this sanctimonious garbage about my prejudices."

"I have a feeling that this is an argument we won't resolve today. Could we perhaps talk about other topics until I have to leave?"

"Of course. The books and radio will be wonderful. Thank you for your consideration of my comfort," she said with only a trace of sarcasm.

"Why is it that I distrust all this gratitude and politeness?" he asked, laughing. "Where's the hellion who so literally and effectively expresses her displeasure? Are you mellowing, *querida?*"

"No, but you're being reasonably accommodating, and I do appreciate it. And you haven't done me in yet. I'm suitably grateful for that, too."

"And I haven't touched you."

The memory of his hands on her body intruded between them, and she wondered what he could read in her face. She realized that in spite of his promise, she had been waiting for him to initiate some sort of repeat of last night, and his power over her physical responses frightened her.

"I did think..." he began, and then allowed the pause to lengthen.

"What?" she challenged, daring him to put it into words so she could deny it.

"I have thought that, in spite of what you said, my touch was not repulsive to you. There are signals a woman's body makes, quite independently of her will. I felt the response in your body, *querida*. Your mouth denies that you enjoyed my caresses, but your breasts and your skin told me something very different."

She wondered if she should bother to lie, but she knew that he spoke only the truth and that he was certainly sophisticated enough to read her body's reaction.

"You're a very experienced man. My body responded to that experience."

"Does that mean that you are experienced, too? How many men have touched you as I did? For how many of them have your breasts lifted and your skin flushed under their lips? Do you like making love or does your body lie about how much it wants to be loved?"

"I can't help what my body feels when you—" she hesitated, unwilling to put those intimacies into words "—do things like that."

"The body is not separate from the mind, Rae, and that's what frightens you. You don't understand what's between us. Your mind can't accept what your body feels, and yet, somehow, you can't make your body reject what it wants. You are in a very difficult position."

Damn straight, she thought, bitter at how well he read exactly what she felt. Her voice, when she answered, however, expressed none of that agreement. "Which you have taken advantage of at every opportunity."

"I've kissed you." His pause was as brief as hers had been. "And I've touched you. You're a very beautiful woman. I don't deny my attraction, but I have not tested the boundaries of that attraction. And I won't, Rae, until you want me to. What is between us goes no further unless *you* decide you want it to. You have my word. I don't make love to unwilling women."

"If you're waiting for permission, don't hold your breath."

"I see," he said softly, but the amusement was definitely back. "While I'm gone, think about how pleasantly we could spend the remaining days—and nights—you'll stay here." Subtly his tone changed again, the sincerity she'd mocked before once more apparent. "I want you, Rae. And you should have no doubt about how much." He paused again, waiting, but suddenly breathless, Rae could manage no response to that confession, and finally he continued, "I'll be back in three days. Try to miss me at least a little. My ego is suffering from all this rejection."

She laughed at the wistfulness he'd managed to inject into his voice. "Somehow I think your ego will manage to survive. Besides, you already have Diego as your willing slave. Why would you want me, too?"

"Try not to take advantage of Diego while I'm gone. You could probably outwit him easily enough, but he would be very upset about any failure in his mission. And his ego is not nearly so secure as mine."

"A nicely veiled threat. If I *do* decide to deceive poor Diego...?"

"Then you will both bear the brunt of my anger. And Diego doesn't deal well with my displeasure."

"I wonder how you inspired such loyalty."

"Diego is my friend. Just remember that."

"I'll remember."

He waited a long time before he asked, "I don't suppose you would like to send me off with a goodbye kiss?"

"Are you serious?" she mocked. "My God, you are. Do you really think that I'm going to let you kiss me after last night?"

"I had *hoped* I was forgiven for last night."

"In your dreams. I don't care if you go, and I sure don't give a damn if you never come back. I don't give kisses to men who tie me up and drug me."

"Definitely *not* forgiven," he acknowledged. And then the voice deepened again, caressing. "I'll miss you, *querida*. I'll think about you every night when I lie down to sleep. I'll think about what you're doing, and I'll know that you're thinking about me."

And now that he had planted the seed, she would.

"Has anyone told you that you don't play fair?" she responded, laughing at his attempt at psychological seduction.

"Certainly not with all the cards stacked against me. Try to be a good little girl while I'm gone. I promise I'll dream about you."

She shook her head, choosing not to answer the velvet stroke of his voice, and finally he called Diego. She bit her lips to keep them closed when the giant reappeared, determined that no word of farewell would reward his master's confession.

"At least tell me goodbye, *querida*," he urged her softly, once more almost as if he could read her mind. "You might not see me again. And in spite of what you've said, I think you would regret that. It's not so much to ask."

She stood at the door, commanding herself not to speak, but she knew that, like Diego, her will was no match for the force of his.

"Goodbye," she whispered finally. She didn't wait for Diego. She turned the handle herself and left, climbing to the room at the top of the stairs and closing its door behind her. Seconds later she listened to Diego engage the lock.

You might not see me again.... I think you would regret that. His words echoed in her mind. She wondered if whatever he was about to undertake was as dangerous as that sounded. Or was he simply using her emotions to get his own way, to make her admit that she was attracted to him? Because there was no longer any doubt that he knew exactly how he affected her.

I'll know that you are thinking about me. And she would be, damn him. She, too, knew that she would.

She lay down across the bed and pillowed her face on her forearms. She didn't raise her head when, much later, Diego brought her lunch. It was only as he was leaving, unable to resist, that she asked.

"Is he gone?"

"Just after you came upstairs."

"Is it dangerous? Whatever he's going to do?"

Diego was quiet so long that she turned over to watch him reach the decision to answer her.

"Everything he does, everything he's ever done, is dangerous. It's an addiction, a drug, to him. A costly one," he said. "It's cost him more than you can imagine."

He closed the door and again she listened to the lock engage. She turned her face back to her arms and closed her eyes to erase the fears Diego had confirmed. When he brought the promised radio and a selection of books with her dinner, not even the possibility of contact with the events of the outside world could break her concentration on willing his safe return.

Only when she finally slept did she release those fears and replace them with the images of assuaging the desires he had suggested she felt for him. Desires she had refused to admit. In her sleep, however, she was powerless to deny what she had known from the beginning. She didn't understand it, but the attraction had been there from the first, as if what she felt were predestined.

She had never believed in reincarnation or love lasting beyond the grave, but she had known from the first time he'd touched her that she wanted him. As if his soul and hers had been joined at some time in the past. As if their destinies had been entangled by the old gods who were laughing at her resistance to what they had ordained. No matter who or what he was, she was tired of fighting what he made her feel. She had never felt this way about any man in her entire life. She wanted his touch, his lips and his strong, sure fingers against her face and body as they had been last night.

As she tossed in restless sleep, dreaming of what he had offered her, she felt the pull of his darkness replacing all the light that had guided her since childhood. And then finally, at least in her dreams, she ceased to fight against that force.

Chapter Seven

The days passed slowly. Rae had found an oldies station that really understood the term, and the music that now filled the room eased the tension of enforced waiting while her mind ran in endless circles around the problem.

Had the courier been what her captor had implied—a suggestion that went against every intuition she had felt about the man? Who had killed the others in the task force and had tried to set her up as the next victim? She composed ten different scenarios to explain the events, but there were too many pieces missing and, locked up in this room, she had no way to solve the rest of the puzzle.

She tried to talk to Diego when he brought her meals, but he gave her as little information as she expected. He was meticulous as far as security was concerned. His routine never varied, and it was safe and practical. He never removed his eyes from her when he was in the room, staying only long enough to leave the tray or the books on the chest near the door.

"Did the cook die?" she asked on the second day of hard-boiled eggs for breakfast and sandwiches for lunch and dinner. "Or maybe her job description includes more than cooking. Maybe she accompanied your boss to provide his fringe benefits," she suggested. *Jealous?* her mind jeered.

"There is no cook," Diego said firmly against her mockery, closing the door sharply.

"Well, at least not anymore," she agreed, touching the unappetizing object on her plate.

She read to occupy her mind, and to forget—both her situation and what Diego had told her about his master's mission. She could not, however, control her dreams, and it was there he tightened his hold on her emotions. In spite of all her best intentions, the long nights became erotic fantasies with a never-changing cast of two. They were so real that she often awoke shivering from the phantom touch of his lips. Then she buried her head under the pillow and thought of her family, her job, anything but him.

On the morning of the fourth day she spent a long time in the claw-footed tub. She had listened for his return the night before and had finally drifted off to sleep without hearing the sounds that she thought would signal his arrival. She dressed in a black sundress that exposed a lot of shoulder and back. She put up her hair, pulling down tendrils that curled in the humidity around her face. She even added makeup.

"Diego will be impressed," she told the mirror image, mocking the care she was taking with her appearance, but the woman in the glass was reassuringly familiar and, in spite of the fact that she felt like no more than a pawn in this game, she somehow still managed to *look* in control of her own destiny.

By the time Diego came with her lunch, she put aside her pretense of indifference. "Is he back?"

"No."

"But it's the fourth day. Surely he—"

"It's possible he was delayed."

"Are you worried?" she asked, wanting his reassurance.

"There's no reason for concern. He'll come back when he's finished," he said stoically as he left her sandwich.

The day passed more slowly than the others. She waited in her room until dinner and knew by Diego's face, knew without asking, that he hadn't returned.

"Maybe tonight," Diego said as he placed the tray on the dresser. "Don't worry," he reassured before he closed the door, revealing exactly how transparent she was.

Rae rejected a delicate lace gown and determinedly put on another of her long T-shirts and lay listening through the dark hours. She never knew when she finally fell asleep. She awoke once to watch the numerals on the digital clock of the radio change until she drifted back into sleep and into the dreams of him that were now always part of her nights.

"YOU'RE EXHAUSTED," Diego accused. The reactive bitterness was briefly apparent in his master's face, and then deliberately replaced by amusement.

"But I know how it was done, Diego. All of it. Money never lies."

"You traced the money in her account?"

"Back to a man named Grajales. What do you know about him?"

"A name," Diego said, shrugging. "Do you want me to try to find out about him?"

"He had nothing to do with the bogus account created for Rae Phillips. The channel for that money is what we're interested in. At least for now, Diego."

"I don't understand."

"Only one man was given information about the courier. One phone call. We've always known that."

"And?"

"The call was clean. The best equipment in the world. No one listened in. There was no problem with the phone."

"Then it comes back to that man."

"So it would seem. But in tracing the money that was deposited into Rae Phillips's account and considering the people who might be involved, I found the record of a highly interesting transaction. And we set the trap." He paused, remembering. He stretched, trying to relieve the aching stiffness of his long day.

"Why don't you go to bed?" Diego suggested. "You can tell me the rest in the morning."

"I'm all right." His master denied Diego's concern. "Did you have any problems here?" he asked simply, but Diego knew him well enough to know what he really wanted.

"She was worried."

"About what? What happened?"

"You told her three days and when you didn't return..." Diego shrugged again.

"Worried," he repeated, shaking his head in disbelief. "My God," he said softly. "Are you sure that's—"

"I'm sure. Why don't you tell her you're back," Diego suggested. "Then you both can sleep."

The soft laugh was also bitter. "I don't think that's a good idea."

"It's what you want to do. To see her. To be with her. For once, think about what you want."

"Why?" he asked. "Why think about something that's not an option?"

"It's an option tonight," Diego reminded him and watched desire battle that iron will.

RAE FELT HIM take her fingers and bring them to his lips. She thought she could even feel their warm texture as he lightly touched the delicate skin on the backs of her hands, and his kiss seemed again too real, too tormenting. She whimpered, trying to escape the web of the dream, and heard him speak into its darkness.

"Diego said you were worried. I'd like to think that was true," he whispered as he turned her hands to kiss the palms.

She responded as she always did in her dreams, raising her body from the cold, lonely tangle of sheets to rest against the hard strength of his. Her fingers found the silk of his hair and felt it curl around them as she caressed the back of his head. Only then did she accept the reality of the body she held, the body of the man who was sitting now on the edge of her bed.

Finally he allowed himself to respond, his arms closing tightly around her slenderness. He crushed her against his chest, against firm muscle and bone, and buried his face in the fragrant, disordered softness of her hair. He lowered his head to touch his lips gently against the hollow of her collarbone, and involuntarily she shivered.

"I'm beginning to believe Diego may have been correct. It's all right, *querida*. I have you."

His lips traced the thin bones of her shoulder and then moved over the line of her throat. Their touch was as light as it had been before on her temple, over her closed eyelids, but she felt his heartbeat accelerate. Her head fell back as he caressed with his tongue the sensitive skin under her jaw. After an eternity, he sought her mouth and possessed it with the sureness she had recognized from the beginning of his bizarre courtship of her.

Rae knew she couldn't match his experience, but felt the strength of her desire should make up for any lack of knowledge. For the first time she held nothing back. She met his heat with her own, and when he released her mouth, her lips clung to his until he held her away from him.

"Like a toothache?" he teased gently, and lowered his mouth again to hers to give her what she wanted. She no longer bothered to deny her need, even to herself.

"I was so afraid."

"Shh. There's no reason to be afraid." He seemed surprised by her confession. He gathered her again against his body. "I'll keep you safe, my heart. I swear it on my brother's grave. No one will hurt you."

She smiled against the stubbled, late-day roughness of his cheek and let him feel the quick shake of her head. "I'm not afraid for me. Diego said everything you do is dangerous. You told me three days. And then, when you didn't come..."

"Someone I needed to see couldn't arrange a meeting until today."

"Someone in the task force?" she said and felt his body react to that question. He moved away from her, but his hands found her shoulders and held her lightly there.

"Do you want to share information with me, *querida?* Do you want to tell me about your friends?"

"You know I can't do that. I would never—"

"Then don't ask me to tell you what I've been doing." He paused and she heard in the darkness the depth of the breath he took. "We find ourselves in what is not a unique situation. We are two people in bed together who have nothing to talk about."

She smiled at the familiar teasing mockery.

"So perhaps we should concentrate on something besides conversation," he finished. And waited.

"Answer two questions," she said finally—and knew by the quality of his stillness that he was considering her offer.

"How do you know I won't lie to you? That I won't simply tell you whatever I believe you want to hear?"

"I don't know how I know. But don't. Whatever it is, tell me the truth at least about these two things."

"You're as trusting as a child. Everyone lies," he said, the dark laughter very soft.

"I won't lie to *you,*" she argued and could only hope that he knew that.

"*Querida,*" he whispered, his tone one that might be used to answer an ingenuous child, but she interrupted whatever he intended to say to ask the first of her questions.

"Did you have anything to do with the courier's betrayal and death?" she asked, her throat crowded with fear and hope.

"No," he said immediately and then added with conviction she could hear. "That I swear to you."

She believed him and breathed again.

"And the deaths? In the task force? Did you order them? Did you have any part in those?"

"No," he answered as quickly as before, and with as much authority.

"Was the courier really what you said? Was he Escobar's accountant?"

He was silent for a long time and, because of that hesitation, she wondered if she would be as certain about whatever he might tell her now as she had been about the other.

"That's the *third* question, *querida*," he said finally. "Our arrangement was for only two, and I've told you the truth about those. The rest we don't talk about unless you're willing to exchange information. There is no more for free. You have had your answers, and now you must decide what we are to do since the limits of our conversation have been reached."

She took a deep breath and put away the convictions of a lifetime. He had answered her greatest fears. And she believed him. Maybe because she wanted to. But she did, and the rest she would live with. Her decision. He had told her that before, and once more she had believed him.

"Take off your coat," she whispered, her trembling fingers beginning to loosen his tie. "You're definitely overdressed for the occasion."

"I didn't know it was going to be *that* kind of occasion," he said, rich amusement touching the caressing whisper, but he obeyed, and she knew by his movements when he had discarded both the coat and tie. Her fingers found the buttons of his shirt and she unfastened enough of them to allow her hands to slip inside the opening. She slid them over the warmth of his chest, spreading her fingers against the hair-roughened skin. She touched his nipples and felt them harden as hers had done under his hands.

He jerked his shirt out of his trousers and, unfastening the cuffs, dropped it to join the coat and tie. His chest was finally completely exposed to her searching hands.

She allowed them to trace upward, skimming across the width of broad shoulders, and then her palms smoothed down the hard, contoured muscles of his upper arms. She could feel his breathing deepen, but he let her explore, enjoying her touch, she thought, her obvious desire to know his body.

"And now I think you're the one who's overdressed," he said softly as he found the hem of her cotton T-shirt bunched over her thighs. He slid the material higher, letting the cool of the air conditioner kiss her skin as he gradually exposed her body.

It was too dark for either to see even the outline of the other, and the necessity of exploring only by touch was more erotic than any visual assessment would have been. His hands stopped their upward journey to cup the fabric under her breasts, and then he lowered his head to kiss the hollow between the still-covered globes. His lips explored that valley, feeling her heart beneath his mouth like a frightened animal's.

"If I take this off, *querida,* there's no turning back. I won't be able to let you go. Not now. Are you sure, my heart?"

"Yes," she whispered, unable to think of anything but how much she wanted him.

"In spite of everything?" he asked, his lips moving over her breast to circle and tease. She could feel the heat of his breath tantalizing the nipple through the thin material. She wanted his mouth against her skin. Over her. Wanted the sweet pressure, wet and so hot.

"I've fought this from the beginning," she answered, her voice husky with need. "I'm not strong enough to fight you anymore. I don't even *want* to."

He reluctantly withdrew his mouth from her breast, the cotton clinging briefly to the moisture on his lips. Slowly he sat back, away from her body, allowing the nightshirt to fall down again against her thighs. He took her hand and pressed a kiss into the palm before he spoke.

"Then perhaps I must do it for you. I want you, Rae. I want so much to make love to you, but to me making love is a pleasant diversion, a spice to what is already a dangerous game. I don't deal in forever-after. There are no promises in what I offer you tonight. I want your body. You must guard your soul. I am still who I am, and you are who you are. There is no magic to change that.

"Don't," she whispered, denying, trying to forget all that lay between them.

"I won't fit into your images of sweethearts and boy-friends. I'll walk away from you tomorrow, and you will be only a pleasant memory. One of many such memories. Can you say that to me? I don't want to take advantage of you, *querida*. Your situation makes you too vulnerable. I'm someone who controls your fate, and perhaps you're offering me the only thing you think you have that might guarantee your survival. I don't want you that way, Rae—as some kind of sacrifice of who you are."

"That's not why," she began, denying his interpretation of her motives, willing him to understand. What was between them here had nothing to do with the other. "I want you. I *want* you to make love to me."

"And I want you. Make no mistake about how much I desire you. But not like that. Not because you're my prisoner. Not coerced by your fears," he said forcefully. When he spoke again she could hear but didn't understand the emotion that colored the voice she loved. "And not as a result of some fantasy of happily-ever-after you've created to give yourself permission to be loved. Only if you're willing to take tonight and be satisfied if we never see each other again. Only as a willing partner in a passionate, if fleeting, relationship. Only if you will have no regrets in letting me love you—only for tonight."

Only tonight whispered somewhere in the darkness. He released her hand and waited a long time for her response. She heard his soft mocking laugh and then he commanded gently, "Go to sleep, *querida*. Perhaps that's better for us both."

"Stay with me," she begged. "Tonight. Even if that's all we ever have," she said, destroying her own pride, and uncaring that she exposed her feelings to him. "Stay with me. Hold me. *Prove* to me that you don't care anything about me, that you can walk away as easily as you say."

"Games, *querida*? I don't play games. If I stay with you, I'll make love to you. Under my conditions. And if I decide it's best, I'll walk away from you in the morning and never see you again. That's all I can offer you. Is that what you want?''

"This is driving me crazy. I don't know why I care about you, but I do. And it's not just... I know you'll think this is insane, but it's like I know you. Like I've known you all my life. As if I recognized that you were...someone I cared about. From the first night you touched me. It should have been wrong that your hands were on my body, but it was *right*. I felt that. I wanted them there. I *knew* you.'' She could hear the desperation in her voice, the plea for his understanding of something that, even to her, made no sense.

"You don't know me. Not even now,'' he said quietly.

"Don't go,'' she begged. "Stay with me. Under your conditions. Under any conditions. Just don't go.''

She waited in the darkness and then she felt him turn away. He sat on the edge of the bed a long time without moving. Finally she reached out and somehow, in the blackness of the night that surrounded them, found his hand. She brought it to her lips and kissed the palm as he had done with hers.

"Just for tonight,'' she whispered.

"Only tonight,'' he repeated. It was a demand, and so she nodded against his hand she still held to her cheek.

"Move over,'' he commanded harshly, and as she scrambled to the other side of the bed, she felt him reach down to remove his shoes. Finally he lay down. Tentatively she moved back until she was on her knees beside him.

"I told you that you're overdressed,'' he said, all the doubt that had been in his voice erased. His hands trailed over her thighs, catching the soft cotton and pulling it slowly up her body. There was nothing hurried about his movements. Slow and sensuous, using the glide of the material as a contrast to the roughness of his palms that occasionally brushed her skin. When she was naked, he pulled her down to lie against his body. She felt the hair on his chest against her breasts, the steel of muscle under her softness.

His lips nudged the tangled strands that covered her shoulder to lie, out of his way, against her neck and then returned to stroke like velvet over the rounded bones and soft curves. He pushed her suddenly onto her back and raised his body over hers so that his lips could trace over the surface of one breast, brushing the nipple that rose of its own accord to deepen the contact. His tongue flicked over and then around the taut peak. And she moaned as heat shimmered through her body like lightning.

"What's wrong, *querida?* Is this what you want?" She could hear the tender teasing in his voice. His hand trailed tantalizingly down her stomach and then between her legs, which fell apart involuntarily, anticipating.

"So wet," he whispered hoarsely, the teasing gone. "So wet for me."

His fingers caressed, stroking the center of her need. The sensations began to gather in her lower body and move upward, flowing molten through her stomach. Her hips arched, wanting to hurry the sweet insanity of the contact between his fingers and her body, but he stopped what he was doing and simply held her, forcing her to lie still with his hand cupped with possessive mastery between her legs, while his mouth explored her breasts until he felt her breathing slow, and she shivered at the falling away from the peak she had almost managed to reach.

She gasped when she felt him begin again the stroking, the demanding caresses, with fingers that seemed to know exactly how to touch her need. She lifted as the pressure built and this time he let her, holding her, surrounding her, until she knew that she had to touch the place her body so desperately sought, and then he again stopped her. He held her as she writhed and sobbed and begged for release. He kissed her neck and shoulders, nibbled her aching breasts, as she pleaded, but he didn't relent until she lay limp and panting against him, sure that she had lost the opportunity he had twice promised and twice denied.

When he finally touched her again, she cried out at the first feather stroke, straining against his hand. And this time he didn't stop, even when she dug her nails into his skin. Then her body exploded, all sense of self lost, all knowledge of anything but how much she wanted him. The waves of pleasure hadn't stopped breaking within her when he turned her, quickly positioning her under his hips. She felt him enter her and fill her, his hands lifting her into him as he thrust deeper than she believed she could bear.

"Don't," she gasped. "You're too big, too deep," she begged hoarsely, suddenly afraid of his possession.

"You were created for this," he whispered, his lips moving against her throat. "You were made for me, to fit together. You knew it with your mind. Now let your body know me, too. Relax, my heart. Relax. Love me. Take me. All of me."

She felt her bones melt and re-form around him. She could feel him in her soul, in her heart, filling every space that had ever been empty in her body, seeking out every atom that had ever dreamed of him, and fulfilling those dreams. He began to move inside her, and she thought then that she couldn't bear the pleasure. Her hands found his shoulders and held as he thrust again and again into the honeyed warmth and tight silk of her body. Her long legs involuntarily wrapped around his driving hips, and she answered every movement until she begged for whatever waited beyond the demanding force. She cried out when his shuddering eruption within her ignited an answering response, and they climbed and then fell together. And lay exhausted, still joined, their bodies slick with the mingled sweat of their lovemaking.

Finally she could breathe, her face against his chest, and the fragrance of his cologne, released by the heat of his skin, filled her senses, soothed her, gathered around her as the familiar scents of home comfort the returning traveler.

He moved to lie by her side, his hands drifting slowly over the trembling muscles of her back. She wanted that contact with this one man she had chosen—against all sanity. She pushed close to his chest and finally felt the rise and fall of his breathing ease. His strong hands were now limp against her body, and she knew that he slept.

And knew that whatever doubts she had had about the rightness of giving herself to this man had been erased by what had happened between them.

She wanted to touch his face, to trace his features, to satisfy her need to know more about how he looked, but she thought that he would wake, and it would be a betrayal. Finally, she ran her hand instead over his chest, moving her fingers through the thick hair, following the line of it down his flat, ridged stomach and found that he was completely undressed. She hadn't even been aware of when he had removed the rest of his clothing. He spoke from the darkness.

"No more. I've had a long and very difficult day. I'm too tired for whatever else you intend."

"'Not tonight, dear'?" she whispered, laughing. "I thought I was supposed to say that." But she obeyed, moving her hand upward to caress the narrow stomach and waist.

"I don't think you would know the meaning of those words. Are you always so responsive?" he asked seriously.

"I didn't know I could feel like that," she answered with the simple truth.

"Go to sleep. You are making me want you again, and I need to sleep. Tomorrow night...will you let Diego bring you to me?"

"I thought you were going to walk away in the morning, and I was just going to be one of your pleasant memories."

"I think this memory will be too pleasant for that." His lips found her temple, and he kissed her gently, without passion, but not without feeling. "Forgive me, my heart. I didn't mean to hurt you. I can make no promises. There are too many problems that can't be resolved even by what we feel for one another."

"We could go away. Somewhere where no one would ever find us."

"Would you do that? Give up your life to run and hide with me? Think, *querida*."

"No, I can't think. If I think, I don't know what to do. I just want to feel. To feel again what we just felt. And then I have no doubts about anything."

"Kiss me," he demanded suddenly, finding her mouth. He tasted her lips slowly, carefully, his tongue seeking hers and engaging in a joining as deep as their bodies had shared.

She felt the tears begin as she thought of the distance that lay between them. He found the moisture when he kissed her eyelids, and he propped his body on one elbow, leaning over hers, and used his thumb to wipe away her tears.

"Why are you crying? God, I wish I could see your face. Don't cry, my heart. We have tonight. Nothing can take away what we've had tonight."

"I'm afraid that's all we'll have. You said—"

"I said a lot of very foolish things. As long as I can. As long as it's possible. And when the time comes—"

"Don't say it."

"And when the time comes," he repeated relentlessly, "you go back into the light. You can't live in the darkness I would condemn you to. You are too beautiful, too fine, to be imprisoned in my world. The choice is not yours, *querida*, but mine."

"And I'll have no say, no voice in that decision?"

"You don't decide with your mind. You make decisions with your heart."

"But that's not wrong, you Latin chauvinist."

He laughed, touching her forehead with his lips. "Not wrong, but not logical. Not reasoned. Not unemotional."

"And you're so controlled," she mocked. "I was here with you, remember? I heard the things you said."

"A man isn't responsible for what he says when he's making love to the woman—" He broke the sentence, but she felt the thought, felt it and wanted him to acknowledge it.

"To the woman?"

"To *whatever* woman is in his arms."

"One of many pleasant memories." She could hear the bitterness in her voice.

"The most pleasant of all. And I think perhaps I am not so tired as I imagined."

He lowered his head to her breasts. His tongue laved in tender spirals, delicately, until she pushed upward into his touch. She heard him laugh, but he took the peak into his mouth, sucking strongly, and then gently nibbling the distended nipple. She gasped with the pleasure and felt her body lift against his, trying to bring herself in contact with the strength that had filled her before.

"Patience. You have no patience," he admonished softly. "You're like a child." The richness of his voice washed over her.

"Love me," she begged.

"I am. All of you. Every inch will be mine." He lowered his head again and his tongue trailed down her sensitized skin to bury in her navel. "Branded," he taunted, and she knew she was. Her fingers moved to lock into his hair, and she held his head as his lips teased and caressed. "Marked," he whispered. His mouth moved lower and lower. "Memorized," he breathed against the softness where her legs met. Again she was boneless, mindless, her resistance melting into his promise, and then his tongue caressed the center of her soul.

This time he didn't make her wait. She writhed beneath him, gasping her need into the night—until she knew that if this was his darkness, then she was lost already, for she couldn't give up what he could make her feel.

Her body became flame, and as the slow fire began to burn along the veins and nerves and arteries that led from the touch of his lips, he moved to turn and lift her. He positioned her quickly over his hips and lowered her body until he entered her, as strong and fierce and demanding as before. She arched and cried out against his strength, but he held her hips as he moved fully into her.

"Show me," he commanded.

She rose to her knees and then lowered along his hardness, hearing the soft growl deep in his throat in response to what she did. She eased from him again, and his hands tried to stop her lifting away from his body, but she knew what he wanted. She almost rose too far and then she eased herself down, millimeter by millimeter, finally sliding her knees away from his straining hips to deepen the contact between them. She lowered her breasts to lie against his chest and increased the tempo of her movements over the steel-hard evidence of his desire.

When she began to tremble above him, it was he who cried out this time, and she felt him convulse again and again under her body. Finally he lay still, the gasping breathing delighting her with proof of what she could make him feel.

"I love you," she said as she held him, uncaring of what she had promised before.

"I know, my heart. I know you do," he whispered, and they didn't speak again.

She slept against the comforting, solid warmth of his side, but at dawn only the fragrance of his body on her sheets was left to assure her that this, at least, had been no dream.

Chapter Eight

"You said you set a trap. What kind of trap?" Diego asked.

"A very simple one. Baited with a great deal of money. Money is obviously what our friend is interested in," his master said, smiling.

"And if he takes the bait?"

"Then he comes to pick up his money. Which should be extremely interesting."

"Here?" Diego asked in disbelief.

"Of course. You don't sound very hospitable, Diego."

"What about the woman?"

"He won't see her. It shouldn't be a problem."

"Who is he?" Diego asked carefully, trying to read past the amusement.

"He hasn't told me his name. I have the impression he doesn't trust me," he said. "Not a very trusting individual at all. Perhaps he's dealt with treachery too long."

"But you know who he is?" Diego asked and then realized the obvious.

"Of course," his master said simply, and smiling, he laid the dark red rose, still misted with dew, beside her plate.

Diego's knock on her door awakened her, and Rae knew by the light from the shaded window that the morning was well advanced. She almost gave him permission to enter before she realized she was naked. She finally found her T-shirt at the bottom of the bed. She pulled the soft cotton over her head and stacked the pillows behind her shoulders. She could still smell his body on the one she had been clutching when she'd awakened.

She straightened the top sheet, and although she realized Diego must know what had happened between them, she was embarrassed to have him see the evidence so clearly revealed in the disordered bed. She ran her fingers through her tangled hair, pulling it back from her face as she attempted to compose herself. Diego knocked again, and she knew she couldn't deny him entry any longer.

"Come in," she called, making one more smoothing motion at the sheet that lay over her body.

When he entered, the aromas from the tray he carried were not those of Diego's gray-yolked eggs. She closed her eyes, savoring the fragrances of real coffee and Canadian bacon, of eggs scrambled delicately in butter, and muffins.

"The cook's back!"

"Yes." And unbelievably Diego smiled at her. "But he spent so long with you last night I thought I wasn't going to be able to get him up in time to prepare breakfast for you."

"He spent so long . . . He's the cook? He's the one—"

"It doesn't make him any less a man," Diego interrupted, studying her face as he voiced the last assurance, lest she mistake his culinary talents as something less than masculine.

Her mind flashed back to the hard body that had mastered both her senses and her physical responses last night, and she was not even aware of the soft smile that Diego correctly interpreted as more than an acknowledgment of his master's essential maleness. Aware finally of the silence that had grown as Diego watched her, Rae glanced up, finding some emotion in the dark eyes she didn't understand.

"Don't let it get cold," she commanded, trying to hide her embarrassment, and reached for the tray. Diego brought it to the bed and placed it across her lap. It was not the simple kitchen tray he usually brought her meals on, but old-fashioned white wicker. And lying between the antique English porcelain plate and its matching cup and saucer was

a long-stemmed red rose. She touched the velvet petals and
then picked it up to hold against her cheek.

"He cut it himself from the garden," Diego said as he
poured her coffee.

She opened her eyes and smiled into his. "If I'd been
awake, I could have seen him. My window looks out on the
roses."

Diego walked to the windows to raise the shades, and
sunshine flooded the room. He looked down on the garden
as if to verify the truth of what she'd said. She watched him
as she sipped her coffee.

"If you had been awake," he repeated, and she wondered at his tone, but he said nothing else.

She tasted the food the silver cover had kept hot and made
such appreciative noises that they evoked a small smile from
Diego.

"I'll tell him you enjoyed it," he said as he crossed to the
door.

"Diego, ask if I can I see him this morning. I want to talk
to him."

He nodded before he stepped out into the hall, engaging
the lock.

When Rae finished, she put the tray on the bedside table.
Instead of getting up, she slid back down into the twisted
sheets. She breathed in the familiar fragrance of his body,
which filled even her bed now, and it evoked all that he
meant to her. She wanted to lie here immersed in the memories and never move, never reenter the outside world to
which they both still belonged, in which they owed such
differing responsibilities. She closed her eyes and like a
movie reel, the images rolled behind her lids. When she
could endure them no longer, she rose to stand by the windows as Diego had.

The garden below was filled with light now, but she knew
that by late afternoon it would be shadowed with the shade
of the trees that blocked the western sun. The roses lifted to
the light as she had strained into his touch last night. She
thought about his walking along the path that wound be-

low her room, pictured him bending to caress the blooms, to choose and cut her rose. He had been on the path this morning, and she knew that she would rise and watch for him from now on.

She carried the rose with her into the bathroom. She didn't have a vase, so she filled the sink and deposited it there. It lay limply against the porcelain. As she bent to turn on the water in the tub, she smiled at the ridiculousness of trying to keep the flower alive. She stripped off the T-shirt and ran her hands over her body as if she could tell the difference his touch had made, could sense it physically.

She stepped into the bath and could feel the pleasant soreness of hard lovemaking. *I won't fit into your images of sweethearts and boyfriends,* he had warned her last night. She thought he might be amused if he knew how few of either she had had. She had been too busy, too goal-oriented to give up time to a relationship. No one had attracted her enough to make the concessions that a successful romance required. And no one had ever made love to her as he had.

Experience counts, she acknowledged, smiling, and slid down so that her breasts were below the level of the scented water. She closed her eyes and allowed herself the luxury of a long soak, adding hot water until her toes were deeply wrinkled. She pulled the plug, wrapping herself in one of the huge towels, and then couldn't resist lying down in the tangled sheets again.

Suddenly the thought of her father, of Paul Hardesty and Kyle Peters and all the men she worked with unpleasantly intruded into the fantasy she was weaving. She wanted out of here. Back into the safety of her old life. Back doing what she was supposed to do. She had always done the right thing, everything that was expected of her. Ridiculously, she found herself hoping that Paul would believe she was dead. She couldn't go back and pretend to be what she had been before.

She climbed out of the bed that held all the memories and dressed, almost frantic to distance herself from what had happened last night, to regain some sense of the woman she had been before.

She realized that she had been walking back and forth across the bedroom only when she heard Diego knock. She attempted to control the involuntary increase in her heart rate—anticipation of being told she could see him, of being told that he might be coming to her room. She took a deep breath, locked her hands together behind her back and gave Diego permission to enter.

"He'll see you. Downstairs."

He allowed her to walk beside him. He even, for some reason, took her hand before he knocked on the library door, and at the sound of the voice that answered from within the room, her stomach turned over like hitting the bottom of a roller-coaster ride.

Diego gripped her shaking fingers and said softly, "It's all right." He opened the door and indicated the chair she had occupied five days ago.

"Thank you, Diego," the voice said from the darkness on the other side of the desk. She looked again into the concealing light and knew only from the sound of the closing door when they were alone.

Neither spoke for a long time.

"Diego said that you wanted to see me, but I see that you have had second thoughts. Perhaps about many things."

She dropped her gaze to study the hands that were twisting in her lap. She thought he would speak again, but he let the silence lengthen until its brittleness strained the very air of the room.

"I wanted to see you," she affirmed when she could stand the quiet tension no longer.

"I'm so sorry, *querida*. I can tell there is regret for last night."

"No," she whispered, shaking her head in denial. "There is no regret for last night. For everything else, but not for that."

"For everything else?" he questioned softly.

"For what you are. For what I am. For what I'm *supposed* to be," she amended. "For the fact that I'm not what I thought I was and can never be again."

"And why not?" The quiet gentleness lessened the hurt caused by the amusement she also heard there.

"Because I can't go back to Paul and the others and look them in the eye and pretend none of this happened. Pretend I didn't make love to you. That I didn't betray everything I've ever been."

"You have betrayed *nothing*," he retorted, the amusement replaced now by anger. "You've done nothing for which you should be ashamed. You've survived. You've been kidnapped, drugged, terrorized, and through it all you have done *nothing* for which you should apologize to any of those men, to anyone, not even to your father."

"I let you frighten me into giving you Kyle's name."

"I knew his name."

"Then why did you show me the picture?"

"To verify it wasn't Franklin. To see your reaction."

"Did you think I would simply admit it? Even if I had been there? Did you think I'd tell you?"

"Why not? If you were the one, you had already dealt with the cartel. Why hesitate to do it again?"

"Then you're sure the pickup team betrayed the courier."

"There was no team. There was only one man."

"And you knew that?"

"No. Not then. I had been told that you and Franklin were the ones."

"Who told you that?"

"And now you're ready to exchange information with me?" he questioned softly, reminding her.

"No," she said, "you know—"

"Then no more questions. Those are the rules."

"How did you get mixed up in all this—with the cartel? Why? You're not like them."

"The cartel has enormous amounts of money to handle."

"And you do it for them."

"Just what do you do for Paul Hardesty?" he asked. "Quid pro quo, *querida*."

She shook her head, knowing that she could never reconcile what she felt him to be with the cold reality, with a reality she had met face-to-face in a dark room in Virginia.

"Your name and Franklin's came to me from within your task force. And the courier was betrayed by someone inside that same group. Compared to the treachery that's already been practiced, you have nothing to be ashamed of," he said harshly. "Go back when this is all over and be what you are. A good cop."

"Who let you make love to her."

"*Querida.*" The tenderness of last night was suddenly back in his voice, and she wished she could read his feelings as clearly in his face.

"I want to see you," she begged. "Please."

"You asked Diego what I look like," he said, his tone carefully neutral.

She laughed, remembering Diego's answer.

"What is it?" he asked, the amusement back.

"Diego said that you looked like a man. He has such a way with words."

"What do you think I look like?"

"I don't believe I'm objective," she whispered, fighting last night's memories.

"That's good," he said, laughing. "You had earlier damaged my ego beyond repair."

She smiled at his laughter and paused before she gave him what he asked for. "You have dark eyes and black hair that feels like silk under my hands. You're maybe six feet tall with broad shoulders, very muscular arms and chest, but you're a little too thin for your frame."

"Go on. What else do you imagine?"

"Am I right so far?"

"Perhaps," he said, his voice still neutral and controlled.

"And handsome," she breathed finally.

He said nothing for a long time, but some infinitesimal change had occurred in the atmosphere of the room. His voice, when he answered, had lost none of its calm serenity.

"I'm sorry you've imagined that. Given the blindfolds and the darkness, I should have anticipated what your mind would create, but I've grown so accustomed to what I am that I suppose I thought you would know as I do."

"Know what?" she asked, recognizing finally, beyond the matter-of-fact tone, some undercurrent of darkness.

"That I am not the prince of the fairy tales, not the handsome prince little girls dream of."

"I dream of you," she said, wanting to remove from the familiar beauty of his voice whatever darkness she heard.

"Of what you had imagined." Again the pause was too long. But finally he said, "Imagine me as you wish. I would like to think you find me handsome. You will never see the reality that might interfere with the illusions we will create during the days . . . and the nights . . . we have."

"Come to my room tonight," she said, wanting to make it right between them again, to destroy the quiet bitterness.

"Will you instead let Diego bring you to me? Without letting that destroy the fantasies we seek to create?"

"I don't think anything can destroy what you make me feel. I don't mind Diego."

"I have a request."

"I'm not sure I want to hear this," she said, smiling.

"I'm afraid I found your gown a little less . . ." He hesitated.

"What? Revealing? Sophisticated? Sexy? I know. Less of everything you're used to."

"I would never be so gauche as to tell you that, my heart. I thought that perhaps you might have something slightly more feminine. If not, I would be delighted to provide you with something suitable."

"Do you have a closet of gowns you just pull out as the occasion arises? No pun intended."

"No," he replied, amusement threaded in the richness again. "What do you imagine I am? I thought Diego might buy something for me to give you."

"And why wouldn't you choose something for me? I don't want something Diego picked out."

He hesitated, so that she wondered what she was missing.

"I avoid public appearances if possible. The fewer people who see my face in any context, the better. I prefer to remain anonymous. My profession requires it."

"I have something suitable," she said stiffly. The distance was between them again—a barrier that would always intrude if they talked of anything outside a dark bedroom, the only place, it seemed, where they could truly find complete compatibility.

My profession, he had said. She blocked the images, feeling guilt over what she was doing. Surely there was some way she could get out of here. They didn't even seem concerned anymore that she might try to escape. Her hands weren't tied. There were windows in this room. Perhaps...

But Diego was outside the door, and she had learned that she couldn't go through Diego. She would have to overpower this man, hurt him beyond his ability to resist in order to escape. She knew that she was not mentally capable of that, even if she might be, given her training, physically capable. She was effectively held prisoner by what she felt for him. She sighed and didn't know that he understood exactly what the sound meant, read in her face exactly what his words had reminded her of.

"Don't," he said. "Don't think of anything outside this house for the next few days. Less than a week, I promise you, and this will be over. You'll be back in your world, and this will seem like only a nightmare. Or a dream. Parts of it. You are my prisoner, taken and held against your will. That's all anyone else will ever know. And it is the truth."

"The facts but not the truth," she corrected quietly.

"The *truth* belongs to us and to no one else. The facts are as I have given them. And as you will give them to anyone who questions you."

"But I'll always know."

"Don't let this destroy who you are, what you are. I don't intend that, Rae."

"I don't even know your name," she realized suddenly.

"What would you like it to be? You may choose any name you prefer. I promise I'll answer to it."

"But you won't tell me yours?"

"One less thing to forget. And you must promise me that you will forget all this. You agreed last night that it would be my way."

"I would have agreed to anything last night to get you to stay with me. And that statement alone should make up for any of the blows to the ego you suffered before."

"It helps. What would you like for dinner? I think breakfast was late enough that we could perhaps settle for an early dinner and then . . ."

"An early bedtime?" she suggested.

"How well you read me. An early bedtime."

"Earl. I think I'll call you Earl. Or Hugo. Or maybe Herbert."

"Those aren't Spanish names."

"How about Juan? As in Juan Valdez. He's from Colombia."

"Who is Juan Valdez?" He seemed puzzled by her amusement.

"The coffee man. With the donkey or the burro or whatever it is. I don't know the donkey's name, so I'm going to call you Juan."

"I suppose it's better than Herbert," he said, and called for Diego to take her back to her room.

THE AFTERNOON WAS long, and finally she walked to the window and stood in the fading light looking down on the garden. The roses were drooping in the late-afternoon heat, and she wondered who cared for the grounds. She hadn't heard the sound of mowers or trimmers, but they could have done it by hand. She realized that she had not been aware enough of her surroundings. Someone who could have helped her might have been below her window at any time during the past week and she had never looked.

She turned away, angry at herself, and vowed that she would not simply drift along in the situation he had created for her. She could not deny herself tonight, but she had made no promises not to escape. She knew escape would somehow allow her to regain her self-respect and might even allow her to go back to what she had always been. *My profession,* she echoed his phrase.

She laid across the bed the nightgowns she had thrown so hurriedly into her bag the day she'd been taken. There were two besides the nightshirts and although she thought briefly of wearing the T-shirt again as a form of rebellion, she rejected the thought almost as it formed. She would do what he asked. Each night held the possibility of being their last, and she wanted no regrets to cloud the memories of whatever time they had together.

She finally selected the plainest and most severe—a white satin cut like a thirties evening gown, long and straight. She tried it on, enjoying the cool fall of the material against her body. She smoothed it over her breasts and looked in the mirror above the dresser. She brushed her hair for a long time and then put it up as she had on the day she'd waited for his return. She wondered where he had gone for those four days and whom he'd met. Less than a week, he had said, and this would be over. Less than a week, and she would be free. Only she didn't want to be free. She wanted to be with him, and the nearer it came to the time to go to him, the more she knew that.

As the sun set, she lost all concerns about fitting back into her former life. She didn't even care anymore. She would ask him tonight to take her with him when this was all over. No one would ever know.

She put her hands on either side of her head and pressed as if she could push all thoughts of the man she was so carefully dressing for out of her brain. But she didn't succeed. He hadn't asked for her help in whatever he was doing. She was not hurting anyone else by being with him. She was betraying no one but herself. As long as that was the case, she could live with it. As long as he didn't ask her to betray others to help him be what he was, to do whatever he was doing, she could live with it.

She was still by the window when Diego knocked. She realized with surprise that it was fully dark; the garden below was invisible in the heavy heat of the summer night.

"Come in," she said, and Diego stepped into the room. In spite of what she had told him earlier, she had dreaded Diego seeing her dressed to go to him, but Diego never looked at her body.

"He's waiting for you," he said softly. "Are you ready?"

"Yes, thank you, Diego. I'm ready."

There was no blindfold, but the hall outside her room was unlighted, so she held Diego's arm as a blind person would hold her guide. He took her a very long way before he stopped to knock on a door. She wondered how he could navigate so fearlessly in the darkness and how he knew which door, and then she heard the beloved voice inside the room give permission and Diego opened the door for her. She wondered if he would guide her to the bed or if...

The door closed behind her, and she was standing alone in the midnight blackness.

Chapter Nine

"Are you afraid of the dark, my heart?" he asked, the seductive caress of his voice coming from across the room.

"Not if you're there," she answered, knowing, in spite of her trembling knees, that was true.

"It is my natural element," he said. As always, she could hear his mood revealed in his voice. He was amused by her fears and anticipating touching her.

"I think I fell in love with your voice first. Before anything else."

"Or perhaps that's all you really know of me."

"That's not true anymore."

"No," he agreed softly. "Not anymore."

She waited for him to tell her what to do and felt the darkness gather around her. *His natural element.* She could smell the fragrance that had haunted her room all day, enfolding *her* in *his* darkness.

"Five steps," he whispered. "Five steps and you will find the footboard. Come to the right side. I'm waiting for you."

"Did you count them for me?" she asked, prolonging the moment before she must step forward.

"For you, my heart," he answered.

Because he was waiting, she commanded her feet to take those five steps. She reached out and the curved footboard of the bed was under her hand. Just as he had told her. She trailed her fingers along the wood until she felt the post and then down to the top of the mattress. She could hear the whisper of their movement along the sheets until his hand grasped her wrist. She gasped, although she had expected his touch, and he laughed, pulling her into the high bed.

He leaned over her, propping his elbows on either side of her arms, imprisoning her so his chest rested lightly over her breasts and his long legs lay beside her body. She waited for his kiss, but instead she felt his thumbs trace both sides of her forehead and then trail down her eyelids, to her high cheekbones, over her nose, across her parted lips. He finally lowered his mouth to hers and whispered before his tongue invaded, "So beautiful."

Then he was inside her mouth, tasting, caressing, demanding. She ran her fingers through the curling hair and down the strong column of his neck and across the broad shoulders.

When he broke the kiss and lifted his head, she brushed her lips along the ridge of his throat and into the hollow below. She felt him swallow against her touch and sensed the slow pulse beneath her lips. "My heart," he had called her, and she felt the reality of that strong beat against her body.

"Did you think about this today?" he whispered into the soft curls piled atop her head.

"About this and you."

"Why did you put your hair up? I want to feel it around me, over my shoulders."

"I don't know. I dressed for you. I put on makeup for you. I fixed my hair for you, and there's only the darkness. I don't know why I did any of those things," she admitted, laughing at her own stupidity. She took out the pins to let the long strands spill over them both.

"Because it made you feel more beautiful," he said. "A woman needs to *feel* beautiful before she *is* beautiful to anyone else. It's not really how a woman looks that's important, but how she feels about how she looks."

"The voice of experience?" she accused, smiling against his shoulder.

"Perhaps. I like beautiful women. And that's a compliment, *querida*."

"If you didn't like the way I look, would you throw me out of your bed?"

"If you weren't exactly who and what you are, you would never be in my bed at all," he said, stopping her questions with his mouth.

It was much later, long after he had removed and discarded the satin gown, as he was tormenting her with the denial and then the sensation of his lips against nipples that he had already made ache for him, that she spoke the thought his words had evoked.

"It's not how a man looks that's important, either," she whispered into the darkness. Her hands were tangled in the dark curls of the head that was bent over her body. She felt him still and then raise his face to look, she supposed, where he knew her to be against the whiteness of the sheets.

"It's how I make you feel," she finished.

"Like the prince," he said.

Daringly, she touched his face and felt the slight indentation in the center of his chin. Her fingers found his bottom lip, and he opened his mouth to capture them gently with his teeth. She let him hold them a moment before she removed them to trace the bow of his top lip and then up to the strong nose, feeling his breath feathering out against her touch. Bolder now, her exploration moved up the bridge of his nose. At that, his hand fastened hard on her wrist, pulling it away from his face to lie prisoner against his suddenly heaving chest.

"No, *querida*. Fantasy and not reality. No more reality tonight. Promise me."

"I promise. I won't touch your face again. Not if that's what you want."

"It's what I want."

"Is there anything else that's off-limits?" she teased, trying to lessen the sudden harshness in the beautiful voice. She touched the hardness that grew into her hand as she caressed him.

"Nothing else. Whatever else you find is yours to explore," he replied, turning onto his back to give her greater access.

She intended to torment him as he had done to her last night—to tantalize and then deny release. But after only a few moments of her somewhat tentative touching, instead he guided her over his body again and, dear and familiar, moved inside her, filling her as she had known all day that he would.

"Do you like this?" he asked, and, not understanding, she laughed.

"Being on top of me," he explained, amused.

"On top. Under. Beside. I don't care. With you. Around you. Surrounding you. You told me last night. Made for you."

His hands taught her how to move against him, to give them both the greatest pleasure. For a long time. As he had done for her alone last night. To the edge of release and then denial, cessation of all movement. Held hard against his heaving chest, her hips stilled by his command, by his hands holding her, cupped commandingly over her slender bottom. She clenched against his hardness, knowing that she alone controlled what happened within her body and felt his teeth against her neck and shoulders. She stopped then, waiting for his permission.

Finally he moved within her, softly at first. And then he released her hips, sliding his hands up to cup her breasts, raising her to sit upright over his sweat-slick body. The shift in position deepened the already powerful sensations, and as he lifted into her, she cried out with her need. He let her control then, setting the tempo for her own release until she felt him join her as she reached the edge of the abyss. Then there was oblivion.

She found his hands still holding her, caressing now in gentle circles her body that shook in the cold she hadn't felt before. The moisture on her skin was his and hers, and she shivered at his touch. Branded and marked, he had promised. And she was.

No one else, ever, my heart, she promised silently, lowering her head to kiss lips that were still gasping slightly for air to fill his tortured lungs. He pulled her down to crush against his strength, hurting her until she whimpered with the pain. He released her then, whispering apologies and love words in Spanish.

"I lose my English," he said in that language, finally. "I have no brain, only a body, when we make love."

She laughed, recognizing its shaky quality in the stillness. "I know. I know."

Time ceased to exist for either of them. He did not plead tiredness tonight and although her bones felt liquid in the aftermath of their passion, he made love to her twice more. As unhurriedly as the first time. Teaching her sensations she had never dreamed existed. Finding places on her body that she had never thought of as being erogenous. Under his lips and his hands, they suddenly were. He wasn't always gentle, but she had learned that his strength was not used to overpower, but to guide, and if she let him control, he could make her feel things that she knew she could never explain. Never put into words. Nor would she want to. She belonged to him and did not even mind the idea of that slavery. She gloried in it. As she did in his touch and the hard force that invaded and owned her body. Made it his own. Claimed it and sealed it forever against anyone else's touch.

"How did you learn all this?" she asked as she lay limp against his side. His hard arm was around her, his hand locked on her breast that he caressed gently now in contrast to what he had done only minutes before.

"A misspent youth," he said, laughing, as he turned his head to kiss her cheek.

"How many women—" she began, but his hand tightened suddenly on her breast.

"Only one. You must know that. Only one," he commanded. She nodded, knowing he could feel the movement against his lips.

"Go to sleep. Diego will come for you before dawn. He will touch your arm, and you will go with him. Don't be afraid when you feel his touch. He'll take you back to your room. Do you understand?''

"My gown," she said in sudden panic at the thought of trailing Diego down the dark halls as she was now.

She heard him laugh, but he fumbled among the sheets at the foot of the bed. She felt the cool smoothness of the satin against her reaching hands. They sat up together in the middle of that vast bed. He helped her put the gown on, smoothing it over her breasts as she had done earlier tonight in her room.

"If. . ." he said into the darkness and stopped as though what he wanted to say was too painful to be put into words.

"What is it?" she questioned, hearing the hesitation in the voice that had always seemed so sure.

"It's possible that we won't be together again. Things are happening more quickly than I anticipated."

"No," she denied, reaching for him. He caught her hands and held them away from his body.

"Listen to me," he demanded. Finally she stopped struggling to hold him and let her wrists rest limp in his strong fingers.

"If tonight is the end. . ." Again he hesitated, but she only waited, knowing that nothing she could say would change his implacable will. "You will always be my heart," he said finally.

She knew it was not what he had begun, not what he had intended, but he put her arms around his neck and pulled her with him to lie down once more in the tangled sheets. He held her as she cried, but he didn't speak to her again.

She was deeply asleep, exhausted by his demanding body, when the soft buzz broke the stillness, pulling her from the dream of making love to him again. She felt him move beside her, to reach for the phone on the table beside the bed. She was awake by the time he had stopped the noise. He had reached with the hand that lay under her body, and his arm automatically returned to encircle her neck. He put the receiver to his ear that had rested against her cheek.

"Yes," he said quietly. Perhaps realizing that the phone was almost as close to her ear as his, he began to turn his body away from hers to change the receiver to his other hand, to his other side, but the speaker on the other end didn't give him time to complete what he had intended. Into the darkness whispered only two words.

"It's Hardesty."

Then he was sitting upright with the phone against his other ear. The hollow quality of the voice that had escaped into the stillness of the bedroom made it unrecognizable, but there had been no mistaking the words. Hardesty's voice or another's—she didn't know which—but the implications of either were frightening enough. It was a name that should not be spoken in this room, into the ear of the man who was now listening so intently.

He didn't speak again and finally leaned against her body to replace the phone in its cradle. She felt him hesitate. She forced herself to lie still, unmoving, her breathing deep and controlled. She didn't know where she found the strength of purpose to carry out the charade that she still slept, but apparently it was convincing enough.

He lay down again beside her, putting his arm across her body, but she turned sullenly away as if irritated in her sleep by the unaccustomed weight. She even managed a soft sigh or two before she finally settled along the edge of the high bed, as far away from him as the huge mattress allowed. He gently touched her bottom, a small caress up the curve of her spine, and then turned away to lie with his back to hers. She waited a long time before the occasional pleasantly masculine snore told her he slept.

It's Hardesty. The whispered words played over and over through her frantic mind. She tried to remember the exact voice to force a recognition, but the distortion was too great to allow her to be sure of anything but the words themselves. Of those there was no doubt.

Either Paul was in contact with this man, was himself the traitor, or someone had just given him Paul's name for some purpose. And because he himself had told her, she knew what he wanted: the person who could be forced to identify the courier who had betrayed the cartel that night in Virginia, the courier who could tell him where Escobar's billion and a half dollars could be found.

She had always believed that Paul would know that name if anyone did, and she wondered if she had told him that under the influence of Diego's drugs, and if that information had just been confirmed by the caller.

However, if the voice had been Paul's, then *he* was the one who had sold out to the cartel. *He* had provided the information that had resulted in the deaths of Frank and the others. Perhaps he had even given this man her name, her picture. Betrayed her to him.

She had no obligation to risk her release. He had promised that no harm would come to her, and she believed him. She could go back to sleep and tell no one until she was safely away from him. And how many people would die before that happened? Would Paul be tortured for the name of the man who had died that night in Virginia? Would they do to Paul what they had done to that man? She had to get out of here, to leave and warn whoever was left alive in the force. She had no choice.

She felt for the floor with her bare foot. Her toes touched the carpet and, resting most of her weight on that foot, she eased onto her palms and then away from the mattress. She waited, ready to lie down again at the least change in that soft breathing, but the sounds from the other side of the bed continued unchanged. She dropped to the floor beside the bed and waited again. Then she crawled in the darkness to where she hoped the door was.

Her reaching fingers found blank wall instead, but she knew she couldn't be that far off. She found the edge of the frame and finally, following it, the knob. She twisted it and it moved soundlessly under her fingers. Not locked. She breathed a silent prayer of thanksgiving and opened the door only enough to slip through. She pulled it almost closed behind her, but didn't chance engaging the latch. Even that noise in the stillness might wake him.

She was disoriented in the dark hall. She couldn't think which way she had turned to enter the room. She had depended on Diego, allowing him to guide her without thinking. *Idiot,* she thought, knowing that she had been anticipating his touch, never thinking about the possibilities of escape that being in his room offered her. She had never intended to escape, had not wanted to and still would not, except for the phone call.

Right, she realized suddenly. She had been on Diego's right arm, and he had turned her right to knock on the door. She had wondered how he knew which door and how many they had passed, but now she must turn left, retracing that long journey to find the stairs. She stood up in the darkness and began moving to her left.

She held her hands before her and couldn't believe that not one glimmer of light pierced the darkness of the hall. *Darker than a tomb,* she thought, shivering at the image of being buried alive. She moved noiselessly on bare feet along the miles of carpet until the blackness faded slightly into gray. Ahead of her she could make out the banister and the stairwell. The moonlight from the uncovered windows of the first floor illuminated this section of the upper story. She moved to the stairs and using the railing, she ran down. This at least was familiar.

She hurried across the cold marble squares of the foyer. Her trembling hands found the handle of the entry door, but when it wouldn't move beneath her fingers, she felt panic building in her chest. She pulled her hands off, fighting to control her breathing. She ran sweating palms down the satin of her gown and then touched the cool metal of the handle again. Nothing.

Dear God, she thought in despair, leaning against the hard wood. *It was locked. With a key, of course. And the key's in Diego's room.*

Something else, then. Closed doors stretched on either side of the halls that ran from the foyer to branch beyond the stairs. The doors on the left—she would simply start there and work systematically until she discovered a room that had an outside entrance.

She opened the first, recognizing even in the darkness the room she had entered several times before. Windows stretched behind the desk where he had sat today. She paused, her eyes locked on his chair. She could almost see him there. Her gaze fell to the top of the desk, and she saw the phone beside the elaborate computer system.

Get out of the house first, she thought, *and then call someone.* First get away from the reach of Diego and from those hard fingers that had tangled in her hair, the same fingers that had so sweetly tormented her body tonight.

She stopped that train of thought and ran across the carpet whose texture she had known before. She had almost touched the handle of the French windows before she saw the grill. Heavy wrought iron, covering all the windows in this room. As her eyes traced the grillwork, she saw, too, the wires along the sills—a security system that would announce the slightest movement of the tall windows. Perhaps even being this close was enough to set off the alarm, so she moved hurriedly away from the glass, listening for any disturbance of the surrounding darkness. What would Diego do if he found her here?

Back upstairs? Back into the bed with the man who wanted information that Hardesty had? With the man who was perhaps willing to kill Paul to get what he wanted? She turned instead to the phone. She picked it up and heard, almost with disbelief, the reassuringly ordinary dial tone.

You have done nothing for which you should be ashamed. No betrayal. Until now. She commanded her fingers to begin dialing, first 1 and then the area code and the number. She listened to the ringing that sounded in her ear as if loud enough to wake those who slept above. She eased down onto the floor behind the massive desk, waiting and praying. There would be no one there in the middle of the night, but she could leave a message. Then she heard the voice—not an electronic voice, but one that was human and comfortingly familiar.

"Hello," he said. She could hear his tiredness even over the distance the wires traveled between them.

"Kyle?" she breathed into the receiver as quietly as she could and still hope he might hear her.

"Who is this?" he demanded.

She wanted to tell him to whisper. She licked dry lips, unable to believe it had been this easy. She fought the unfamiliar urge to cry, swallowing the emotion building in her throat. Finally when she thought she could push a sound out past the hard lump, she whispered, "It's Rae."

"What the hell?" he demanded. "What is this, some kind of sick joke?"

"Kyle, it's Rae. I need you."

"Rae." She heard him breathe against the mouthpiece and knew that he believed her, that he had recognized even her hoarse whisper.

"Where are you?" he asked. Only with his question did she realize that she didn't know.

"I don't know. A house. I don't know, but I can't get out. It's wired."

"My God, Rae, we thought you were dead."

She shivered against the impact of the word, although it was only what she had assumed they would think.

"Not yet." She forced herself to laugh.

"Paul thought that you'd—"

"Kyle," she interrupted, realizing she hadn't warned him against the possibility that Hardesty was somehow involved in this. "Don't tell Paul where I am."

"What? Why not? What's wrong with you?"

"I think Paul might be working with this man. I overheard part of a phone call. I heard Hardesty's name."

The silence was too long, and then she heard his softly breathed profanity.

"Okay. We're tracing. I'm coming for you. Hang on."

"Talk to me," she begged.

"I'm right here, and soon I'll be there with you. Don't worry. I'm not going to let anything happen to you. I'm coming to get you, Rae. It's all right. Everything is going to be all right now. My God, how did you manage this call? Where are you?''

"I'm downstairs. They're asleep upstairs."

"But how—"

"A slipup," she lied. "They got careless."

"Good girl. Hang on, hang on, we're almost there." She knew he was waiting for the word on her exact location, so she swallowed her fear, hoping that soon . . .

It wasn't good. She knew as soon as she heard his voice. "Rae, listen to me. It's going to take several hours before I can get to you."

"No." Her mind denied what he was telling her. She shook her head as if he could see, knowing that she couldn't stay here for hours.

"You're too far away," he said.

"Call somebody. The locals. Call them, Kyle," she demanded.

"No, listen. You know they'd screw it up. It's a little town, Rae. They don't have the people to handle this. How many are there in the house with you? How many right now?"

"Only two," she whispered.

"Are you absolutely certain of that?"

"Yes. No. I think only two. That's all I've seen."

"Okay. This is what we do. You go back upstairs—"

"No," she said harshly, too loudly.

"Yes, Rae, back upstairs. Don't let them know you've been downstairs. Don't leave any traces. Fix everything like it was and go back to where they expect you to be. I'll be there. With lots of help. I promise. Do it, Rae," he commanded.

"Don't hang up," she said in panic. "Don't leave me, Kyle. Why can't I wait down here? I could hide," she argued, knowing rationally that he was right, but unable to explain the difficulties he was asking her to undertake. To find his room among all those doors and to climb back into his bed and wait for Diego . . .

Diego, she thought. *What time was it? Was he there now? How many minutes had passed?* She turned to look out at the reassuringly dark windows and then wondered in quick panic if they weren't a lighter gray than they had been when she had first entered the room. Or maybe her eyes had simply adjusted.

"Rae?" Kyle said into her silence. She could hear the effort he was making to control his impatience with her arguments. "Go now before they discover you're gone. If they realize what you've done, they'll kill you and get away. Go back upstairs," he said very deliberately, trying to impose his will on hers. "We can't chance losing them now, sweetheart. I'll be there with you in a few hours. I promise. Do it, Rae. Promise me. Swear to me."

"All right. I promise—" And she heard the connection broken. She almost cried out with the pain of it, but instead she leaned her forehead against the smooth wood of the desk, finally putting the softly humming phone back into its cradle.

She turned to stare into the grayness of the night, knowing with certainty that it was lighter than it had been before. She felt the copper taste of fear in her mouth, so she bit her tongue hard to bring her back to the reality she had to face.

Back upstairs. She stood, examining the top of the desk, trying to see if she had disturbed anything he would notice in the morning. She hadn't touched anything but the phone. She moved across the floor to listen at the door before she opened it, slipping out, the marble of the hallway cold under her bare feet. She looked up the stairs and wondered if she could climb them with her knees trembling. *How many minutes? How long? Was he still asleep? And Diego? Where was Diego?*

She put her hand on the railing and climbed into the everincreasing darkness at the top.

Chapter Ten

To the left, she told herself as she climbed, using it as a mantra against her fear. She wondered if she could simply slip inside the door of her own room and convince them that she had found it in the night.

Think! she screamed silently to a brain that persisted in offering any solution other than the one she had promised to carry out. She reached the top and, taking a deep breath, began to walk, concentrating on how far the journey had taken with Diego. How would she know which door? What if she walked into Diego's room, crawled into his bed? In spite of her fear, she couldn't prevent a brief smile at the thought of Diego's reaction.

His reaction before or after he kills me? she asked herself, forcing her mind back to the reality of who and what these people were.

She had never imagined when she left his room that she would have to find it again in the dark. She had intended to be out, gone, before they woke. She knew logically that Kyle was right: if they discovered she was missing, they would disappear.

The thought pierced her blind obedience to Kyle's instructions. *They'd be gone.* He'd be safe. She would have accomplished her purpose, and *he would be safe.* She had already warned Kyle that Hardesty could be mixed up with them, so Kyle would follow up on Paul's involvement. And if he wasn't involved? If someone else had given Paul's

name, then she had condemned him to the authorities
without a shred of real evidence against him—only his name
whispered into the darkness.

She wished she had explained that to Kyle, had told him
what made her question Paul's connections here, but it was
too late now. She could explain when Kyle got here. She
could hide and then give them time to get away before Kyle
and whoever he brought arrived. Surely Diego wouldn't take
time to search this enormous house if he thought she had
given the alarm. How long would she have to stay hidden to
ensure they would give up their efforts and leave, and would
they be gone before Kyle's arrival? She had promised to return to his bed and not let them know, but she didn't want
him hurt.

*He's a drug lord and I'm plotting to allow him to escape.
No, not allow. To warn him. To warn him by my absence.
To make sure he escapes punishment for what he's done, for
whatever part he played in what was done to the man in
Virginia that night.*

She knew in her heart there was something wrong with
that argument, and she steeled herself against anything but
the promise she had given Kyle: to go back and never let
them know she had called.

She heard a sound somewhere in the darkness, and she
froze, her fingers against the wall. A door closing? Or only
the creaking of an old house?

Her mind screamed at her to hurry, but she forced herself to stand silent for several long minutes, listening to the
darkness. She could hear nothing else and finally she began
to move. She touched each door her fingers encountered,
remembering that she had not engaged the latch on his. It
should push open, and then she would know. If only all the
other doors on the long hall were securely fastened. If only
Diego had not already opened his and was waiting for her
in the black bedroom.

Too far, too far, her fear whispered, but she walked on,
touching each door on the right side of the hall, until one
swung open under her hand. And in spite of the fact that

Only a Whisper

this was what she was looking for, it was unexpected. She had touched it and then it wasn't there any longer. It had moved away from her reaching fingers. Her hand sought the door again, only slightly open, and it swung a fraction more before she finally gripped the edge. She waited in the doorway, listening, and eventually she heard, above the pounding of her own heart that threatened to drown any outside noises, the soft rhythm of his breathing.

She dropped to the bedroom carpet, gently pulling the door almost closed, and then she caught the knob and turned it. She waited, listening to the even tempo of the breathing of the man who slept behind her before she eased the knob back until the latch rested silently in its niche in the frame.

There was no change in the quality of the sound from the darkness. She crawled across the floor and knew that getting back into bed, the pressure of her weight against the mattress on which he slept, would be the deciding factor, the most difficult part of all she had done.

She reversed what had worked before. Her weight on one foot, she lowered her body to touch down in breathless stages. And finally she was there. She enjoyed for a brief moment the cold smoothness of the sheet against her burning face. Then she finally pulled her foot up off the carpet and onto the mattress.

She almost screamed when his hand touched her. She bit her lips to keep them from gasping with the shock. His hand lay on the curve of her lower back and then he turned toward her body. She felt his breath against her shoulder, heard him sniff and the soft noises of waking. He rubbed his palm up her spine, and when he took her upper arm to pull her to spoon against him, she offered no resistance. She eased into his body and heard the sleepy whisper, his breath stirring her hair, "You're cold. Come here, *querida*. Let me warm you."

The muscular arms that had tightened lovingly around her body finally slackened into sleep, and she lay, staring into the darkness, feeling the regular rise and fall of his chest against her back.

She never could have guessed how long or how short a time it was until she felt Diego's hand on her wrist, freeing her from his arms. It had seemed an eternity that she had lain against the body of the man she had betrayed. Like a prisoner being removed from his cell, she welcomed Diego's touch as he guided her back to her room without speaking. When she heard the lock engage on her door, she knew that the decision she had made was now irrevocable.

SHE WAS STANDING by the window when dawn broke. Dry-eyed and unseeing, she stared into the garden below. She had done what she was supposed to do, what she had been raised and trained to do, what was right; but it felt only like betrayal. Against all the treachery that had already been committed, add one more. In the name of law and order. In the name of her father's memory. In the name of…betrayal.

There was nothing in the morning light that climbed over the house to touch the roses to signal that this day was any different from those that had gone before. And still she stood watching the shadows edge across the dew-wet grass. A figure appeared on the outer rim of her vision, and she almost missed him in her inner contemplation—Diego with garden shears in his hands. He moved among the roses and touched with his huge fingers one and then another. He bent his head to breathe against the crimson-black of their petals, and suddenly the scene below her blurred.

She watched his hands gently select and touch a long stem and then cut. He held the rose up to the light, turning it slowly in his outsize fist, examining it from every angle as if ensuring its perfection. He moved back along the path and disappeared around the corner, and she could taste the salt of the tears that covered her cheeks as she licked them from her lips.

Finally she used her palms to rub them from her face and turned away from the window. She walked to the mirror. The makeup she had so carefully applied last night was smeared, and her neck was beard-burned by his lovemaking. And the eyes of the woman reflected in the glass were dead.

She left the mirror and spent a long time under the hottest water she could endure, letting it pour down over her head and body until there were no more tears, no more shuddering sobs left, and then she carefully dried off and dressed. She lay across the bed in the sunshine and waited.

It was Diego who came for her. When he didn't knock, but opened the door and walked in, she knew that whatever she had set into motion was already taking place.

"You have to go downstairs," he said, and she nodded.

When she rose to follow him on the last journey down the stairs, he was standing with a pistol on his outstretched palm. The immense size of his hand made it look like a toy, a child's gun.

"He said to tell you that this isn't a rescue, *querida.*"

"I don't understand," she said, but he slipped the pistol into the right-hand pocket of her pleated slacks and pulled her arm behind her back and pushed her out the door. She led the way down the stairs to the room where he had taken her before, and again Diego didn't knock.

His master was seated in the chair behind the desk while Kyle Peters, looking blessedly efficient, held a gun against his temple. The fingers of Kyle's left hand were locked into the curling blackness of his hair, pulling the dark head back against the padding of the high-backed chair. The right profile of Diego's master was highlighted against the wall of windows behind the desk, as clean and pure as the faces on old Greek coins: the nose strong and high-bridged, the chin still arrogant even against the pressure of Kyle's fingers.

"Check your escort, babe," Kyle ordered. "I told him if he wasn't back with you in under a minute without any tools he'd picked up on the way, I'd kill his friend here. Make sure."

Rae ran her hands down Diego's body, feeling the tension that corded the muscles bulging under his clothing. She stole a glance at his master's profile as she touched Diego, her mind locked on the two men silhouetted against the light from the French windows.

"He's clean," she assured Kyle, knowing where the gun Diego had carried was, but she didn't understand why he had given it to her or the cryptic message. *Not a rescue.*

Kyle turned his body slightly. The desk chair and the seated man swiveled with the movement, out of the glare from the morning sun, and she could see the bloody gash that marred his right cheekbone.

"What have you done to him?" She could not have prevented the question had her life depended on it.

"He said something to the big guy, something in Spanish. I just reminded him that I don't like messages I don't understand. It still doesn't quite match the other side, however."

Kyle's laugh struck the wrong note, jarring against her senses, but then he swung the chair another quarter turn so the face of the seated man was squarely before her eyes, and she was no longer aware of Kyle or of anything else in the too-bright room. Only of the horror of what had been revealed.

The left side of the darkly handsome visage was ridged with two scars, brutally illuminated in the summer light. The top one ran across his eye so the lid was slightly distorted, drooping over the dark iris that was barely visible under the damaged flesh. The other traversed the cheek, pulling the skin. The bottom of that slash touched the corner of his upper lip.

He watched her impassively. She could guess what her face had revealed, sickened by how much he had been hurt. Now she knew the reason for the darkness. *My natural element,* he had said.

"Not a very appealing sight this early in the morning," Kyle mocked, but the figure under his hands made no response and finally Kyle released his head with a jerk and removed the gun from his temple. He motioned Diego closer to the man behind the desk so he could cover both of them.

Just Kyle. No one else.

"Where's your backup?" she asked, watching him move around to the front of the desk to pull her against his side in a quick embrace. Kyle didn't take his eyes off the two men, and the gun never wavered.

"On the way. I couldn't wait for it all to be coordinated. I had to get to you, so I came on alone. Are you all right? They didn't . . . hurt you, did they?"

She knew what he was asking and what the hesitation conveyed, just as she knew that she had to answer him.

"I'm all right. I just want out of here. How long before help arrives?"

"Not long," he reassured, still holding her lightly against him, his left hand caressing down her upper arm. She thought of the pistol that was in her pocket, and she moved away from him, crossing her arms over her chest as if she were cold in the brightness of the sunlit room.

"This is stupid, Kyle. Let me call the sheriff. We need to get this wrapped up."

The man in the chair and Diego were too quiet, too calm. Something wasn't right here. She hadn't looked at him since Kyle had shown her the damage to his face, and she didn't dare. But she could feel the force of his and Diego's eyes on her, and she suddenly realized that they must know what she had done.

"How did you get in?" she wondered aloud, remembering her failure and frustration last night. "How did you get past the security system without setting off the alarms?"

When Kyle didn't answer, she knew it was because he had no answer. There was no way he could be here unless someone had let him in, and if they had, it was for a very good reason.

"Kyle," she said, trying to think what that meant, "there's something wrong here. They're waiting for something. They let you in, didn't they? They were expecting you." None of it made any sense.

"Not unless you told them I was coming. You said there were only two. I found a window and surprised them. It wasn't hard. They're not as tough as they're cracked up to be."

"I don't like this," she said, trying to convince him of the reality of her premonition that this was some kind of trap. What she knew of these men did not fit with their calm acceptance of Kyle's control. They were waiting. She could sense Diego listening, expecting. She looked at Diego's master and couldn't read his expression, but his dark eyes were locked on her, not on Kyle. He disregarded whatever threat Kyle might pose, and she suddenly knew that, as always, he was the one in control. She wanted the gun Diego had given her in her hand, wanted the tangible reassurance of its protection; the problem was, she wasn't sure exactly whom she needed protection from.

Diego's eyes flicked to the window and even that small movement telegraphed a warning. She followed his gaze to the stretch of lawn revealed beyond the glass, but there was nothing there. The pleasant morning calmness was unbroken. And then she heard what had attracted Diego's attention, what he had been aware of before any of the others except possibly the man who sat so calmly behind the desk, the one who was closest to the windows. The man whose gaze was fastened intently on her face.

Not a rescue, querida, he had instructed Diego to tell her. To warn her.

She felt Kyle stiffen beside her and knew that finally he, too, had heard the unmistakable thrump of the chopper that was moving through the still, summer sky to touch down on the velvet of the manicured lawn beyond the glass.

"Damn," Kyle said, and she turned to look at his face, which had suddenly gone gray under the tan. He moved to the window, but his attention on his two prisoners never wavered. Rae slipped her hand into the pocket of her slacks and felt the satisfying coolness of the pistol. She knew that it didn't have the stopping power she was used to, but she was an excellent shot, at least on the range. Although her father had taught her to shoot when she was a child, she had never shot a man, never killed anyone.

The chopper was down, and she could see figures jumping out, moving across the lawn, guns drawn. Paul Hardesty's white hair was unmistakable, and she felt nothing but relief, in spite of the name spoken into the darkness last night.

"It's Paul," she told Kyle, whose continued tension didn't fit with her own overwhelming sense that help was at hand.

"You know he's one of them. You told me that."

Rae could hear the strain in his voice. Diego shifted slightly, and Kyle's gun trained on the center of that broad chest.

"I told you I heard his name. That there was some connection," she said. "I don't know that he's involved in this. I just wanted you to be careful who you contacted."

She watched the people advancing carefully across the lawn and knew that they couldn't see inside, were unaware how closely three pairs of eyes were watching their every movement. She recognized another figure and knew then that her suspicions about Hardesty must be unfounded.

"That's Stewart," she said to Kyle. "Dell Stewart. You know Stewart's straight." Stewart was DEA, one of their top men, and they had both worked with him before. If Stewart was here, then Paul was clean, still operating within the system, not a renegade.

Which meant that someone else was the weak link in the task force, the betrayer. Her eyes moved from the men on the lawn to the figure of her colleague outlined against the light.

You can do better than Kyle Peters, he had told her. She didn't know why or how, but all at once she was absolutely certain that Kyle was the key to the puzzle—to the deaths, even to the betrayal of the courier who had died to bring down the cartel. His reaction to the arrival of the chopper had just revealed his guilt.

Her eyes found the face of the man in the chair and spoke her conviction aloud, "He's the one who knew the name. You let him in because he could lead you to the man who gave us the information."

"No, *querida*." The beautiful, familiar voice washed over
her, and she wanted to lay her head on his shoulder and have
him touch her as he had last night. Last night. A lifetime
ago. "I let him in because we were expecting him. He came
here to sell me that information, but he doesn't know the
name, and now the game is over. And he has lost. But then
so have I, my friend, and we must all learn to accept our
fates," he said, his mockery clear.

He was deliberately goading Kyle Peters, who stood behind him, watching the end of his options approaching
across the peaceful green of the summer lawn beyond the
windows.

"You son of a bitch," Kyle said, hatred deep and harsh
in his voice. "You lying son of a bitch."

From the time the man in the chair had begun to speak,
to answer her question, Kyle had also begun to move away
from the window, the muzzle of the heavy revolver he held
tracking downward at the beautiful, taunting, slightly accented voice. By then Diego was moving too, but not, of
course, quickly enough. No one can outrun a bullet.

Kyle swung his weapon, and Rae saw red blossom across
Diego's massive chest and his forward motion checked almost before the report of the gun echoed in the closeness of
the room. She could smell the cordite and watched as Kyle
fired again into Diego's body. She heard her own voice
screaming against the second report, and then Kyle turned
and pointed the revolver again at the man still seated behind the desk.

She shouted Kyle's name, as if she could stop him with
words, and the pistol was in her hand now. Kyle's attention
was diverted, and as she had intended, the black eye swung
toward her, away from its target to focus like an accusing
finger at her body. As on the range, she raised and fired
smoothly, the motion practiced so many times that her body
performed what her mind had no time to command.

A small dark circle appeared in Kyle's forehead, and she
could see the surprise in his glazing eyes before he fell forward onto the top of the desk. But his finger had com-

pleted its own well-trained and automatic squeeze of the trigger. She was aware of the blow and the heat, but there was no pain. She felt her legs melt, and the gun dropped from her nerveless fingers.

Please, God, I don't want to die, she thought, and then her cheek was somehow against the rough wool of the Oriental rug.

She wondered why it was taking Paul and Dell so long. Why it was so quiet and why the air was dead in the room. Her head began to swim and the last thing she thought was that she could smell his cologne, so she closed her eyes to savor it.

SHE WAS NEVER SURE of the sequence of events after she fell. She felt the shock wear off and then the burning pain in her shoulder, and she knew she had cried out when they moved her.

She wanted to ask about Diego, but nothing would come out, no words would form that ever reached her lips. Dell Stewart's face floated before her once and Paul's, but they were like figures in a dark dream. Their mouths moved, but the sense of whatever they asked her never reached her brain.

She awoke again in the chopper, and the paramedic was with her. She didn't know who else, but she felt the rhythm of the rotor vibrate through her body and she relaxed against it, knowing she was being taken to help.

"I don't want to die," she said, quite clearly she thought, but she couldn't understand the words that answered her.

The ride through the halls of the hospital to the operating room was just like on the television show, whatever it had been, where the ceiling flashed overhead. She was sick with the motion, so she closed her eyes and didn't wake up again until much later, after the surgery, in her own room.

Paul Hardesty was sitting beside her bed, and he smiled at her when he realized she was awake.

"How do you feel?"

"Like I've been run over by a freight train," she managed to whisper. "You see all those people in the movies get shot and then jump up and fight and swim rivers and all kinds of stuff. I'm not sure I can manage the next breath."

"I'll let you in on a secret, kid," he said, reminding her suddenly of Frank. "They don't use real bullets."

She closed her eyes and smiled. "That makes me feel lots better."

She heard his laugh. They sat there together in the quietness. She didn't have the energy to ask for details, but there were two questions she had to know before she could rest.

"Diego?"

"Dead," Paul answered, and she clenched her eyes against the rush of tears.

"And the other man?" she asked, not even having a name to call him.

"He's all right. In custody."

She nodded and wished for the oblivion of unconsciousness again. Finally Paul took her hand, and she wasn't aware she had been crying until he gently wiped her face. All she'd seemed able to do lately was cry. Paul didn't talk, but he stayed until they gave her another shot that let her drift back into the whiteness where she didn't have to think about what she had done.

Chapter Eleven

She floated through a couple of days, welcoming the co-
coon of drugs that smiling nurses periodically provided. Her
surgeon assured her that there should be no permanent
damage from the bullet that had slammed into her shoulder.

"You're either lucky or, more likely, I'm simply very tal-
ented," he told her, smiling. "It's a good sign that everything works." She cooperatively wiggled her fingers for him
again. "Do your rehab like a good girl, and you can have
plastic surgery in a few months that should take care of most
of the scarring. It could have been much worse," he finished, making notations on her chart.

She thought of Diego's chest, of the two hits dead center, and knew he was right. She wondered if Kyle had found
it difficult to shoot her, or if she had come up before he was
ready, had literally gotten the drop on him. And then she
couldn't imagine that it mattered. He was dead and she was
alive, and she infinitely preferred it that way.

Although he hadn't explained, Paul had reassured her as
soon as she was lucid that Kyle had indeed been the seller of
information, the killer of Frank and the others. He hadn't
wanted her to spend even one minute worrying about the
rightness of her actions.

"If you hadn't shot him, he might have taken out any of
us coming across the lawn or into the house. We knew we
were going to be targets, but we wanted to get to you as

quickly as possible." He wouldn't give her any details of the operation, telling her there would be plenty of time to sit down and explain all the loose ends. But for now...

"I know. All I have to do is get well. Did you guys practice that line beforehand? Everybody that's been to see me has said it. I don't know what else you think I'm going to do in a hospital but get well."

By the second week she was tired of being charming to the staff. She hated the restrictions of her injury, she hurt, and she'd had to call her mother.

"Get out of this business," her mother ordered, her anger apparent, and suddenly Rae wanted to be at home in El Paso so badly she could taste the dust storms and the enchiladas. "It killed your dad and now it's almost killed you. Let somebody else do it. Come home and finish your law degree. We'll manage somehow."

It was tempting. She was burned-out in more ways than one. Paul worried about the effect on her of having shot Kyle, but it was Diego she saw falling again and again, whenever she closed her eyes. Interposed with scenes of him picking the rose for the breakfast tray he'd never gotten a chance to deliver. She had killed Diego with a phone call and had imprisoned the man she still, in spite of everything, knew she loved.

She cradled her elbow with her left hand and leaned back against the too-hard hospital pillows. She wanted her down ones. She wanted her nightshirt. She wanted to go home. Maybe even home to Mother. And she had *never* thought she'd say that.

She began badgering her doctor until finally they rolled her out in a wheelchair, dressed in her own clothes, or almost her own clothes. The nurses had pulled an oversize T-shirt over her head, and she had her left arm through its sleeve with her right arm in its harness underneath. She found in the next few days that was the easiest way to dress. She lived on microwave dinners that Paul had stocked in her tiny freezer and take-out Chinese he brought as a treat about three times the first week she was home.

It was the Friday night of that week when she knew she
was ready to hear the details of what Kyle Peters had done.
Not really ready, but she needed to know, needed to have her
questions answered. Especially one.

She and Paul had eaten off the coffee table, which was
now littered with take-out containers, and finally Rae
stretched out by careful stages on the couch. They both
dreaded, she knew, rehashing things they would rather forget, but putting it off wouldn't make the pain go away.

"Kyle came to the task force highly recommended," Paul
began, "like the rest, and, believe me, we checked you all
out. I think he was still a good cop then. I don't know
whether it was having access to more important information that turned him, or if someone finally made the offer
on a level that was at last appealing enough, or if there were
personal factors. And I guess we'll never know."

"Stop blaming yourself, Paul. There's no way you could
have known he'd go bad. That danger's always there. Everybody makes up his own mind. Nobody comes with a
guarantee."

She thought of the decisions she had made that were not
the result of her moral code, but the result of her emotions,
her feelings, about a man who was, as she had called him,
"the scum of her earth." She hoped Paul didn't realize how
closely she had walked the line between doing what good
cops do and selling out. And in her case it hadn't even been
for money.

"For whatever reason," Paul finally continued, "at some
point Kyle began collecting information he could sell, could
pass on in return for...whatever's enough to buy a man's
soul. He didn't realize how important the courier in Virginia would be because, frankly, I didn't realize it. And that's
another regret I'll always have to live with. I sent one man,
Jeff Reynolds, to meet the guy. Jeff was late, but his unexpected arrival interrupted what had been going on, and he
did get the courier out alive, so I had no reason to suspect
him. And thankfully he'd had enough training to *keep* the

guy alive until I could get help. The rest of that night's activities you already know.''

"Why was Jeff late?"

"Because he'd had a message telling him the location had been changed. He waited there awhile before he had sense enough to go to the original location.''

"Who left the message?"

"I did." At the shocked widening of Rae's aquamarine eyes, he smiled. "At least, it was my voice. The bits and pieces of the message had been put together electronically, using our own equipment.''

"Kyle," she said.

"Apparently during all those extra hours he put in after work that impressed the hell out of me," Paul admitted.

"But if Kyle wasn't to be in on the pickup, how could he have known about the courier in the first place? You're not that careless.''

She could tell by the dull flush that Paul was embarrassed, and she wished she hadn't asked. He obviously had enough regrets about all that had gone wrong with the operation. How Kyle had gotten the information wasn't important. She started to let him off the hook, when he took something out of his pocket and laid it down among the leaking white containers on the table between them.

"What in the world?" she asked, and then she knew. "A hearing aid? That's a hearing aid.''

"I have some nerve deafness from flying choppers in Nam. Kyle noticed it and suggested a friend of his could help. The friend was legit. I checked him out later. Kyle was nice enough to offer to pick the thing up when it was ready. Apparently, he added a very sophisticated bug.''

"That's fiendish," she said, "and so damn good. We have millions of dollars' worth of scramblers, high-tech debuggers, and he sticks it right in your ear." She glanced at Paul's face and laughed. "Sorry, but you have to admit it was ingenious.''

"Just stupid on my part. I had no reason to doubt Kyle at that time, and I didn't want to admit I needed this damn thing. I probably didn't wear it a week. It didn't seem to help, and I just left it on the bathroom shelf. It must have driven him crazy. He even asked me how it was doing a couple of times, and I lied. I didn't want to offend him because he'd recommended the audiologist."

Finally Paul joined in her laughter. "A real comedy of errors, until you think of everyone who suffered as a result of it."

"Why did he kill Holcomb? Frank was thinking about retiring. He said that night in Virginia he was getting too old for all this. He was going to leave it to us young ones." She shook her head. "I'll never make it like you guys. Like my dad. I don't have whatever it takes to stick it out. Not thirty years."

"Things have changed since your dad's days. It's all dirtier and the stakes are higher. The temptations are so damn great." He touched the hearing aid on the table with one finger. "Get out, Rae. Run home to Mama. Get your law degree. Get away from this filth."

She didn't respond to his advice, and finally he went on with the story he had been putting together for her.

"When the rumors started floating around about Escobar's lost billions, Kyle apparently remembered our conversation about the courier's having had access to the cartel's financial records. He reasoned that the man would know where Escobar's private fortune had been hidden. Or maybe...somebody suggested it to him. If that man could be found, he could be forced to tell—"

"You told me the courier died. That night. Are you trying to tell me—"

"Kyle couldn't know that. He didn't know the outcome of his original sellout. All he knew was that the cartel had been interrupted and that we'd gotten the information."

"How could Kyle know about Frank's involvement? You told us not to talk about Virginia."

"Frank liked to tell war stories. Maybe he'd let slip he'd been involved that night. Kyle would have been a very interested listener. And maybe later, when he believed the courier was the way to Escobar's money, he thought back to Frank's story."

She remembered their dinner together and the almost-irresistible urge she'd had to share her knowledge about the man in Virginia.

"Kyle and I discussed Frank's death. And Jeff's. We thought you had something to do with them. At least Jeff's. Kyle suggested you'd used Holcomb's death to cover up your assassination of Reynolds because he'd sold out the courier."

"My assassination? What the hell were you thinking, Rae? If I'd thought Jeff Reynolds had sold out, he'd have been sweated for every piece of information he might have had tucked away in brain cells he didn't know existed. I don't have hit squads. That's the other side. The guys in the black hats."

"I sat in that room and listened to a man die," she said softly. "Slowly and painfully. If Jeff was responsible, I could probably have killed him, and that scares me. You think I regret shooting Kyle, but the really scary thing is I have never had one moment's regret about pulling that trigger. I have lots of regrets, but none about that."

"I don't suppose—"

"My regrets are my own business," she interrupted. "I have nothing I need to confess to you. I didn't compromise us."

"I know that, Rae. I know you too well for that. I never doubted you."

She laughed at that misplaced vote of confidence and then, realizing she shouldn't have, asked the next question.

"Did Frank give Kyle my name?" Given what she supposed Frank had been subjected to, she couldn't blame him if he had. It would at least explain why she'd been kidnapped.

"I don't think so, or you'd have been next on Kyle's list. I think, somehow, Frank protected you, didn't reveal that you were with him in Virginia that night."

She shook her head, thinking how grateful she was for that protection, given under circumstances and at a cost she could only imagine.

"When Frank couldn't provide any information about the courier," Paul continued, "Kyle went on to someone else he had always known had been involved that night. He'd heard me instruct Reynolds on the pickup during the time I wore the bug. When Jeff was finally dead, Kyle hid the body. It was sheer luck it was found."

"Then . . ."

"What's the question?"

"Kyle said Jeff's body had probably been mutilated *after* he was killed to suggest the cartel."

"Jeff was tortured for information, cartel-style. Bullets carefully and deliberately placed to cause the most pain and the most damage: first the ankles, then the kneecaps—"

"I know the drill," Rae interrupted, sickened. "I just can't see Kyle doing that. He must have been insane."

"I told you. Get out. They're all insane," Paul said, and she nodded her agreement.

"After Jeff's body was discovered," he went on, "I put Drew Gates on the two murders. I gave him *all* the facts and turned him loose. He had informants in Miami from his days with DEA who were very reliable. He's the one who told me that someone was putting out feelers about what had happened that night, trying to find the courier's identity."

"Cali. The uptown boys. Trying to find Escobar's money," she said softly, remembering. "Kyle must have heard those rumors and decided if *he* couldn't find the courier and the money, he might still make a profit out of this. If he led Cali to believe he could supply them with the courier's name—" She stopped, suddenly aware of Paul's focused intensity on her face.

"What is it?" she asked.

"It's not just Cali, Rae. There are a lot of sharks circling in that water."

"Are you trying to tell me that even with Kyle dead and with…" She paused because she didn't want to say it. "Just what *are* you trying to tell me, Paul?" she asked.

"That you can't forget the possibility that someone else, someone just as determined and just as ruthless, will be interested in finding out about the courier."

Paul was trying to scare her, she realized. Into quitting? she wondered. Trying to protect her because he'd been a friend of her father's and because she'd been hurt. Or maybe because, somewhere deep inside, he didn't believe this was a job for a woman.

"Gates was good," Paul said, picking up the thread of his explanation, and she brought her attention back to the narrative. "And he was starting to get some nibbles, whispers that suggested a leak in the task force itself, and then he was gone. I don't know what he did that tipped Kyle off, but I'd lost three of my people in a matter of weeks. I don't think I've ever felt as helpless as I did when Gates disappeared."

"Who did you assign next?"

"I decided that since it was my force, my people, I was responsible for finding out what was going on. I went to Dell Stewart for help, and he's the one who suggested that whoever had originally sold out the courier to the cartel could be traced through the financial transactions—through the money the traitor had been paid. Every transaction leaves its footprint, no matter how carefully it's hidden. If you're smart enough to read the footprints, you can follow the trail back to the person who took those steps. So we… called someone out of retirement. Someone very good at untangling records, at seeing implications in things that look perfectly normal to the rest of us. Someone who can remember all the other little bytes of information scattered in all the other computers working all over the world."

"A hacker? You called in a hacker?"

"Everybody uses hackers."

"*Nineteen Eighty-Four*. Big Brother of the peripherals."

"And then you disappeared. I didn't know how I was going to tell your mother."

She smiled at the idea that Paul's biggest worry in the middle of all those deaths seemed to have been a ninety-five-pound Texas redhead.

"And while I was missing," Rae said, "your expert figured out it was Kyle from some electronic footprints and you followed him to his meeting with the cartel."

"Kyle was under suspicion. You all were. And all calls in and out of the office were taped, but by the time we listened to yours that night, Kyle was gone. We followed, and you were there for the rest."

"But they were waiting for you. I swear they knew you were coming."

"Not us. They were waiting for their own people. We got there first. They were expecting Kyle. Your phone call just put him there ahead of schedule."

"Why did he come? He knew I was still alive, which should suggest they hadn't bought his story about my involvement."

"Kyle's ego made him believe he could carry it off. He planned to collect his money, and then kill all of you, get rid of anyone who could connect him to what was going on."

"His money. His payment for giving them *your* name, Paul. That's what I heard that night. Kyle giving them your name." She stopped because she didn't want to explain to Hardesty the circumstances under which she'd heard part of that conversation.

"The call that made you think I was the one working with your captor?"

Your captor. She had tried not to think about him at all. She didn't want to remember what she had felt, what she had done.

Paul apparently didn't pick up on her distress. He was still explaining the events of that morning.

"They hoped Kyle could eventually tell them who the courier was, but all Kyle really knew was about the warehouse meeting. He *was* smart enough to know they would never have let him get away with it because he had just been stringing them along. Selling them bits and pieces that didn't add up to anything. He didn't *know* anything. No one knew the name of the courier.''

"That's twice you've lied to me about that, Paul. I even understand. But don't tell me again that you don't know who he was. I don't believe you. I'm sure I told the cartel that. They used drugs to pick my brain. I've always believed you knew who he was. Why didn't Kyle come after *you?* He must have known you were the logical one to have real information.''

"I think he tried, but I've been in this business a long time, Rae. After Frank's death, after what you suggested about the cartel, I took precautions. I didn't give anyone an opportunity. Kyle couldn't take me at the office, and I made it real hard to find me anywhere else.''

"All those tricks of the trade,'' she observed, thinking of the weeks they had worked for her.

"*I* didn't go back to water my plants,'' he said, smiling at her.

"Kyle couldn't find the name, even after murdering three people, so he gave them me and tried to convince them with a doctored picture that I was the one who could supply them with the courier's name.''

"He didn't have any real information, and he wanted their money. So he manufactured some evidence: the picture and the money he had electronically had deposited to your account.''

"But he couldn't have taken that picture. He was in it. And that in itself seems—''

"He took it out of my files.''

"Your files?'' she repeated, not understanding. "Why would a picture of Kyle and me having dinner out be in—'' The realization of what that meant was shocking. "*You* had us under surveillance. You were following and taking pictures of your own people.''

"At that point, there weren't that many of my own people left. And obviously one of them was extremely dangerous to the rest. When the two of you started meeting, especially since everybody knew how you felt about Kyle—''

"Everybody knew what? What are you talking about?"

"That you thought he was a jerk. It was obvious. I imagine, obvious even to Kyle."

"Paul," she said softly, thinking of the number of times she'd rejected Kyle Peters's advances, "do you think that's why he tried to make them believe I was the one? Because I'd damaged his ego? Did he set me up so they'd torture me for information I didn't have?"

"I don't know. Judging by what we know he did to Jeff... Forget him, Rae. He was sick. A rogue. And you ended the harm he could do."

They didn't say anything for a few minutes. She watched Paul examine a couple of the cartons for another bite of food they might have overlooked. She guessed that was what made him a good cop. He could discuss all this mayhem and still have an appetite.

Now there was only one question she had to ask. No matter what Paul thought.

"What will happen to him now?" she asked and watched the blue eyes come up to examine her face. He didn't question who she meant, and she knew that Paul, at least, had guessed that more had gone on during the week she was missing than she had told him, than she would ever tell anyone.

"He'll be tried in Colombia. We decided that was best. Otherwise, we could be called to testify."

"Did you agree to his deportation because of me? Were you protecting me? You know it's possible he'll escape the full force of what we'd give him. Their judges have reason to be leery of dealing too harshly with the cartels. Did you allow him the easy way out because of me?"

It took him a long time to answer, and when he finally met her eyes, she knew what he was saying was hard.

"You do what you have to do because you make promises or because you think it's in somebody's best interests. You walk the line between doing what you want to do, what you feel is right and what's . . . necessary. I just do the best I can, Rae, given the circumstances. Sometimes I screw up, but they pay me to make decisions. It's my job. I took the job, and I'm going to do it."

She eased up off the couch. She sat on the arm of his chair and put her good arm around his shoulders. Finally she kissed his forehead. "I guess we all just do the best we can. Thanks, Paul, for everything. I'm glad you came for me. I'm glad I'm alive, and I promise you I'm going to be all right. I may do what you said—go back home and finish my degree. I don't know about that right now, but I want you to know that I'm going to make it. I promise."

"Your dad would have been very proud of you, Rae."

She smiled at the thought of her father. "I don't know about *that,* but I think he would have understood. I guess that's all I can ask."

He hugged her carefully and stood, apparently embarrassed by their display of affection. He began to gather up the containers.

"Leave them," she said. "I'll get high smelling them in the morning. It'll give me something to do to loosen up this shoulder."

"Aren't you supposed to do some therapy?"

"Yeah, and it's probably going to hurt like hell, but I do hate being left-handed."

Paul laughed. "You do it. The doctors assured me you'd have no problems if you'd do everything they tell you."

"I *always* do what I'm told. I'm the good little girl my daddy raised. I worry over keeping library books out too long. That's why I'm a cop. I doubt I'll make a good lawyer."

"Be a prosecutor. Work for the state. It's the next best thing."

"The next best thing?" she asked, smiling, knowing what he meant.

"To being a good cop. That's the best thing there is, Rae. The very best."

She kissed him again, and she locked all the locks, just as he'd ordered her to when he left. She still slept with the lights on, but it didn't help the dreams. *Darkness is my natural element,* he had said, but he invaded her lighted bedroom every night, and she wondered how long it would take before she didn't dream about him anymore.

THE PHYSICAL THERAPY was every bit as bad as Rae had thought it would be, but at least it gave her a goal, something to focus on besides what had happened. She worked like a dog, pushing herself hard during the next weeks. The physical exertion helped her sleep at night. With the gradual but steady improvement in her shoulder, however, she knew it wouldn't be long before she would be physically capable of returning to work. Whether she would ever want to do the kind of work she had done for Hardesty and the task force remained a question. She was on leave until her specialist dismissed her, and she knew that day was approaching faster than she really wanted it to.

When it came, she went back because they were dissolving the task force anyway. Nobody believed they could be effective, given what had happened. All they would be doing was a mothballing operation, closing up shop and transferring information. Rae could do that without thinking, and most days she did.

Paul had given her credit in front of the team for putting an end to Kyle's activities. She knew he had deliberately built up her role to prevent questions about the week of her disappearance. Nobody asked, but occasionally she would detect speculation in a pair of eyes that would slide hastily away, or a conversation would just die when she approached. She could live with that. She had told them the facts. Not the truth, but the facts.

She was looking out into a cold December rain, preparing to make a dash for a cab after working late, when she felt a hand on her arm, preventing her from stepping out the revolving door.

"I thought it was you," said the deep voice at her elbow.

"Dell Stewart," she said, glancing up into the smiling brown eyes of the man she hadn't seen since that summer morning. And she hadn't seen him too well, then.

"How are you, Rae? I heard you were back at work. How's the arm?"

"I'm fine. We're closing up shop. I know that doesn't come as a surprise to you."

"No, Paul told me. Looking for a job?"

"Why? Do you have one?"

"Yes." There was no hesitation in Stewart's offer. "Just say the word."

"I appreciate it, but I really think I'm going back to law school."

"Well, I can't blame you, but I hate to see it happen. You're not letting Peters's death influence you?"

"No, although Paul thinks I am. It's just the culmination of a lot of things."

Dell studied her a minute and then nodded his understanding. "Why don't you let me give you a lift home? This stuff will chill you to the bone."

"Are you sure? Will it be out of your way?"

"You're on my way home if you're still at the same place."

"Then I'm on your way, and I hate cold rain. Lead on, Macduff," she said, joining him under his outsize golf umbrella.

During the ride they talked about football, the weather, some social events, although Rae, having been holed up like a hibernating bear throughout the fall, was really out of touch. She enjoyed being with Dell and told him how much she appreciated the lift.

"Anytime, Rae. Just call me. I'm still at the same place. Still doing the same old things."

She had wanted to ask Dell all along, because she was sure he would have heard, but she had forced her mind away from the questions until they arrived at her complex. *Why not?* she finally decided. *After all I went through, I have a right to ask.*

"Is this the one? Or the next set?" Dell asked, trying to find the right building in the driving rain.

"This is it. This is great. I really appreciate the ride."

"It was good to see you, Rae. Take care."

When she didn't open the car door, Dell turned to look at her.

"What finally happened with the guy you arrested that morning?"

He didn't answer for a long time, so she waited, thinking she was probably going to regret having asked.

"What the hell," he said softly. "I'm not Paul Hardesty. I don't owe anybody anything in this. Except maybe you."

"Me?"

"Yeah, because I think it was a raw deal."

"A raw deal?" she repeated when he didn't go on.

"And maybe dangerous. Dangerous for you *not* to know."

"What the hell are you talking about, Dell?"

"Look, we didn't arrest anybody that morning. Kyle was dead. The big guy was dead. But there were no arrests."

"Wait a minute. I don't get this. The other man. He was there. He was there when I was shot. You guys were just outside. Are you trying to tell me he escaped? With all you big-time lawmen surrounding the place?" She allowed her disbelief to color her questions.

"I'm not telling you anything other than the fact that we didn't make any arrests that morning," Dell repeated, almost challengingly.

"Paul told me he was in custody. That they were going to deport him to Colombia for trial."

Dell didn't say anything, but he met her eyes without flinching.

"You're telling me that was a lie?" Rae asked.

He waited a long time, maybe regretting what he had revealed, but finally he nodded. "I might as well be hanged for a sheep as for a goat. That's what I'm telling you. You make Hardesty level with you. He owes you that."

He stopped talking and looked out the windshield into the night and the rain.

"Is that it?" she said finally. "Is that all you're going to say?"

"You ask Paul. *Make* him tell you why he lied. I didn't even visit you in the hospital because I was still burned. Tell Hardesty I said to stick it if he doesn't like me telling you the truth."

"Trust me," Rae promised softly, "that's going to be very *mild* compared to what I tell Paul Hardesty."

Chapter Twelve

Paul was on the phone when she knocked on his open door the next morning, but he motioned her in. She walked across the room to the chair in front of his desk and waited for him to finish his conversation. Finally he hung up and turned, smiling, to greet her.

She didn't give him time to speak, wanting to catch him off guard as much as possible. "I talked to Dell Stewart last night. I want to know why you lied to me, Paul. Why you've lied to me from the beginning."

The impact of her words touched his eyes, flickered briefly in the clear blue, and then he shook his head. "I don't understand, Rae. What are you upset about?"

"God, you do that so well. Doesn't it even *bother* you anymore? You've lied and lied and lied to me. From the very first, when you lied about the courier. You look at me out of those innocent baby-blues, and like a fool, I always believe you." She stopped for a breath, and then went on, trying to at least sound rational. "You told me that the man you arrested the morning I shot Kyle had been deported, sent to Colombia for trial. Stewart told me there *were* no arrests."

"Did you want him arrested, Rae?" he asked softly.

The question stopped her. Could Paul possibly know what had happened between them? She had felt so much guilt for loving him; it was a betrayal of the person she was, of her father's memory, a betrayal even of Paul and the task force. But despite the depths of those feelings, the heaviest guilt had been that, in finally doing the right thing, she had betrayed her captor. Why, then, had she been so furious last night to find out he hadn't been arrested?

"I wanted what was *right*," she said angrily—an explanation of her own emotions as much as an answer for Paul. "I got Diego *killed* trying to do what was right. I took a bullet, Paul, doing what good cops do. Then I find out from Dell—"

"Stewart shouldn't have told you," he interrupted. "It wasn't his *place* to tell you anything."

"Why not? Because Stewart doesn't lie? Or because that's all *you* know how to do? Why wasn't that man arrested? And damn it, don't you lie to me again."

She waited a long time, breathing deeply, again fighting for control.

"I can't tell you that, Rae."

"You owe me, Paul. You at least owe me an explanation. You know you do."

"Yes." He acknowledged the truth of her statement.

"Did they pay you off?" she demanded, wondering if she could have been so wrong about Hardesty. "How much does it take to buy a man's soul? You asked me that about Kyle. How much did it take for the cartel to buy yours?"

"Do you think I'd still hold this job if Stewart thought there'd been a payoff? Did he even suggest that, Rae?" Paul asked, seemingly as angry now as she.

And, of course, Dell hadn't. It had simply been one of the scenarios that had occurred to her in the sleepless night during which she had tried to figure it all out.

"Then what else? What possible reason could there be for *not* taking him in? Why would you just let him go? Give me something that makes sense."

Paul's lips tightened, and he said nothing for a long time, weighing what to tell her, she guessed. Deciding, maybe, on the next lie. Wondering what she would buy. When he did speak, it was obvious he wasn't even going to attempt an explanation—believable or otherwise.

"Sometimes we don't have choices about what we do. I told you it went with the job. Sometimes we just have to do what we have to do."

"That's *it*? *That's* your explanation for letting him go? 'We have to do what we have to do'?" she jeered. "God, you make me sick. This whole business makes me sick. Did he cut a deal? What the hell went down, Paul?"

He sat there behind his desk, meeting her eyes, but she couldn't read anything in the clear blue depths of his.

"I slept with him, Paul. I let him make love to me," she told him, trying to make him understand. And then she knew the rest was more important, so she said it, too. "And I loved him, more than I've ever loved anyone in my life. But because I'm a cop, I gave him to you. I betrayed him. And I've lived with that every day for the past five months. Because it was the *right* thing to do. I could live with that guilt because, somewhere inside, I *knew* I had done the right thing. And then last night Stewart told me you let him go. All I'm asking is that you tell me why. Make me understand," Rae begged.

Finally, the slow negative movement of the white head provided his answer.

"I can't work for you anymore, Paul. I can't live anymore with the lies and deceit."

She got up and walked toward the door of his office.

"Rae," he said softly.

She turned around in time to see him close a desk drawer. He held an object almost hidden in his hand.

"When I was packing up, I found this. I made you a promise, and I've kept it, but since we're shutting down, I can't guarantee what will happen to this if I put it in the case file. I think you should have it."

He opened his hand to reveal a tape. The tape Franklin Holcomb had made that night in Virginia. The agonized whispers of the dying courier.

"Escobar's accountant," she said softly. There was nothing left. There was no truth or honor left anywhere.

"What the hell are you talking about?" Paul said, the blue eyes reflecting now what appeared to be genuine puzzlement.

"He told me that. He said the courier knew so much about the money laundering because he was Escobar's accountant."

"Then *he* lied to you, Rae."

She shook her head, her small smile very bitter. "*Everyone* lies. He told me that, too. And he was certainly right about you. He said it was probably in your job description. So who do I believe, Paul? Who can I ever trust again?"

"Listen to me, Rae. The man in Virginia was everything you thought he was. And he wasn't part of the cartel. I swear to you on my soul that's the truth."

"I'd be surprised if you have any soul left. You've probably sold it all through the years in little bits and pieces. Little dishonors that you did, although you knew they were wrong. Expedient, maybe, but wrong."

"Take the tape, Rae."

"I don't *want* it," she said, feeling sickness coil inside her. "If he was what you say he was—" She stopped because she didn't know anymore. She would probably never know. "Burn it," she said finally. "I told you then. If he was what you say, it shouldn't be the only thing that's left."

"I thought you might want to listen to it. To remember—"

"I don't want to remember anything I ever did for you. You're not the man I thought you were, and you used me. You lied to me and you used me. I won't ever forgive you for that."

"Rae," he said, and for once the mask was down. For once the regret was clear in the blue eyes.

"Burn it," she said again. "At least do one right thing in this whole mess of lies and deception. Do one thing right," she ordered bitterly, as she turned and left.

IT WAS A FEW DAYS before Christmas, and Rae had fought off her mother's determined efforts to have her on a flight to Texas to spend the holidays there. Rae didn't know why she hadn't gone, why she was sitting in a dirty apartment alone, eating day-old pizza out of the refrigerator. She put the half-eaten piece she held down on the coffee table. She ought to be home where there would be a tree and decorations. The only decorations here were a pair of panty hose draped across the back of a chair, and they didn't look at all festive.

She stood and began gathering up newspapers, dirty dishes, and stray garments. She had made a dent in the mess when the doorbell rang.

She found herself looking at Paul Hardesty across the short length of her security chain. She tried to close the door, but he had already put his foot in place.

"You damn well know better than to open your door without asking who's out here," he said. "It's dangerous, and you know it."

She didn't understand his anger. Unless he was embarrassed about showing up here after what had happened in his office. Unless he was trying to give her something to think about besides his lies and deceptions.

"Maybe I like living dangerously," she said. She turned to walk across the room. "Let me know when you get tired of standing there."

"We have somewhere to go," he said, "and you really don't have a choice, Rae. Your presence has been requested at the Colombian Embassy reception tonight. I gave your regrets to State, and they were very annoyed. If you don't show up to receive the grateful response of the Colombian government for your role in exposing the money-laundering operation and in Kyle's death, then it's a slap in the face to those people who are trying very hard to control the trafficking, against odds we can't comprehend. Murder of Supreme Court justices, ministers of justice—anybody who gets in the cartel's way is brutally killed and still there are people willing to fight them.

"So, get off your butt, Rae, and unlock this door. You just smile and receive their thanks, and then I'll bring you back. They didn't do anything to you. Hate me if you want to, but do this, because it's right.''

She was halfway across the room before she realized what argument he had used. "I *always* do what's right," she said bitterly, but she closed the door and undid the chain so he could come in.

"How long do I have?" she asked, looking at his tux.

"How about thirty minutes?"

Thirty minutes later she was standing in her bedroom with her evening gowns spread across the bed. One was strapless and the other had narrow straps that crossed behind her neck.

"What's wrong?" Paul asked from the doorway. She was glad she had taken time to throw a robe on over her underwear.

"Come right in," she said sarcastically. "Don't mind that I'm not dressed."

"That's what I'm concerned about. What's the holdup?"

"I don't have anything to wear," she explained and saw the disbelief on his face.

"Is that a joke? Put something the hell on and let's go."

"I can't wear these because they don't hide this." She pulled her robe off her shoulder to expose the scar Kyle's bullet had left. "State Department or not, I am not going around looking like Frankenstein's monster at this party. You can forget it."

"The scar's not that bad. Hell, flaunt it," he said. "Let them see—"

"Like you said, Paul, it's not these guys."

He took a deep breath. "What about a coat, a jacket?"

In spite of herself, she laughed. "Over an evening gown? Give me a break. God, if that's not just like a man."

He ignored her mockery and began systematically going through her closet.

"This is it, Paul. These are all the evening dresses I have."

Her words didn't slow his methodical examination, and finally he pulled from the back of the closet a black velvet dinner dress. It was old, but cut on classic lines, with long sleeves and a high neck.

"That's not an evening gown," she began.

"Look, they won't care if you wear a uniform. Put it on, Rae, and let's get this over with."

The dress worked. The black was a contrast to her ivory skin and dark red hair. She wore no jewelry, except the diamond studs her dad had given her when she'd graduated from college. She had expected a new rifle.

When she walked into the living room, Paul's eyes were reassurance that the black velvet would do. She had good legs. Maybe if they were the only ones exposed at the party, people would think she was just trying to attract attention. She didn't really care what they thought. Like Paul, she just wanted to get this behind her.

At the embassy Rae stood beside Paul with a barely touched drink in her hand, the noise and the color, the mingled scents of expensive perfume and good cigars, swirling around her. Since nobody had paid her the slightest attention, she had begun to wonder about all this grateful-government crap Hardesty had used to get her here.

It was at least a couple of hours after they arrived before Paul touched her arm, whispering, "The ambassador wants to see you in private. Come on."

She wasn't even nervous by this time, just ready to get it over so she could go home. Maybe really go home. She wondered if she could still get a flight out in the Christmas rush.

His eyes tracked the movements of the woman in the black velvet dress. Her hair alone was enough to mark Rae Phillips's passage through the throng, but Paul Hardesty's equally unmistakable coloring and military bearing made the two people walking toward the ambassador's private library even more distinctive.

There appeared to be no lingering effects from the bullet she'd taken last summer. At least no physical ones. It was surprising that she had come here, surprising she would respond to any invitation issued by this government. It had seemed she would want to put it all behind her.

The lips of the man hidden in a curtained alcove of the balcony lifted in a slight smile. Rae Phillips apparently hadn't learned the true meaning of fear, despite what had happened to her. She was a woman of courage; and everyone admired real courage, except that sometimes being so brave could lead to disaster. The smile faded as the couple disappeared behind the closing door. A private conversation with the ambassador.

He could have arranged, had he desired, to listen in on that conversation, but then there was always the chance he might be discovered. Besides, he already knew what would be said. And more important, what would not. It was better this way. Better only to watch.

PAUL ESCORTED HER into a small library. The ambassador—dark, slightly overweight and nearing middle age—rose from one of a pair of ivory couches arranged before the welcoming fire. He kissed Rae's hand and led her to sit on the opposite sofa. Paul had discreetly disappeared.

The ambassador said nothing until he was again seated, and then he smiled at her.

"Ms. Phillips, I am Carlos Ramirez, and on behalf of my government, I wish to thank you for your role in the last round of what has been a very discouraging war with the criminals who are trying to control our country."

"I really think my part in those operations has been highly exaggerated. I did my job, or at least I tried to. That's all."

"I understood from Mr. Hardesty that you would feel this way, but I wanted you to know how much we appreciate your efforts. So many people assume that all Colombians have their hands out for the money the cartels generate. That is not true. Many have fought and continue to fight against what is happening in Colombia. My own brother was mur-

dered by the cartel. He was one of those who was determined to destroy them, and it cost him his life.''

''I'm sorry. I didn't know.''

''Do you have brothers or sisters, Ms. Phillips?''

''No,'' Rae said, ''but my father was a police officer who
was killed on duty. I *do* understand.''

He nodded, and then went on, almost as though lost in
the past, working through his own emotional response to the
story he was telling.

''I had two brothers. One I told you about. Always it was
duty, responsibility. But the other,'' he said softly, shaking
his head. ''He was the beauty, the light of my mother's life.
She spoiled him because he was charming. He always got
what he wanted. Always.''

Rae waited, wondering where this was all leading, wondering where Paul was and how she was going to get out of
here. She wasn't good at social chitchat, and she had lost the
point of this conversation. *Come on, Paul,* she pleaded silently. *Get me out of here.*

''Fast cars and expensive polo ponies, beautiful women.
Too much money. Everything came too easily. We didn't
understand, until it was too late....''

The ambassador's soft, accented voice faded. His eyes
were lowered, as if examining his hands, which were clasped
tightly together in his lap, their paler skin a contrast to the
fine black wool of his evening dress.

What am I supposed to say about his playboy brother?
Rae wondered. She didn't understand what this family history had to do with the cocaine wars or with the Colombian government's appreciation of the Americans who had
been involved in this phase.

''I'm afraid, Ambassador Ramirez, that I don't understand exactly what—''

His eyes lifted to her face.

''No, of course, you don't. I apologize. Sometimes when
one feels strongly about something...'' Again he paused,
and then he smiled at her. ''I wanted to meet you, Ms.
Phillips, and I'm glad I have. We truly appreciate all that

you've done for our country. And now, Mr. Hardesty tells me, you're thinking about going home.''

"To finish my law degree. I think maybe that's best.''

"Why? Why is it best to give up a job you do so well?'' he asked, smiling at her again.

"Because...'' She couldn't explain to this stranger why she could no longer do that job, could no longer work for Paul Hardesty. Carlos Ramirez was a man who still believed in the values she had been taught, the same values her father had held.

"Because going home seems to be the right thing to do,'' she said finally. Even to her own ears, it sounded as ridiculous as the excuse with which Paul had answered her questions. "When there's nothing left, you just go on. You just keep doing the things you *hope* are right.''

"That sounds like something my brother might have said,'' the ambassador replied softly, with feeling too deep for those simple words.

She smiled at him because she didn't have any response to his comment and then was immensely grateful to feel Paul's hand on her shoulder. She made polite noises of goodbye and did all the things she was supposed to do.

As Paul was putting her coat over her shoulders in the embassy foyer, she saw the ambassador standing in the doorway of the room where they had met. She understood then the almost-eerie feeling she'd had of being watched. His dark eyes were on her, and he smiled as he saw her notice him.

All the way home, Rae tried to decide what had been wrong about the meeting. She knew instinctively that she had missed something. There had been far more going on in that small library than she'd picked up on.

Paul insisted on checking her apartment for her. He did it methodically and thoroughly, opening every closet and even peering under the bed.

"Looking for the bad guys?'' she asked sardonically, watching the practiced routine. Whatever else Hardesty was, he was professional.

"You never know," he said, ignoring her sarcasm. "And lock the door behind me," he ordered.

"If you *arrested* all the crooks instead of letting them go, we wouldn't have to be so careful."

"Don't start, Rae. Just lock the damn door."

Out of habit she obeyed.

It wasn't until after Paul had gone, and she had begun to take off the black velvet, that it hit her—what she had missed tonight. Maybe if she hadn't been so concerned with her own problems, she might really have listened to what the ambassador had told her. She would have put it all together then.

The man in Virginia, the courier, had been the ambassador's brother. She had always known the original contact had been made through diplomatic channels. Ambassador Ramirez had told her that the cartel had murdered his brother, but in her hurry to get past his gratitude, she hadn't realized the significance. And that was why he had wanted to meet her. She was the one who had been with his brother at the last.

Which meant, of course, that the courier had been exactly the kind of man she had thought him to be that night. She had *not* been mistaken. At least Paul hadn't lied about that. Somewhere inside, a little of her bitter disillusionment eased.

She knew then that she would have to see Carlos Ramirez again, to tell him how much she had admired the courier—his courage and endurance. She owed him that. She owed them both. She didn't know if it would ease the ambassador's pain, but it would help her to finally express what she had felt about the bravery of the man she'd met that night in Virginia.

But if she were successful tomorrow in getting a flight out, she wouldn't have a chance to tell him. The way she felt about Washington and Hardesty, about everything she'd done, she would probably throw what she could fit into her suitcase and leave. Just get away from all that had happened.

Which meant that if she wanted to tell the ambassador
what his brother's sacrifice had meant to her, she would
have to go back tonight. There was time to grab a cab and
get back before the party dispersed. She still had the invitation Paul had handed her on their way in. She slipped the
zipper of the black velvet back up. This was really the best
way. To say what she needed to say to Ambassador Ramirez and then get the hell out of Dodge. Permanently.

When she arrived, there were a few people waiting under
the embassy portico for their cars to be brought around. The
staff, however, was politely reluctant to admit her. Most of
the guests had departed, and Mrs. Ramirez had already gone
upstairs. Rae's smiling insistence that she needed only a
quick, private word with the ambassador eventually paid
off, and she was directed to the same library she had visited
before.

The rooms that had earlier been filled with elegant women
on the arms of their influential men were now almost deserted. The servants were moving among the few isolated
clusters of people, unobtrusively beginning the task of
cleaning up, which would probably go on for hours after the
last guest had departed.

Rae debated whether or not to knock on the library door.
Finally, she simply turned the handle and eased it open
enough to see into the dimly lit room. If the ambassador had
already gone upstairs, she would leave. She could always
write to him. It really didn't matter how she conveyed what
she felt—as long as she did so.

Carlos Ramirez was standing beside the fireplace. In his
hand was a tumbler of liquid, its contents ambered in the
dying firelight. His black tie had been loosened, and she
could see the tiredness in his dark, heavy face.

She opened the door wider and stepped inside.

"Ambassador Ramirez," she said.

He was not alone. Rae wasn't sure when she became
aware in the room's firelit dimness of the other occupant.
Another man. Sitting on the ivory sofa she'd occupied earlier as she had listened to the story of the ambassador's

martyred brother. And this man's dark eyes were focused on her face as intently now as they had been on the day she had killed Kyle Peters to prevent his being shot, the day she had more than willingly taken the bullet that had been meant for him.

"Hello, Rae," he said softly.

Her heart stopped. And then, of course, it began again in the familiar, unchanging rhythm.

She heard the ambassador's startled, inarticulate response to her presence, but it was as if the sound came from a great distance. It had no real connection to what was happening here.

She had thought she would never see him again. And then, where she should least expect someone like him to be...

"What are you doing here?" she asked.

Her first thought. Not her first reaction. That had been physical. Hot and jolting. Sensuous. Nothing had changed. He still had that power over her senses. The power to make her want him, to want to touch him, to feel his skin moving against hers in the darkness. His mouth over her body, sweet and hot and so achingly tender.

"I think a fairer question might be, what are *you* doing here, *querida?*"

The beautiful voice hadn't changed, and in response to its pull, she found herself advancing over the rich Oriental carpet that covered the space between them until she stood, looking down into those midnight eyes.

During the intervening months the scarring she had seen that morning had been surgically repaired. The left side of his face almost matched again the beauty of the right. *So damn beautiful,* she thought.

Aloud she said something very different—some thought that had formed in the still-functioning, coldly rational fragment of her brain. In the minute part that was not examining his features, that was not storing every dark, near-perfect detail, every memory.

"I thought..." she began, realizing how ridiculously wrong she had been. "When the ambassador told me tonight about his brother, I thought *he* was the courier. The man who died in Virginia."

She had returned to sympathize with Señor Ramirez, to tell him how much she had admired his brother, and had caught him entertaining the cartel. And she knew she shouldn't be surprised, considering the current rumors about corruption at the very top of this government. *People think all Colombians have their hands out for the money the cartels generate*—the ambassador's words echoed bitterly.

"And instead... I find he's no better than the rest Such *honest* Colombians," she mocked.

Her former captor's mouth tightened briefly. The ambassador also made some movement, and the dark eyes of the man on the sofa lifted, met and held Ramirez's. As Rae watched, the ambassador subsided, leaning back against the mantel, the same implacable will that had dominated Diego again directing, ordering—this time, without words.

"He wasn't the courier, *querida*. The brother Carlos told you about was a judge. In Medellin. A judge the cartel couldn't bribe, couldn't control, so they killed him with machine guns. Along with his wife and daughter. They were ambushed on the way to mass one Sunday morning. The baby was three years old. An *honest* Colombian, Rae," he said.

She fought against the impact of the story. It didn't change what was going on here.

"Then why is his brother doing business with scum like you?" she challenged.

"Rafe," the ambassador intervened.

The man on the sofa raised his hand, palm out to command his silence.

"Rafe?" Rae questioned softly. It was right. It fit.

"I am Rafael Ramirez," he said. "Forgive the belated introduction. And don't hold Carlos too responsible for offering me refuge. In Colombia, we still believe blood is thicker than water."

"The other brother," she said. Finally something made sense. "The playboy who needed a lot of money for all his little games. The charming one," she mocked.

"The black sheep," he agreed, the hard mouth tilting slightly at the corners. "Every family has one, *querida*."

"Diplomatic immunity," Rae realized suddenly. "That's why Paul couldn't arrest you. Carlos protected you. He provides you with total immunity, no matter what you do, simply by putting your name on the list of diplomats accredited by his government. Of course," she said sarcastically. "How convenient."

"A very convenient relationship, all things considered," Rafe agreed softly, and he smiled openly at her this time.

Congratulating her, maybe, for finally figuring it out.

"How can you protect him?" Rae asked, glancing at the silent figure standing beside the fire. "Knowing what he is, what he does."

"I handle their money," Rafe said simply, drawing her gaze back to him. "That's what I do, *querida*. Nothing else."

"Is that how you justify it? You and Carlos? Does that make it all right?"

"I don't try to justify it."

"Rafe," the ambassador protested again.

"You're upsetting Carlos, *querida*. I think you owe him an apology."

"I don't think so," she objected bitterly. "You told me once I didn't owe *anyone* an apology. I think that's still true. Certainly not Carlos. He knows what you are, and still he protects you. Paul lets you go because your name's on some piece of paper that he knows is a lie. The courier I came here tonight to express my admiration for is probably in witness protection, retrieving the dirty millions he hid for Escobar. And they all still sleep at night."

"And you, *querida*, would punish us all," Rafe said, smiling at her again.

"It's wrong. All of it. No matter what you say, what justification you use, none of it's *right*," she argued.

"That's true, *querida*. And there are so few things left in this world that are *right*. Those you should hold on to," he suggested quietly.

When he spoke again, the dark voice had changed, becoming less personal, more businesslike. And remembering his business, she was sickened.

"Carlos tells me you're going home."

"I'm going back to Texas."

"To finish your law degree."

"Yes."

"Then you'll be able to lock up all the bad men," he said. The familiar gentle amusement colored his tone. "You'll put them away, and the world will become a safer place. For *your* babies."

"My babies," she jeered softly, mocking what she felt.

Suddenly, unexpectedly, her eyes filled, the tears hot and stinging. Unwanted, all the memories imploded. And through the blur, she watched his eyes change at what was happening in hers.

"Rae," he whispered.

She controlled the tears, the hard lump that blocked her throat, the pain of the memories, so that she could tell him.

"You *told* me to guard my soul. I should have listened. I accused Paul of selling his in little bits and pieces through the years. Doing things that he knew weren't right because they were expedient or necessary or because he had to. And then lying about them. Lying to me. Maybe even to himself."

She paused, but he said nothing. The black eyes had never left her face. She felt a tear slip down, against her control, and she brushed it angrily from her cheek with the back of her hand.

"And Carlos," she went on. "He sold his soul for blood—in spite of knowing what you are—because you're his brother."

The silence in the room was complete. It seemed that no one even breathed. And no one denied what she was saying.

"But I *gave* mine away. And that's the worst sin of all. To destroy *yourself*. To destroy who you are. Until there's nothing left. No guides through the darkness."

He didn't attempt to offer, this time, any comfort in the night she had created for herself, and so she told him the rest. The real reason she had known, somewhere inside, that there was nothing left of the good little girl her father had raised.

"Even now, Rafe, if you asked me... Even now, knowing what you are..."

And she found herself waiting. Still, in spite of it all, waiting for him to ask.

"Go home, *querida*," he said, too softly, his eyes very dark in the shadowed firelight.

"I should hate you," she said.

"If it helps."

"It might. If I could manage it. But all I seem able to manage is to hate myself."

She turned and made her way back across the expanse of luxurious carpet, the journey endless to the door, and then closing it behind her, she moved through the now deserted rooms of the Colombian Embassy.

Chapter Thirteen

The following morning Rae listened to the carefully concealed impatience in the voices that answered her inquiries. There was no space available on any flight from Washington to El Paso, they assured her. Or to Dallas. Or anywhere else, as far as that was concerned, one harried, disembodied voice had confirmed. It was, after all, Christmas Eve, for heaven's sake. Of course, she could come to the airport if she wanted to take a chance on a cancellation, but the waiting lists for those were already miles long.

When she had reconciled herself to being stuck in Washington until after the holiday rush, Rae decided that those days could at least be productive. She would have to sublet her apartment and the cleaner it was, the easier that would be. And it wasn't as if she had exactly been spit-shining the place lately. There were areas of her housekeeping that could certainly stand improvement.

When her mother called Christmas morning, Rae was scrubbing the grout in the bathroom tiles with bleach and an old toothbrush. She tried to imbue her voice with some seasonal cheer as they exchanged greetings. Her mom's description of the dishes she was carrying to dinner at Aunt Molly's created a tightness in her throat, and determinedly she fought off the emotional response. If she gave way just once, she knew, it would all come tumbling down—this house-of-cards control she'd been rebuilding since her confession last night.

She knew she hadn't fooled her mother when, at the end of the conversation, she asked softly, "Rachel, baby, you are all right, aren't you?"

"I'm fine. I just miss you. I just decided to come home."

"It's not—"

"Nothing's wrong," she interrupted. "Stop worrying. I'm a big girl now. I'll see you as soon as I can get a flight out. I'll call you. I love you."

"I love you, too, Rachel. Have a Merry Christmas."

"Merry Christmas, Mama," she said softly. The tears had welled as she listened to the dial tone.

SHE HAD FINISHED the tile and had even scrubbed away the black stuff that grew behind the faucets. She cleaned out the refrigerator and then turned to the stove. There wasn't much to worry about there, no cooked-over pie juices like in her mother's oven. And finally, when she couldn't find anything else to clean, she sat down in the only comfortable chair in her tiny living room, letting her sweatpants-clad legs dangle over its overstuffed arm.

She picked up the remote and surfed through the choirs singing carols and old black-and-white Christmas movies, trying not to think. Only a couple of days and she would be home. She held on to that promise like a lifeline. Once back home, back in law school, she would manage to find her emotional equilibrium. She wouldn't always feel like this. She never had before. *This, too, shall pass,* her grandmother had always reminded when some family crisis loomed so large as to obscure the good. This, too, would pass. The bitterness and the disillusion.

The phone interrupted, and she fumbled to find the Mute button on the remote. She didn't even recognize the people on the screen, now silently mouthing their lines. She hadn't been watching, lost in this endless emotional fog. The caller was probably her mother, worrying about what Rae hadn't been able to hide this morning. Her mother always knew when something was wrong.

"Hello," she said, working to keep her voice light.

"Rae?"

It wasn't her mother.

She knew immediately to whom the deep voice belonged, despite the slight, unfamiliar distortion caused by the phone. She would have recognized his accent if nothing else, although the electronics had changed the dark richness subtly, altering the texture, so that something fluttered at the back of her mind. There was something—

"Rae?" he said again.

"Yes," she whispered. Her eyes closed. This was the last thing she needed. And the last she'd expected.

"I thought maybe you'd already left."

"I couldn't get a flight. The holidays."

There was too long a silence, and she fought the urge to fill it up. *His nickel.*

"I'd like to see you," Rafe said. "Before you leave."

"No," she replied, her mind and not her heart controlling.

"There are some things I'd like to tell you. Things that I think—"

"I don't want to hear anything you have to say. You and I have nothing to talk about."

She had remembered even before she heard his soft laugh.

"I know. We never did. That's why we decided—"

"That wasn't an invitation," she told him.

"I know, *querida.* I know it wasn't."

Again the silence grew. She bit her lip to keep from saying anything. She had confessed enough in the embassy that night. She had laid bare her innermost feelings, and it hadn't made her feel any better. There was no need to rehash it all.

As if he had read her mind, Rafe spoke again.

"There was something you said . . ." He paused, and she waited. "Something that *wasn't* true. In all the truths you told us, there was one thing that—"

"It doesn't matter," she interrupted. She didn't want to hear excuses or explanations. She thought she had made that clear.

"I told you from the beginning I couldn't make any commitments, Rae. I never lied to you."

Everyone lies, he had said. Suddenly she was furious to hear him deny it.

"You *lied* to me every time you put your hands on me. Every word you whispered into the darkness was a *lie.* Every time we made love your body said you cared about me, and *that* was a lie."

Another silence. Prolonged.

Why couldn't she just keep her mouth shut? Rae wondered. *Why did she have to reveal all the pain?*

"I never meant to hurt you."

There was nothing to say to that. Maybe it was even true.

"I'll survive."

"I know you will. I never doubted it. I'm only concerned that what I've done has—"

"You want me to absolve your guilt for taking me to bed?" she interrupted again, still angry. "Is that what this is all about? Is that why you called? Okay, you're absolved. It was my fault. My decision."

Again, silence.

"I'd like to tell you about the courier. I think we owe you that."

"The courier?" she repeated. *What the hell did that mean?*

"I'd like to tell you the truth about the man you met that night in Virginia."

She didn't know what to say. She remembered Paul's assurance. Had Hardesty, for once, not lied to her? And it mattered, she thought. For some reason, it still mattered that her impressions about that man had been correct.

"Escobar's accountant?" she asked bitterly.

"No."

"That was a lie?"

"Yes," he admitted. "And I need to tell you the truth. I think you deserve to hear it."

His brother, she thought. *Her guess had not been wrong. Then why—*

"There's no one here. Carlos and Elena have gone back to Colombia for the holidays. The staff has the day off."

"The embassy?" she asked, her body already reacting to the thought of being with him. Just to see him again before she left. Without Carlos. With no one there.

"There's a buzzer on the column. Ring, and I'll open the gate for you. The front door's unlocked. Come to the library where we were that night. I'll be waiting, *querida.*"

Suddenly, the connection was broken. She held the phone in her trembling fingers, once more listening to a dial tone.

Did he honestly believe she was going to go running across town to see him? What kind of idiot did he think she was?

"Bastard," she said very softly. The people on the muted television made no response. "You rotten bastard," she whispered.

SHE BUZZED THE gate, and it opened immediately. He'd known she would come. She walked inside the embassy grounds, pulling the gate inward. Her hand hesitated just before the lock engaged. She might decide she needed to leave before she'd listened to whatever else he wanted to say, besides the truth about the courier he'd promised. And she didn't want to be dependent on his permission.

She let the gate rest against the fence, but she didn't pull it together. If she decided to walk out, she could. At any time.

The front door was unlocked, just as he'd promised. She stepped inside and closed it behind her. The huge house was silent, but she waited in the foyer, listening. She could see the entrance to the small library, where Carlos Ramirez had stood and watched her and Paul's departure the night of the party.

She walked toward it, her running shoes making little noise on the gleaming marble floors. She stood for a moment before the door, again hesitating over whether to knock or just enter unannounced. He'd said he would be waiting, so she turned the handle and stepped inside.

There was no welcoming blaze in the fireplace today, and
the room was slightly chilled. Rafe was seated on the same
ivory sofa, wearing a navy crew-neck sweater and worn
jeans. On the table beside him was a decanter and an empty
glass that matched the one he held, half-full, in his long dark
fingers. He was looking down at its contents, and although
she knew he must have heard the door, it was a moment before the midnight eyes lifted to meet hers.

"Thank you for coming," he said.

"I didn't have anything else to do. I'd finished scrubbing
the bathroom."

She hadn't even changed clothes. She wore the same ratty
gray sweats she'd slipped into after her shower this morning. No makeup and her hair pulled back into a ponytail.
Defiantly, she hadn't dressed for him. She hadn't even allowed herself to look into a mirror. It didn't matter how she
looked. That wasn't what she had come for. She just wanted
to hear what he'd promised to tell her. Hear some truth and
then leave.

His eyes drifted slowly down her figure in the oversize
sweats, all the way down to her running shoes and crew
socks.

Not how the women he associated with dressed, she
thought. *But then, it's about time he realized I'm not one of
his women.*

His lips quirked suddenly.

The bastard was trying not to laugh, Rae realized.

"You look about sixteen," Rafe said, finally allowing his
lips to move into the smile he'd been fighting. Rae could
hear the teasing quality of his voice, could feel it inside,
curling through all the places he had ever touched. And it
was as if he were touching her again. She controlled the responses in her body that just his voice could cause.

"Yeah? Well, I feel about a hundred. So let's get this
show on the road—whatever it is that's so important I had
to come over here to hear it."

"Would you like to sit down, *querida?* This may take...a
while."

"Don't call me that," she ordered and saw the reaction in his face. He hadn't liked it. Her request or her tone. She wasn't sure which, but what she'd said had definitely had an impact. His eyes fell again to the tumbler in his hand. He lifted it and drank, a long, deep pull on the alcohol.

"Dutch courage," he said, smiling, when he looked up to find her watching him. "Sit down, Rae."

She didn't move, trying to decide if she wanted to be that close to him, until he added softly, "Please."

She walked away from the door and toward the other sofa. She stopped before it because, from across the expanse of the Oriental rug, the faint fragrance of the expensive cologne that had always surrounded him invaded her senses. Again, she fought the memories and the automatic responses of her body. The scent evoked the nights they'd spent together, but the darkness in her memory was cold, somehow, and frightening. Involuntarily she shivered.

"Please, forgive my intrusion," a voice spoke from the doorway.

Rae turned to find a small man standing there. No one she'd ever seen before. Colombian, she thought, judging not only by his coloring, but by the marked accent. She might never have seen *him* before, but she was familiar with the .357 he was holding. Very familiar with what it could do.

"Allow me to introduce myself," he continued softly, his smile still in place, very pleasant, except for the deadly threat he held in his hand. "I am Enrique Grajales."

He paused, waiting for some response.

"Despite a natural vanity, I suppose I should be grateful my name means nothing to you, Ms. Phillips. Perhaps I should tell you simply that I am a former employer of a colleague of yours. Kyle Peters worked for me," he told her, smiling again.

It took a second for that to sink in—for all the implications to filter through her brain that had been paralyzed by the unexpected sight of the gun. She had come here today prepared to face a very different kind of threat.

A former employer of Kyle's, she thought. *Which meant he was . . .*

Slowly she turned her gaze to the man on the sofa. Rafe hadn't moved. His eyes were locked on the figure standing in the doorway. And their focus didn't shift, not even when she spoke to him.

"You sold me, you bastard. You set me up. That's why you called—to get me here, so you could give me to the cartel."

It was the last, most bitter disillusionment. In spite of what she had known about Rafael Ramirez, she'd never dreamed he would betray her.

"No, *querida,*" Rafe denied softly, his eyes still on Grajales.

"No, Ms. Phillips," the man at the door agreed, amused by her anger, perhaps. "Your name was given to me by Peters. A long time ago. Apparently the only worthwhile information he ever provided."

"*Kyle* gave you my name?" she asked, stalling for time, trying to figure it out. *What the hell was going on?* Paul had told her Kyle had been dealing with Rafe, trying to sell him information. If that were true, then who the hell was Grajales?

"Unfortunately, before we could make use of that information, you disappeared," the man with the gun continued, apparently enjoying his role at center stage. "And then you *reappeared,* rather miraculously, considering what Peters had done to the others. There had to be some significance to the fact that *you* didn't die and Peters did. I felt all along you might be the key to what we sought. All I had to do was be patient, and eventually you would lead me where I wanted to go."

To the courier, Rae thought. He believed she would lead him to the courier, but of course, she had never known—

The revelation was instantaneous, like a cartoon light bulb going on over her head, but there was absolutely no doubt in her mind. *Oh, dear God, Rafe. Lead him to the courier,* Grajales had said, and that was exactly what she'd done. She had finally led the cartels to the courier. *It had come full circle,* she thought, remembering that cold night and the man she'd never forgotten.

This was why she'd trusted Rafe from the beginning, had believed him when he'd denied responsibility for the deaths in the task force. This was the reason Paul hadn't taken him into custody. It even explained Carlos's reaction the night she'd made her bitter accusations. And, of course, Carlos had been the diplomat who had made the original contact with Hardesty.

Rafe had been the man in Virginia. And with that information, all the pieces of the puzzle shifted into place. Of course, Hardesty wouldn't have arrested him. *Not* because he had diplomatic immunity, but because—and her heart lifted at the thought—because he had never been what she had thought him to be. This was what Dell Stewart had wanted Paul to tell her, what he had thought she had a right to know, because it was dangerous for her *not* to be told. That Rafael Ramirez was the man who had whispered into the darkness that night in Virginia—and that someone was still out there searching for him.

Rae fought not to look at Rafe again, fought to keep her eyes focused on Grajales's face. Maybe he hadn't figured it out. It had certainly taken her long enough. Maybe she could still protect Rafe, convince Grajales he had nothing to do with the man he sought, that he was just a competitor with the same goal.

"And where is that?" she asked. Her voice sounded remarkably steady. Considering the stakes.

Grajales simply smiled at the bewilderment she'd tried to inject into the question. "You know very well what I'm looking for, Ms. Phillips. The man who has a very special expertise," he explained patiently, "which he employed with great effect against my former competitors. The man who gave Hardesty the money-laundering information about Medellin."

"Then you and Ramirez are looking for the same thing," Rae lied calmly. "I really hate to disappoint you, but I don't *know* anything about that man. Ramirez can tell you. He used drugs to pick my brain. To get his name. I don't *know* the name of the man you want. You're wasting your time," Rae said.

"I must admit I was a *little* slow in figuring it all out, Ms. Phillips, but the time for deception has passed. I truly didn't understand until I saw Señor Ramirez, but *now*, of course, it's very obvious."

Obvious. Why hadn't she known? Because she hadn't listened to her instincts. To her heart. Because she'd believed all their lies, his and Paul's. Because they both had lied to her from the beginning.

"The clues were all there, but the role was completely out of character for the man you had always appeared to be," Grajales said, his attention directed now to Rafe, away from her, and she tried to gather her resolve. To think of something, anything, to get them out of this.

"You have the ability, of course," Grajales went on. "Well documented. And the financial background. Your title is . . ." He paused, but when Rafe didn't provide the answer he sought, Grajales simply smiled at his refusal to cooperate.

"Investment counselor?" he guessed. "For all your family's very legitimate and extremely profitable businesses. Your disappearance from both the playing fields and the social scene should also have been pointedly coincidental, but, still, I'm afraid I never put it together. Whatever made you decide to become involved?" he asked, his tone almost taunting.

For the first time, Rafe allowed his eyes to find Rae's and it was to her that he spoke. Explained the reason he'd begun the deadly game that had now reached its climax.

"They killed my brother," Rafe said. "And his family. His baby. I thought that wasn't *right*," he added softly.

Slowly she nodded. *In Colombia, we still believe blood is thicker than water.*

It was almost as if the threat of the man in the doorway no longer existed. Or at least had become unimportant. Rafe had told her the truth in this room that night. Not all of it, of course, but at least the truth about his brother. Why, then, hadn't he confessed the rest?

"Why didn't you tell me?" She asked the question aloud and knew by his slight smile that Rafe understood.

"That's the reason I asked you to come today. To explain *all* the whys. After what you said, I knew there were explanations I had to make."

"An impulse to confession for which I'm very grateful," Grajales interrupted the quiet exchange, reminding them of his presence, of the continued threat he represented.

"You've been following me?" Rae asked, trying to buy time. Time to think. There had to be something she could do.

"On occasion. Mostly I've listened to your phone conversations, which have been remarkably dull. Until finally, today, my patience was rewarded. A call from someone who promised to tell you all about the man in Virginia. This has been a long and frustrating search, but I am a very patient man, and the promised reward was . . . *extremely* high."

"You'll never get away with it," Rae said.

Movie dialogue, she thought in disgust. *B-grade.* He would get away with it unless she thought of something. Her brain was racing, but nothing that occurred to her was much better than the empty threat she'd just made.

"And who do you think will stop me?" Grajales questioned, letting his amusement show. "I don't believe Hardesty's cavalry will show up for the rescue *this* time. However, I do think it's time we were on our way—just to prevent any chance of an unexpected interruption. I have a car outside. Mr. Ramirez, if you would."

He smiled at Rafe, who made no move to obey. The big gun slowly traced toward the man still sitting calmly on the ivory sofa. When the eye of the revolver finally arrived at its target, nothing in his dark features had changed.

"No," Rafe said simply.

The blood in Rae's heart congealed, a thick, cold knot in her chest. *Please, God,* she prayed. *Please, don't let him shoot. Don't make me watch him die. Not now. Now that I finally know what he is.*

Even as she prayed, she was measuring the distance to the door, calculating how quickly she could cross it. *Do something,* her instincts screamed, but she knew that if she did the wrong thing, she would only trigger a response she didn't want, one she had just prayed wouldn't happen.

Grajales wouldn't kill Rafe, she told herself. *Rafe was safe because he was the man who could find the treasure. Rafe was safe, so that left...*

"It won't do you any good," Rafe said. "I won't do what you want. You've *wasted* a great deal of time and energy."

"Do you think so?" Grajales asked politely. His eyes moved slowly and deliberately to Rae. "*I,* on the other hand, believe you will do *exactly* as I want you to. Because now I have Ms. Phillips. You may be very willing to die, however slowly and painfully I could arrange for that to happen, but somehow..." His gaze returned mockingly to Rafe. "Somehow, I don't think you'll be so willing to watch *her* suffer. You *do* remember how painful that suffering can be, don't you, Señor Ramirez? The savages from Medellín almost killed the goose that could provide the golden egg—the man who could find Escobar's money. What a shame if they had succeeded. I suppose we should all be grateful to Mr. Hardesty for his intervention."

Grajales had come to the same realization Rae had reached. She was the key to making Rafe do what he wanted. He began to cross the room toward them.

Closer, Rae urged the advancing figure. *A little closer. Just give me some kind of opportunity,* she thought. A chance was all she asked for.

He stopped finally, facing the fireplace, the third point of the intimate triangle they formed. He was too near now to adequately cover them both, but his gun had shifted to Rae during his journey, its muzzle aimed at her body like a pointing finger. She was the one standing, the greatest threat. And the greatest leverage. Leverage to use against the man who still sat, unmoving, on the ivory sofa.

The .357 shifted slightly to focus on her left shoulder.

"The other shoulder this time, I think," Grajales said. "I'll try for a flesh wound, Ms. Phillips, but I can't really promise that. It's difficult to be that precise, as I'm sure you know."

Rae remembered the day she'd taken Kyle's bullet. The fear she was going to die. The pain. It was all there in her head, but she tried to allow none of what she felt to show in her face. Rafe didn't need to know how afraid she was.

"Now, Mr. Ramirez," Grajales ordered again. He never even glanced at the seated man, his attention completely on Rae, a small satisfied smile playing about his lips.

Rae forced herself to be patient. The opportunity was Rafe's. He would have to make the move because he wasn't covered by the big gun's threat. And when he did, she would be ready to dive out of the line of fire. He would never let Grajales shoot her, and whatever action he decided to take, she would be ready, she thought, feeling the adrenaline kick in. She certainly wasn't going to get into a car with this bastard. And neither was Rafe.

"Or do you need help?" Grajales asked, his politeness blatantly false now, the small smile broadening. "I'm sure Ms. Phillips would be very willing to assist you."

"I don't need assistance," Rafe said.

He bent down for something lying on the floor at the end of the sofa. Something hidden in the shadows between the couch and the table that held the decanter.

The eyes of the man holding the gun never wavered from their focus on Rae, but again she had almost forgotten him. She watched as Rafe gripped and fitted the metal forearm crutches he'd picked up. Watched him use them to lift himself off the couch. He was so tall, she thought irrelevantly, when he was standing, leaning slightly on the sticks.

He looked up to find her eyes on him.

"I told you, Rae. Not the prince of the fairy tales," he said softly.

She defeated the sudden blur of tears, but she couldn't seem to produce an answering smile. Paul had warned her so long ago about the scope of the injuries the courier had suffered. He hadn't lied about that. And at last she knew why Rafael Ramirez had not intended her to know who he was or at what cost he had avenged his brother's death.

"The truth," she whispered. This was what he had planned to reveal today. This is why he had asked her to come. *All I seem able to manage is to hate myself.* Because she had told him that, he had finally decided to tell her the truth.

And now it was up to her, she realized suddenly. Whatever hope she'd had that Rafe might stop Grajales was lost in this reality. Any action taken toward getting them out of this would have to be her call and her responsibility.

"I didn't mean to hurt you, Rae. I would never willingly do that, my heart," Rafe said. "I *did* try to warn you. A long time ago. So you'd know—this is not a rescue, *querida.*"

It was the same message he had sent through Diego. To warn her about Kyle.

Even as she was making that connection, Rafe swung upward the metal crutch he held in his right hand, a blur of motion, to impact under the wrist of the man with the gun, the man who still had his entire attention concentrated on Rae, discounting entirely whatever danger Rafael Ramirez might be to his plans, because, of course, he had never seen Rafe as a threat.

The weapon discharged, the sound too loud in the stillness of the room, the bullet whining into the wall behind Rae's head. The force of Rafe's unexpected blow had dislodged the gun, which flew out of Grajales's hand. Without pause, Rafe swung the stick sideways, like a scythe, to catch him full in the face.

By that time Rae was moving. She launched herself, her shoulder aimed at Grajales's midsection. She could hear the breath leave his lungs when she hit. They went down together, landing hard, her body slightly cushioned by his.

She recovered first, raising her torso to drive an elbow into his face, not particular about where it landed because she could feel him already beginning to stir beneath her. His cheekbone, she thought, judging from the surprisingly satisfying sensation of cracking bone. The next driving blow, with all the force of her body behind it, was more accurately landed on his nose, and he slumped back to the floor, eyes closed, his body no longer moving.

Far easier to handle than Diego had ever been, she thought.

Rae crawled off Grajales, panting a little. She rested a moment, still on her hands and knees, watching his face for any signs of returning consciousness, infinitely grateful that there didn't seem to be any.

She was still congratulating herself when the unmistakable clatter of an automatic weapon erupted from the open door. Instinctively, she dropped flat, pushing her body against the floor beside Grajales as shards of stone from the fireplace flickered over her, stinging hard where they struck.

Rafe, she thought. *Where the hell was Rafe?*

Just as that thought formed, she heard the deep-throated answer of the .357 from behind her. Somehow, Rafe had gotten to Grajales's gun.

There was another barrage from the doorway, spewing death across the room. She heard glass break and more debris rained down, a drift of white-plaster snow from the walls or the ceiling. She put her hands over the back of her head as a primitive shield. Again the single cough of the heavy revolver echoed through the room. An answer.

And then nothing. In the sudden, shocking silence, Rae waited—as long as she could force her heart to wait. The entire exchange of gunfire had probably lasted twenty seconds. She waited at least twice that long before she carefully raised her head enough to check the entrance to the room. She could see bodies sprawled in the open doorway, but no one standing.

She glanced toward the fireplace, which had taken the brunt of the damage. Rafe was sitting on the floor, leaning back against the stone facing, the .357 he'd knocked out of Grajales's hand still trained competently on the doorway.

She could see above his head the sweeping pattern of damage from the automatic weapons. *No blood,* she thought. He was down, but she didn't see any blood. His eyes were open and trained, also waiting, on the door.

Finally, because she couldn't make herself delay any longer, she began to crawl across the debris-littered rug that stretched between the two couches. She stayed low, out of the immediate line of fire of anyone entering the room. When she was near enough, she touched Rafe's left hand, and the long fingers closed tightly around hers, steadying ones that were still shaking with reaction.

"I think that's all of them," Rafe said, "but you'd better call Hardesty."

She glanced across the room. From this vantage she could clearly see that there were two bodies before the open door. Grajales's henchmen had apparently reacted to the discharge of the revolver by rushing into the room, prepared to launch a rescue or to help in whatever assault their boss had undertaken.

She turned back to Rafe.

"Are you hurt?" she asked, her concern for him instinctive.

Rafe met her gaze and held it for a long moment. He allowed the gun to lower until it lay flat against the worn denim that covered his thigh.

"Nice shooting," he said.

"What?" she asked blankly.

"I think that's what you would have said to anyone else."

"Nice shooting?" she echoed. *What the hell was he talking about?*

The black eyes were cold. She realized suddenly that he was angry. Because she hadn't complimented his marksmanship? What the hell kind of reaction was that?

"Call Hardesty," he ordered again. His gaze had shifted to the open doorway, but the gun didn't lift.

Knowing he was right, she got up to find a phone.

She couldn't just leave him here, she thought, *sitting on the damn floor.*

"Let me help you up," she suggested, and watched the cold black eyes meet hers again.

"Call Hardesty, Rae. There's a phone on the desk."

"Are you sure that I can't—"

"I'm very sure. Thank you."

HARDESTY SENT the cops, and they arrived first. Rae was relieved when Paul himself appeared minutes after their arrival. She hadn't brought any ID, and she could tell by their attitudes that the uniforms weren't thrilled about being called out on Christmas Day to handle a shooting at the Colombian Embassy.

On his way into the library Hardesty bent to check the bodies that still blocked the doorway.

"Nice shooting," he said, looking up to smile at her. "Your daddy taught you good, Rae."

"It wasn't me. It was Mr. Ramirez."

Paul made a quick survey of the room. Rafe was still sitting on the floor, eyes closed, his head back, resting against the shattered stone facing of the fireplace behind him. Retracing the damage with her gaze, Rae again wondered how he'd escaped injury.

Hardesty glanced at her, for guidance maybe, and she shook her head. She had said nothing else to Rafe after she'd made the rejected offer to help him up.

Hardesty walked over to Rafe and squatted down, blocking her view. Whatever he said was too softly spoken for Rae to hear, and she knew that was deliberate, so she turned back to watch the police put the cuffs on Grajales. It appeared she or Rafe had broken the man's nose, which was streaming blood. Whatever his injuries, he certainly wasn't putting up any resistance. All his fight had dissolved when Rafe had separated him from the gun. *Little men, big guns,* Rae thought derisively.

She was aware when Hardesty stood. He walked back to the Oriental carpet in front of the ivory sofa and bent down to retrieve the crutches.

Rae turned back to watch the cops finish up. There wasn't much going on in the room now. Not much else to pretend to watch.

Suddenly Hardesty's arm was around her shoulder.

"Come on," he said, applying pressure to pull her with him. "You can tell me what happened."

"Now?"

"Right now. Outside," Hardesty said.

She looked up into the clear blue eyes. He squeezed her hard, holding her close against him, and said it again, an order.

"Come on, Rae."

Obedient as always, she let Paul take her outside.

Chapter Fourteen

"Is he all right?" Rae asked, as Paul led her across the foyer.

"He's fine," Paul assured, adding another squeeze with the arm that was still around her shoulders.

They stood in the chill of the December afternoon watching the cops load the bad guys, living and dead, into the appropriate vehicles. They didn't say much to each other while the officers were around.

The cold felt good, making her know she was still alive, fighting the effects of the adrenaline rush. She breathed in several lungfuls of the winter air and said a couple of prayers. Her dad had told her that you never had time to be afraid while it was going down. The real fear came before and after. While things were happening, it all was crystal clear and in slow motion. Every move.

She shivered suddenly, rubbing her hands up and down the sleeves of her sweatshirt.

"I think you owe me some explanations," she said to Paul.

"Where do you want me to start?" he asked.

"How much of what you told me that night in my apartment was true?"

"Most of it. The man Stewart suggested we call in to find the traitor was Ramirez, of course."

"Rafe was your hacker?"

"Don't let him hear you call him a hacker. He doesn't believe in invading systems. The cartel's he did for obvious reasons—to avenge his brother. And he agreed to try to find the traitor in the task force because he had a vested interest in discovering who was trying to locate the courier."

"Because he *was* the courier."

"To protect his family. The cartels would have used anyone he loved to force him to find Escobar's millions for them."

That was what Grajales had threatened. To use her to make Rafe locate the hidden money.

"Grajales was Kyle's original employer," Paul went on, "but Kyle had strung him along about as far as he could. Peters didn't really know anything, and Grajales would figure that out eventually. To trap our traitor, we had discreetly put the word out that another player would pay big for the name of the man who'd revealed the money-laundering operations. Because he knew Grajales was bound to get wise, Kyle was more than eager to take our bait."

"You were the voice on the phone," she realized. *It's Hardesty.* Paul had been working with Rafe, and his name had been identification, not another betrayal by Kyle.

"Making arrangements to take Peters when he showed up the next day for his money, his payment for giving Ramirez your name. Only, your phone call warned him things weren't what they seemed. So Peters came early to the rendezvous to find out what was going on. To kill you all."

"Rafe and Diego weren't waiting for the cartel. They were waiting for you."

"If you hadn't shot Kyle, we would have been too late."

"Who's Grajales? He seemed to think I should recognize his name."

"A wannabe. With the Colombian government making arrests at the top of Cali, there are a lot of guys hoping to step up to take their place on the gravy train."

"You knew he was still out there, still looking for the courier, and you didn't tell me? What the hell, Paul?"

"Kyle had already broken off with him to sell to Ramirez, to us. The best-case scenario was that, having lost his link to the task force, Grajales would give up, sink back into the slime. The Colombian government was finally coming down hard, and we thought whoever was involved in trying to find the courier would back off the search that had led them nowhere. And Grajales *did* disappear. We tried to find him after Ramirez gave us his name."

"And what about the worst-case scenario?" she asked. "That he'd come after me. You left me hanging, Paul."

"I kept you under protective surveillance for a long time, Rae. While you were in rehab, and even after you came back to work. But then it went so long, almost six months, and there was nothing. No hint that anyone knew your name, that anyone was even looking for the courier anymore, so we felt the threat was over. It seems we were wrong," Paul admitted.

"Yeah," Rae said. "*Real* wrong."

"You know I'd never deliberately put you in danger, Rae. You know that."

And she believed him. She always believed him, so she let it go. Besides, she wanted to ask something else—something that hadn't been explained by what he'd said before.

"Was it part of your plan for Rafe to abduct me?"

"No," Paul admitted. "Ramirez, as you can imagine, didn't trust any of us. He wanted to protect his family from reprisals, but he wasn't willing to play by our rules, given the fact that we'd admitted we had a traitor on the force."

"He took me because he thought I might be the traitor?"

Paul didn't say anything for a moment.

"You want the truth?" he asked finally.

"That would be nice. For a change."

A small flush crawled into the smoothly shaven cheeks.

"I guess I deserve that," he said. "I think the truth is that when we told him what had been happening in the task force, about the deaths, he was afraid you'd be next. You'd been closest to the courier. The nearest link. He knew that.

He knew what would happen if the cartel discovered that fact.''

And Kyle had already given Grajales her name. If Diego hadn't taken her that night, she *would* have been next, she realized. She shivered again, thinking about what had been done to the others.

''And,'' Paul continued, ''I think maybe he just wanted to see you again. The deal we'd set up gave him an excuse.''

''He accused me of selling out the courier.''

''The first thing Kyle did was try to convince him you were the traitor. He provided the doctored picture and a record of a supposed payoff as proof.''

''So, at least for a while, he believed I might be the one.'' She stopped, thinking again about what he'd said to her. *Did you enjoy the sounds he made? Did you watch?* How could he have refrained from hurting her if he thought she was the one who had betrayed him? And that was why, of course, poor Diego had injected her with the drug. To find out the truth for the man he served, the master he loved.

''Why didn't you tell me who he was? After it was all over.''

''It was the only thing he had ever asked me for, Rae, in return for all he'd done. We owed him. I gave him the promise he wanted because I didn't have any choice.''

''Did you know...'' She hesitated. ''Before I told you, did you know what had happened between us? Did he tell you?''

''It wasn't hard to figure out how he felt when you were shot. I thought he was going to kill me and Dell for letting you get hurt.''

''You could have given me some hint, Hardesty. Something.''

''I *tried* to give you the damn tape. I thought you might recognize his voice. I thought that—''

''On the phone,'' Rae interrupted. ''That's what almost happened on the phone today. I *almost* recognized his voice.''

Was that why she had trusted him from the first? Because burned somewhere into her subconscious was the memory of the courier's whisper? And even of the elusive scent of his body? Had her heart made the connection her mind had never remembered?

"You want some advice?" Paul asked. The flush was back and he didn't meet her eyes.

"About him?"

"Yeah. I guess. I never saw myself as 'advice to the lovelorn,' but in this case, I feel like some inept, middle-aged Cupid."

Rae laughed. "Okay. What's the advice?"

"He won't tell you how he feels."

"Go on," she said, knowing that was probably true.

"You're going to have to take that on faith. And if you want it to work, Rae, don't treat him . . . any differently."

That was what she'd done after he'd shot Grajales's men. That was why he'd been angry.

"You even sound like Ann Landers," she said, but Paul's eyes were on hers, and they didn't respond to the gibe. They were clear and open and sincere.

She stood on tiptoe and put her arms around his neck. He hugged her tightly and then stepped back.

"Good luck, Rae," he said softly. "I really hope you get what you want for Christmas."

PAUL AND THE officers had left in the gathering twilight, the gate and the front door securely locked behind them, and in the darkened embassy Rae again stood, apprehensively, before the library door. She had reason, she supposed, to be a little paranoid about opening this particular door. Except now she *knew* the fear that made her hesitate. A fear that she wouldn't say or do the right thing.

Someone killed my brother . . . and I thought that wasn't right. She had not been wrong about the man in Virginia. All the things she had believed about him so long ago were true, despite the lies that had surrounded that night. And finally she knew the reason for those lies.

When she entered the library, Rafe was seated again on the ivory sofa. She walked across the room until she was standing in front of him, just as before, looking down again into those midnight eyes that were wary now, awaiting her reaction.

Suddenly she raised her right hand and slapped him, as hard as she could, holding nothing back. His head turned with it, the force of the blow enough to rock the strong man she knew him to be.

The imprint of her palm was already forming on his cheek when his eyes, full of angry shock, came back to hers.

"That's for making me think I was nothing to you but a one-night stand," she said.

Something cold and bitter softened in the midnight depths.

"You were *never* a one-night stand," Rafe replied.

"But that's how you treated me," she accused softly. "Like someone who didn't deserve an explanation."

His lips tightened, but he didn't defend himself. He never had, she realized. He had chosen at the beginning the path he had thought was right, and he had never deviated from it. Except when, at her invitation, he'd made love to her.

And remembering, she asked, "Now what?"

Involuntarily her thumb touched the trace of blood at the corner of his mouth. She wiped it away, but she didn't remove her hand. She let her palm rest against his cheek where the mark she had made was changing from livid white to red.

"I think this is where you tell me that...what I am doesn't matter to you."

"What you *are* matters a great deal to me," she said. "Now that I finally *know* what you are. The kind of man you are."

"That's not what I meant."

"You meant physically?"

"Yes."

"Would you believe me if I said it doesn't matter?"

When he smiled, she could feel the movement under her hand.

"I'd believe that you *think* that's true."

"But you don't?"

He said nothing in answer to her question. After a moment she removed her hand and sat down on the littered floor at his feet, cross-legged, to look up into his face.

"What can I do to convince you?" she asked when the silence stretched too long. "To make you believe me?"

"I told you what I want you to do, Rae. Go home to Texas."

"No," she said, shaking her head.

"Nothing's changed."

She laughed. The sound was wrong, a contrast to his seriousness.

"*Everything's* changed. I know that you're not what you pretended to be. I know that all the things I felt about you weren't a betrayal of who I am. How can you say that nothing has changed?"

"Nothing's changed about how *I* feel."

And that hurt. Could she be mistaken? Because she loved him, was she assuming he felt the same way? *You'll have to take it on faith,* Paul had warned, but if Rafe continued to deny that he wanted her, continued to try to send her away, what could she do to break through that resolve?

"How *do* you feel?" she asked. She couldn't ask if he loved her. She knew that wasn't a question he'd answer, but maybe, if she only asked for what he'd given her before...

"Are you telling me you don't want me? That you don't want to make love to me?"

She waited a long time, long enough that she had begun to be afraid, before he told her, the black eyes no longer wary, as open now as Paul's.

"Unlike Hardesty, I can't lie to you, *querida.* I want you very much. More than you can imagine."

"Then...I really don't understand the problem. It doesn't seem there's anything else to talk about."

She smiled when she saw the remembrance touch his eyes. He studied hers a long time, and she let him look, let him see what she felt. Finally his gaze moved away from that examination to fasten on his hands, the long fingers lying open, spread against the denim-covered thighs.

"That *was* an invitation," she said softly.

His lips moved slightly, but he didn't look at her when he answered.

"I can't make any commitments, Rae. That hasn't changed. Someone else may be looking for the man who can find Escobar's treasure."

"Could you find it?" she asked, really wondering.

The dark eyes met hers again, and he smiled.

"Probably. Given enough time."

"Grajales admitted he hadn't figured it out—who the courier was. No one knows your name."

"That won't stop the search. And I don't want you involved."

She laughed. "I think it's a little late for that. I've been involved since the beginning. *I'm* the one whose name Grajales did know."

"Go home, Rae. Get away from all this."

"Only if you'll go with me," she invited, smiling. "For protection."

She didn't realize what he thought until the black ice reformed.

"*My* protection," she corrected gently. "You were right. That was some *very* nice shooting. And that *should* have been the first thing I said. Which brings us back to the other reason you're trying to get rid of me."

He didn't pretend not to understand.

"This may be as good as it ever gets. *Physically*," he said, employing her euphemism with a bitterness he didn't hide.

"Well, I never had any complaints. Certainly not *physically*," she said softly.

The memories rushed between them. All the touches in the dark.

"I haven't asked you for any commitment, Rafe. I just want to be with you. And I can't think of a single reason why we can't be together."

He shook his head.

"At least here. At least today," she whispered.

"Rae," he said, a denial.

"I could build a fire," she suggested. "I've always wanted to make love on a rug in front of a fire. Doesn't that sound romantic as hell?"

He waited a moment, still watching her eyes, before he gave in, remembering, she hoped, all they had shared and could share again.

"And about as comfortable," he said. "Especially on *this* rug."

"You're not supposed to consider comfort. You're supposed to be swept away by the passion of the moment."

"I must be old-fashioned. I've always preferred beds with soft, useful pillows, clean sheets—"

"So much easier to fall asleep afterward," she mocked.

"I thought you didn't have any complaints," he reminded. His fingers touched a tendril that had escaped the ponytail's confinement and tucked it behind her ear. His hand moved slowly to the back of her head to urge her upward to meet his descending mouth.

All the feelings he had created in the long-ago darkness came back to her. Nothing here had changed. Or ever would. *You will always be my heart.*

When the kiss finally ended, Rae found herself kneeling between his thighs, her hands on his shoulders.

"Come upstairs with me," he said. "I don't want to make love to you in this room."

She had forgotten the violence, forgotten everything but the promise of his body holding hers.

"No fire?" she whispered.

"I don't think you'll notice," he promised.

SHE TOOK A shower in his bathroom. He had suggested she use one of the guest suites, but she'd refused, not wanting to be that far away from him. When she noticed the accommodations that had been added to the room, she realized they were probably why he'd not wanted her here.

He had hidden everything from her before, and now all the tricks he had played in the darkness were exposed, and there was no way to lessen the reality. She had recognized his discomfort with the continued revelation of that reality on their way upstairs.

She put her forehead against the glass and closed her eyes. How could she know it would never matter to her? How could she really guarantee something like that? Was he wiser than she in wondering how the reality of what had been done to him would eventually affect her feelings?

She straightened and looked at the woman in the mirror. If she could doubt the depth of what she felt, why shouldn't he? Why should he believe her when she said that none of it mattered?

You'll have to take it on faith. Paul's words echoed through her doubts. Every relationship, every commitment, every marriage was based only on faith. Faith that feelings didn't change, that vows really were forever. *If you could know it for fact,* her mother had always said, *then they wouldn't call it faith.*

The aquamarine eyes of the woman in the mirror swam with sudden tears.

"Damn it," Rae whispered to her reflection. "You cry, and it's over. You let him see you cry, and he'll have you on the next flight to El Paso."

Angry with herself, she pulled the robe off the hook behind the door and slipped it on, belting it with fingers that trembled. She took another look in the mirror. There was no evidence of the fear, the sudden doubt that she might be wrong. The woman reflected there seemed serenely sure and, Rae realized with wonder, despite the total absence of makeup, almost beautiful. Simply a woman anticipating being with the man she loved.

Rafe was leaning back against the stacked pillows, wearing only the bottoms of a pair of black pajamas, his chest

and shoulders broad and dark against the white of the bed
linens. He looked perfectly relaxed, completely masculine,
and she wondered suddenly how many times he had waited
here for someone as he waited now for her.

"What's wrong?" he asked when she hesitated beside the
bed.

"You look so...practiced," she said finally.

"Practiced?" he questioned. He caught her hand, pulling her down to sit beside him. His fingers gripped her
shoulders.

"Like you wait for someone to come out of that doorway every night." She could hear the wrong note in her
voice. The playboy brother. Suddenly she was jealous of
anyone else who had ever touched him.

"This is my brother's house. I have never brought anyone else here. I swear that. There has *never* been another
woman here with me. Do you understand?"

"I'm sorry," she said, reaching to touch her lips to his. "I
know I don't have the right—"

"You have the right," he said, opening his mouth under
hers. She felt the response course through her body like a
current.

He finally broke the kiss and leaned back to look at her.
"I've lain in this bed so many nights and thought about you.
I thought that never again would I be able to touch you, and
now you're here."

"You made the decision to keep me away, in the dark
about who you were."

"I thought I was doing the right thing. Maybe I was."

"Are you regretting—?"

"No," he interrupted and she heard the depth of emotion. "Whatever happens, I can't regret having you here. I
thought it was better for you to send you away, but I want
you so much."

He took her face gently between his hands and studied her
features a long time, as if memorizing them, and finally he
lowered his mouth to hers again. She put her arms around
the hard, bare shoulders and could feel the muscles move

under her fingers as he tightened his hold on her body, moving his hand down her spine to force her closer.

He kissed her until she couldn't breathe. Finally he raised his head and lightly touched her mouth and eyelids and then her forehead with his lips.

"You are again overdressed for the occasion," he whispered and competently, with the fingers of one hand, began to undo the knot she'd tied to belt the robe.

"Rafe," she said, trying to remember why she should resist this. The image from her mirror flashed in her head, and she put her fingers over his.

He shook his head. "No more, *querida*. No more hiding."

She let him slide the robe off her shoulders, and it fell around her as she sat before him. She watched the dark eyes find the scarring, the ugly mark of the bullet she had taken to save his life.

And then they lifted to smile into hers.

"Whenever you're ready to have this done," he said, lowering his mouth to trace lightly over the scar, "I know a very good plastic surgeon."

He looked up, still smiling, to let her examine his face.

"Yes," she said after she had looked a long time. "Yes, you certainly do."

"I didn't like your eyes that day, *querida*," he said.

"Why hadn't you had it done before?"

"They always wait until a scar has healed as much as possible on its own, and at that point I didn't care. I'd had a couple of operations on my legs, been in and out of hospitals for months, and I was tired of it all. And I had believed, until I saw your eyes that day, that I would never again care what a woman thought about my face."

He lowered his mouth to her throat, and she closed her eyes. She had dreamed so many nights that he would touch her like this. His lips found the smooth, fragrant valley between her breasts, and his tongue made languid patterns against the ivory skin. She wanted more, so she found his hand and cupped it under her breast. He looked up and smiled at her.

"No patience," he whispered, but he didn't remove his hand. It caressed with the old sureness, with an almost-instinctive knowledge of what she wanted. Finally he touched her there with his lips, and she felt as if her skin were on fire and only his mouth could stop the burning. When he took the peak into his mouth and suckled hard, she gasped at the pleasure.

He turned her so that she lay on the bed, her body fully exposed to him for the first time, and his slow smile curved. He lay down beside her, propped on one elbow, and ran his palm lightly from her breasts to her stomach and as far as his long arm could reach down her legs. Then he moved his hand up again, its callused strength trailing against the silken texture of her inner thigh, gently smoothing skin that tingled with the anticipation of his destination. He watched her face as he began to touch her where she had known he would, where she ached for his touch.

Her eyes closed as he made her respond with all the authority he had always had over her body, over her emotions. His mouth moved against her throat and down again to nuzzle softly over the pearled nipples. Her breathing deepened, her lids drifting open to watch him stroke her breasts with his tongue. She began to move under his fingers, and he looked up to find her watching him, her blue-green eyes locked on his face, and he smiled at her.

"I want you," she whispered. "Make love to me. Please."

He guided her until she was astride him as she had always been before, helping him move into the emptiness that had been inside for so long.

She saw the deep breath that racked his body as she slowly took all of him into her soul, and then he whispered, "I think *I'm* the one who will not be able to have patience. I want you so much. Forgive me, my heart."

But he didn't leave her behind. She watched the desire build in his face and knew that he loved her. She smiled above him and, feeling his urgent hands against her waist, she moved to give him the most pleasure, the deepest joining, the strongest answer to his need. Finally the sensations began inside her body that corresponded to the convulsions jolting through his. Too soon she lay against his chest, still joined, but exhausted by what they had shared. She stretched her legs out atop the long length of his. His lips lightly touched her forehead, which rested beside his chin.

"Again?" she suggested and felt the small spurt of laughter shake the broad chest she lay against. Instead his arm tightened around her, his hand finding her hipbone. He ran one caressing finger over its protrusion. When he pulled her to lie beside him, she wanted to cry out at the separation. She moved her hand over his stomach and into the darkness below that was exposed by the opened pajamas.

He let her touch him, and eventually she felt him grow hard against her fingers. There was nothing tentative about the way she caressed him now. When he began to again position her over him, she resisted his direction.

"No. On top of me," she whispered. "I want to feel your weight against me. I want to feel every inch of your body over mine."

She felt his breathing pause, the skillful hands hesitate, and she knew something was wrong. Suddenly, dark fingers locked on her upper arms to hold her body prisoner against the bed, as forcefully as the black eyes held hers. She waited, wondering, and eventually the tenseness of his hands eased.

"Indulge me, *querida*," he suggested softly. "The other's easier for me."

Her stomach lurched with the realization of what he'd just confessed—the reason he had always wanted her on top. She could hear what his honesty had cost in the rawness of the whisper she had loved before she had loved him.

But into her mind came the memory of when he'd first made love to her. She had never forgotten the hard strength of his body over hers, driving, controlling, commanding her responses with such tender surety.

"The first time..." she began and then wondered why she was questioning. It didn't matter how they were together. It had never mattered to her.

"Not impossible, *querida,*" he explained, the same remembrance caught in the seductive caress of his voice. "I'm still mobile enough to make love to you, my heart," he said, finally smiling at her before he added, "any way you desire."

She swallowed against the lump that suddenly crowded her throat as he dropped a kiss on the very tip of her nose.

"It doesn't matter," she whispered. "I'm sorry I—"

"No," he said. "No apologies. I told you. No more hiding in the darkness. For either of us."

She nodded, still meeting his gaze.

"It's just...easier," he said again, "if you're willing to take the more active role. And you were always so willing."

Easier. Another euphemism. Less painful for the brutally damaged legs.

She reached for his mouth, and he let her kiss him, but then he lifted his lips from hers and loosened the pressure of his hands against her arms. She lay very still, forcing her eyes to hold his, fighting tears he would never be allowed to see.

"Don't ever pity me, *querida,*" he ordered, his voice as soft as before, but she recognized the depth of emotion behind the warning. "*That* I won't tolerate. Not even from you."

"No," she whispered. "I promise."

Only when he smiled at her again, did the tightness in her chest begin to ease.

"You never wondered?" he asked, his thumb smoothing a curling strand of auburn hair away from her temple. His lips lowered to trail along her throat.

"I never thought about it."

When he spoke again, his breath was skimming teasingly over the moisture that had gathered between her breasts.

"Good," he said. "Don't think about it now."

And after a while, she didn't.

THE SHRILL ALARM threw her back into a panicked response to dangers that no longer existed. She woke instantly, mouth dry, heart pounding, her body automatically preparing to meet whatever threat was there. She felt his arm tighten comfortingly around her, holding her and holding back the fear.

"It's all right, *querida,*" Rafe said quietly. "I have you. There's nothing to be afraid of."

He reached for the phone that had already pealed again into the dimness of his bedroom. He didn't release her, even as he answered it.

She felt her tension ease as she listened to his soft Spanish. Carlos, calling from Colombia, she realized after only a few sentences. His family wanted to check on him, of course. She waited for him to explain that he wasn't alone, that they no longer needed to worry about his spending Christmas by himself, but the conversation continued without any mention of her. And still he held her, occasionally smiling down into her eyes as he talked, his thumb making small, caressing circles over the soft skin inside her elbow.

Rafe didn't intend to tell them she was here, she realized. Not even Carlos, whom she had met, who had been kind to her. And why should he? Maybe she *was* only one of his many pleasant memories.

She wondered if she could live with that. Her dreams had always centered around white lace and babies. That was how she'd been raised. To take someone home to meet her mother. And to be taken home. Instead, it seemed, he wasn't going to mention her. Not even, *Oh, by the way, don't worry. I'm not spending Christmas alone.*

When he hung up, he pulled her closer, his mouth against her forehead.

"I'm sorry the phone woke you," he said.

"Were you asleep?" she asked, trying to let the pain of the other go.

"I've just been watching you."

"Great," she said, embarrassed. He had always seen her at her worst. Mouth open? Snoring, maybe? "Do you know that you snore?" she asked, remembering the night she'd lain awake listening. The night she'd betrayed him. The night she'd warned Kyle he wasn't dealing with the cartel.

"No," he said, leaning to kiss her, "but I know that you don't. You sleep beautifully, like an angel."

"And lines like that have really worked for you?" she mocked. There was something wrong with her tone—the pain covered over, perhaps, but still there. And of course, he knew.

"What's wrong, *querida?*" he asked.

She shook her head.

"Rae?" he questioned.

"Why didn't you tell Carlos I was here?"

He didn't say anything for a moment, but his eyes never left her face.

"Why do you think I didn't say anything to Carlos?"

"Because it wasn't important enough to mention?" she suggested bitterly.

"Is that what you think? That I don't consider this important?"

"Then why didn't you tell Carlos I was here? Are you embarrassed I'm with you? That I'm in his home?"

"Embarrassed?" he repeated. "Why the hell would I be embarrassed that you're with me?"

"Because I'm not like the others," she admitted. She had always known that, from the time he'd sent Diego with the black silk. That's what *his* women wore.

"There are no others, Rae," he said.

She nodded, but her eyes fell. He touched her chin, lifting her head until again she met his gaze. "There are no others, *querida.* And whatever there might have been before..." She waited, hoping for something. "Having you here, Rae, is the most important thing in my life."

"Then why didn't you tell Carlos? They're worried about you because they think you're spending Christmas alone."

"This is a private line, direct to my bedroom. He knows where I am. If I told him you're here, he'd know you are in my bed."

"I don't care if he knows," she argued, but somewhere inside she knew that she did.

"I care, *querida*," Rafe said softly. "I'm a little old-fashioned when it comes to you."

"So you don't kiss and tell, Mr. Ramirez. That's very nice to know." *A little old-fashioned*. Like white lace. *Maybe someday*.

"And besides, Carlos has already told me I'm a fool. I didn't want to listen to my big brother say 'I told you so.'" From somewhere a thread of amusement had crept into that confession.

"A fool?"

"For letting you go," he acknowledged softly.

"I *knew* I liked Carlos."

He smiled at her.

"So, are you going to?" she asked.

"Am I going to what?"

"Let me go?" she whispered. She turned her head to kiss him, giving the lightest brush of her lips against the corner of his mouth.

"*Querida*, there's so much—"

"I don't care, Rafe. None of it's important. Nothing you can say matters against what I feel."

"Rae—"

"No commitments. I'm not asking you for anything but to be with you. Whatever rules you want."

"Damn it, Rae, I don't want rules. I just don't believe—"

"Faith," she interrupted, turning against him to push her tongue into his open mouth. "Just take it on faith." She felt the tension of their argument in his body, and she fought it, trying to convince him with her kiss that this was right and inevitable, no matter what problems he imagined might interfere.

"Until you *do* believe," she whispered. Her breasts touched the muscled contours of his chest, and she smiled at the depth of the breath he suddenly took. She moved until once more she was over him, watching the midnight eyes close as she tried to convince him that what she had said was true. Nothing else mattered. Nothing but this. Nothing but what they created together in the darkness.

Chapter Fifteen

They drifted through the week he had promised her before the return of his family. There were literally no outside distractions to their rediscovery of each other, and the chains that had bound her to him from the first tightened through the long days.

They spent hours talking, recounting childhood escapades, family stories. Their worlds were so different, and she began to recognize the vastness of the gulf that his wealth, education, and family's position put between them.

Rafe was lying beside her one rainy afternoon, drawing patterns on her skin with his finger dipped in the wine he was drinking. At first, he had written messages that he teasingly demanded she interpret, but they had become so increasingly suggestive that one thing had led to another. Now they lay together in the twisted sheets, as he lazily moved one dark finger over the ivory skin of her stomach.

"When..." she began and found she couldn't put her fear into words.

"What?" he questioned at her hesitation. He bent his head to lick the wine from the design he had drawn.

"When will you go back to Colombia?" she asked, and saw the surprise in his eyes as they lifted to meet hers.

"Colombia? Why would you think I'm going back to Colombia?"

"Grajales said you handle your family's investments. I just assumed..."

"There's no reason to go home to do that. And I'm still involved in therapy, working with people I'm comfortable with, have confidence in."

"You're still in rehab?"

"Of course," he said. "Did you think I'd given up, *querida?*"

"I didn't think about it," she admitted. And she hadn't. She had blocked from her mind the grueling weeks she'd spent getting her shoulder back in shape. And Rafe had now devoted more than two years to that same kind of pursuit.

"It's just that it's been so long," she said. She knew the chances of improvement lessened dramatically with the passage of time.

She touched his face, running her finger lightly over the faint evidence of the surgeon's repair. When he spoke again, she thought it was to ease the strain that had grown from her comment.

"Do you ride, Rae?"

She laughed, welcoming the change of subject. "You're talking to a Texan. Since I was born."

"Ski?" he asked, and there was no answering laughter in his eyes.

"Yes," she said softly. Not a change of subject, she had realized.

"Climb?"

"No."

"Run?"

"Not competitively."

She wished she hadn't started this. The cold darkness was in his voice, and she had put it there.

"Do you like to dance, Rae?"

And this time she didn't answer.

He spoke very deliberately. "I will never do any of those things again. I'm very grateful to walk across a room. No one gave me any hope that I ever would, but I didn't intend to spend the rest of my life in that damn chair. And as long as any possibility exists for further improvement, I'm going to pursue it. And *then* I'll go home. Do you understand?''

"Yes."

"All those things I used to do, that you still can do—"

"I don't care about any of those things," she interrupted vehemently.

"You're a liar, Rae. *I* care about them. And so will you. Eventually you'll get tired of doing nothing together but making love."

"I hope you don't have any money riding on that," Rae said gently, and the black eyes came up to find hers. "Don't hold your breath, Rafe, waiting for me to get tired of making love to you."

"I need you so much," he whispered, his fingers threading through the disordered tangle of her hair to pull her closer to the caress of his lips. "I need you to hold off the night that's just waiting for me to give up."

"I can make a different kind of night. Do you remember Scheherazade?"

"A Thousand and One Nights," he replied.

"I am very creative."

"I know," he said, smiling.

She pushed him to his back, taking the wineglass from his hand. He closed his eyes in anticipation of whatever she intended. She tipped the remaining trickle of wine so that it ran slowly in a golden stream along the dark trail of hair that led down from his chest across his navel to its inevitable end, and then she began, as he had done, to remove all traces of it from his body.

THEY HAD THEIR first fight when she told him she intended to accept the job Dell Stewart had offered. It seemed the perfect solution, one that would allow her to stay in D.C.

"Doing what?" Rafe asked.

"I don't know. We didn't get that far. He just offered me a job. At the time I was planning to go back to Texas, so I didn't bother—"

"With the DEA?" he interrupted.

"Yes." She kept her voice calm and reasoned. What the hell did he expect her to do?

His lips tightened, and his eyes were almost as cold as the day she'd hit him. Almost.

"Back to the same dangers." It wasn't a question.

Probably a lot more dangerous, but she didn't tell him that.

"Why?" he asked.

"To make a living?" she suggested, her voice tinged with sarcasm. "I have this bad habit. I enjoy eating."

"You know damn well you don't have to work."

"Really?" she said, one eyebrow rising as if she had never considered that. She knew what he was suggesting. It just wasn't an option. She could imagine her mother's reaction.

"I think I have enough for both of us."

"And we'll all live together in Carlos's happy home. I don't think so, Rafe, but thank you for the thought."

"I won't have you involved in that again. Enough, *querida,* and you know it."

"*You* won't have it?" she repeated softly. "I'm a cop, Rafe. This is what cops do. Chase the bad guys."

"You were planning to go back to law school."

"If I went home. If I lived with my mother, I could probably manage the tuition. Do you want me to go home, Rafe?" she challenged.

The midnight eyes held, cold and hard, but behind them were the memories, old and new. It was an idle threat, and they both were aware of that, but she needed to hear him say no.

"That's my choice, *querida?*" he asked. "You go back to again being somebody's target or I tell you to go home? That's the decision you're asking me to make?"

"No," she replied. "That isn't fair. I'm sorry."

"If that's my choice, then go home," he continued over her withdrawal of the ultimatum, his voice tight with anger. "I don't want you working for the DEA. For any of them."

"I'm not going home," she said. "That's not even an option."

"And what options are left?" he asked.

She didn't answer. There were some things he would have to figure out on his own.

IT WAS ALMOST worse telling her mother. She offered all the same arguments Rafe had used.

"You don't have to go back to work, Rachel," her mother had argued. "Not if you'll come home, live with me."

"I can't come home."

"Why not? At Christmas you'd made up your mind. It was all settled. What's changed, Rachel?"

"Everything," she admitted. *I know who he is, what he is. Everything's changed.*

"Such as?" her mother asked.

"There's a man."

"A man?" her mother repeated. And said again, in a different tone entirely. "A *man,* Rachel? A cop?"

"No."

"What, then? What does he do?"

"He handles money. Investments. For his family."

"Investments," her mother repeated. "Legitimate?" she asked sharply.

Rae laughed. "Very."

"Then what's wrong? Something's wrong. I can tell from your voice."

"I think he's probably...very well-off."

"He's rich?" her mother asked. "Is that bad, Rachel? You sound as if that's a problem."

"There are *lots* of problems, Mama."

"Do you want to tell me about them?"

"Not especially. I just wanted to tell you that I love him. And I can't leave Washington right now."

"Are you going to get married?"

Rae smiled at the question. A natural progression in her mother's mind.

"If he asks me."

"And you're afraid he won't?"

"Yes," she whispered.

"Don't you settle for anything less, Rachel. You won't be happy, honey. Not you."

"I know, Mama. Everything's just so hard right now."

Her mother didn't say anything for a moment.

"I'd like to meet him," she said finally.

"I'd like for you to. Maybe soon. I'll call you."

"I love you, Rachel, baby."

"I love you, too."

THE WEEKS gradually turned into months—five months that she treasured, storing the memories of each day in her heart, trying to prepare for a night when he would no longer seek her body in the darkness and touch her into flame.

Rafe had moved out of the embassy and into a town house not far from her apartment. Their belongings had gradually scattered between the two: a toothbrush in both, a few of her dresses hanging in one of his huge cedar closets, a drawer of clean shirts and underwear in her bureau. Their nights were spent in either place—almost always together.

And then one Monday Elena called to invite her to dinner on Friday at the embassy.

"Just the four of us," she said. "There's no need to dress."

Which was good news, Rae thought, mentally reviewing her wardrobe. When she mentioned the invitation to Rafe, his response was so casual that she realized she shouldn't attach any significance to the evening. Elena and Carlos simply wanted to get better acquainted, Rafe explained. His attitude was definitely no big deal, and she tried to put it out of her mind.

She spent the week dreading the evening and wondering why. She was working hard, helping Dell put the finishing touches on an operation they were fine-tuning. Rae wouldn't be in on the takedown—something Dell had made clear from the start. And she had to admit she was glad. DEA agents were supposedly addicted to that rush, but Rae had already had enough adrenaline highs to last a lifetime. She hadn't mentioned what she was working on to Rafe. Her job was forbidden territory. The less he was reminded of what she did for Dell Stewart, the better.

On Friday, she had hoped to have time to go home and change, but just in case, she'd worn a simple black dress, and as the hands of her office clock crept past seven, she realized it would have to do. A change of earrings and shoes, both of which she'd brought to work, and she would be able to make it.

Carlos was charming, welcoming her, and Elena seemed to be as warm and friendly. It wasn't until after dinner, over coffee served in Carlos's small library, that Elena brought in the presents.

"What's the occasion?" Rae asked, wondering why Rafe hadn't warned her. Her budget would have stretched far enough to buy something. A token, maybe, but it was the thought that counted.

"Rafe's birthday," Carlos answered. "Didn't he tell you?"

"He forgot to mention it," she said. She glanced at him, a little embarrassed that she hadn't known.

"Because you would have worried about a present," Rafe said.

"I would like to have gotten you something," she admitted.

"I already have everything, *querida,*" he said softly. "Everything I need."

"I know. It's just that birthdays are special. I wish I had known."

"Birthdays *are* special," Carlos agreed. "Especially Rafe's."

Especially Rafe's. Each birthday a miracle. A gift. Considering.

"And for that reason," Carlos went on, "I have a very special present. Something I know is perfect."

He handed Rafe a long package wrapped in foil and tied with glittering ribbon. Elegant. And expensive, Rae guessed, judging by the wrappings. She watched as the dark fingers that knew her body so well dealt with them. Rafe finally opened the box to reveal his brother's gift: a magnificent ebony cane, its L-shaped head and ferrule of worked gold.

Rafe glanced up to smile at his brother, but Rae's heart ached suddenly, wondering what Carlos had intended. It seemed almost a cruelty, she thought, a mockery of the endless effort.

"Thank you," Rafe said softly in Spanish.

"It's nothing," Carlos replied, "compared to what you've given."

"Enough," Rafe said, changing back to English, his embarrassment obvious.

"Try it," Carlos urged.

"*Querida,* would you like to see me try Carlos's present?" Rafe asked.

"Maybe later," she suggested, smiling at him.

"And why not now?" he questioned, holding her gaze. "*I* think the attempt is long overdue."

Using the curved wooden arm of the ivory sofa and the cane, Rafe pushed himself up. She held her breath as he limped slowly across the expanse of carpet, leaning on the cane, until he stood before the sofa where she was seated.

Using only the single, slender cane. He had come so far, and she knew suddenly that the evening's surprise had really been intended for her. This was why she'd been included in the family celebration.

"A nice present, *querida,*" he said, smiling down at her. "Don't you agree?"

"A very nice present, you show-off," she returned, standing to put her arms around him. "Happy Birthday, Rafe," she whispered against his cheek. "A very Happy Birthday, my darling."

And in her heart, the hope that she'd tried so hard to bury took new life.

She was still at the embassy when the call came from Colombia. Carlos had arranged it, of course. Rafe used the library phone, and she eavesdropped on his conversation while pretending to concentrate on whatever Carlos was saying.

Rafe's responses to his mother's questions reminded her of her own careful evasions during the past few months. It took a moment for the sense of the most important words to register. Rafe was going home. He had just given his family in Colombia that message—that he would see them next week. Apparently that, too, had already been arranged.

And why not? He'd come as far as possible with physical therapy, further than anyone had ever believed he would. And now it was time to return to his own country and his family, to go back to his life. It was nothing her mind hadn't accepted months ago. She had gone into this with her eyes open. He had certainly warned her. *No commitments, querida.* No commitments.

"I'm so sorry," she said softly, breaking into whatever Carlos had been saying. She really had no idea what he'd been saying. And it didn't matter. The only important thing was that she got out of here before she made a fool of herself. "I'm afraid I have an early day tomorrow."

She was standing by then, her hand held out to Carlos, who took it automatically. She saw Rafe glance up at her from across the room, the phone still against his ear.

"Thank you both for a lovely evening," she said. She gathered up her purse and began to walk toward the door. She was aware of Carlos's protest, aware that he'd made one, but she needed to get away.

Rafe said something to her from across the room, his hand over the mouthpiece of the phone, but she shook her head. She turned and walked the rest of the short distance to the door. Once she was outside, where no one could see her in the concealing darkness, it would be okay. Just not here. Please, just not here.

She'd walked a few blocks, hurrying in the near-summer heat, before she managed to find a cab, and in its dark interior she finally relaxed the tight control she'd demanded of herself for so long. All the tears she had denied for weeks found release. All the emotions she'd hidden in the day-to-day routine of work and in the night-after-night wonder of being with him. It was over, and Rafe had simply chosen a rather oblique way of letting her know.

Oblique, but effective. His physical therapy had ended, and now he was going home. She had always known it was inevitable, but still, she hadn't been prepared.

Rafe was sitting on the landing of the steps leading up to her apartment when she got out of the cab. As she walked up to him, she found herself hoping the darkness would hide the evidence of the tears she'd shed. Old habits.

"I didn't think the party was over, *querida*," he said softly.

"Didn't you?"

"Why did you leave?"

"I don't know. It just seemed . . . I just needed to leave."

"Would you sit down and talk to me about why?" he asked.

She sat beside him on the stairs. The new cane was between his knees, held loosely with his right hand. After a moment, he put his left arm around Rae's shoulders and pulled her against the solid strength of his body.

"I thought this was *so* important," he said, turning the cane in his fingers. "And finally I'd accomplished it. But when I looked up, you were gone. What I'd worked for for so long didn't mean much, *querida*, without you there."

"I'm sorry. I didn't mean to spoil it."

"You didn't spoil anything. It was just no longer as important as I had thought. When I saw you leave, my heart," he said— And then he stopped, the beautiful voice faltering suddenly. "I would willingly have gone back to the wheelchair, Rae, to sit again in the darkness, watching you sleep . . . just to have you still there."

He was looking out into the night, but the fingers of his left hand smoothed up and down her arm, comforting. "I was right before, *querida*. I *already* had everything. I didn't need this." He lifted the ebony stick slightly. "The other didn't matter to you."

"No," she whispered. None of it had ever mattered. And finally he knew.

"Why did you run away, *querida?*"

"I heard you talking about going home."

"I haven't been home for more than two years."

"I know," she whispered.

"Is that what's wrong? You don't want me to go home?"

"I know you have to go home," she said.

His lips touched her temple and lingered there for a moment.

"I just wasn't expecting it to be so soon," she admitted.

"You could come with me," he invited softly.

"I haven't been working for Dell long enough to ask off," she said. "But thank you. I would like to have seen your country."

"Colombia. Where everyone works for the cartels," he said.

"Don't. I may have deserved that at one time, but I know better now."

"And would you also have liked to meet my family, *querida?*"

"Yes," she said.

"They would like to meet you. I don't think they really believe there is a woman willing to marry their black sheep. At least . . . not anymore."

She said nothing, the tears threatening again.

"*Are* you willing to marry me, my heart?"

"As long as I can have all the trimmings," she promised. *White lace and babies.*

She turned her head to rest her cheek against the fine material of his suit.

"I have another present for you. I know now I should have given you this one first. It's by far the more important."

He propped the cane against his leg and reached into his jacket pocket. He removed his arm from around her shoulder to open the jeweler's box.

"Left hand, *querida*," he commanded, holding out his own, palm up.

She placed her hand in his, and he slid a ring on her third finger. It was a huge emerald, rectangular, and surrounded by diamonds. With a timelessly feminine gesture, Rae held her hand up to allow the jewel to catch the faint light.

"If you don't like it, you may choose another. Whatever you wish. My feelings won't be hurt, but I should warn you, my father's probably will be." The teasing note had returned to the richness of his voice.

"Why?" she asked cooperatively, very willing to again be teased.

"Because he owns the mine."

"An emerald mine?" she asked.

"Emeralds are Colombia's third-largest export product."

"And you invest the money your family makes from mining emeralds?"

"And from the coffee."

"Coffee?" she repeated softly.

"Our second-largest export."

"What's the first?" she asked, laughing.

"That, *querida*, my family does *not* deal in." There was no longer any amusement in his voice.

Cocaine, she realized. Not a subject for laughter. Not this man.

"Then you *are* Juan Valdez," she said.

"My father," Rafe assured her, smiling again. "I don't even own a donkey."

"Am I marrying money, Rafe? Is that what you're trying to tell me?"

"You're marrying me. That's all you get. But I don't advise not liking the emerald."

"I love the emerald."

"Good. It's always nice to have peace in the family. Now I think we should go inside. I have to warn you that sitting on these steps is not going to be conducive to my successfully making love to you."

"No complaints," she said, standing. "I never had any complaints."

Rafe held out his hand. "You'd better help me up, *querida,* before I make a liar out of you."

He had never before asked for her help, and she would never have dared offer it. She took his strong, dark hand and held it tightly a moment in both of hers before she laid her cheek against it.

"No more tears, my heart," he ordered softly because he knew her so well.

"No," she agreed. "No more tears. I have to call my mother, and she always knows when I've been crying."

RAFE WAS WAITING in her bed when she got off the phone, the white pillows stacked again behind his broad shoulders. He had been massaging the muscles in his left thigh. His fingers hesitated when she entered the bedroom, but then, deliberately, he allowed them to continue the slow, rhythmic movement.

She sat down beside him on the edge of the bed and watched for a moment.

"What's wrong?" she asked.

"The cane requires a different set of muscles. It's just a cramp."

She put her thumb on the hard quadriceps and pressed downward. She could feel the tightness.

"Here?" she questioned gently.

His hand hesitated over hers, and then he directed her fingers lower.

"There," he said.

She pressed both thumbs along the length of the cramping muscle and heard his small, sighing groan. She massaged deeply for a long time, using all the strength in her hands, working to relieve the tightness. When she glanced up, his eyes were closed, his head resting back against the pillows.

"Better?" she asked.

He opened his eyes and smiled at her, but instead of answering, he inquired, "What did your mother say?"

"That she wants some grandbabies before she gets too old to enjoy them," Rae admitted.

He didn't say anything else for a long time, and she continued to work on his leg. Gradually, she felt the tension relaxing under her hands, and she knew that the pain, too, would ease.

"Grandbabies?" he repeated finally.

She nodded, her eyes still on her hands, moving over the hair-roughened thigh.

Suddenly his long, dark fingers closed over hers.

"Querida," he said. It was a command.

She looked up. Her fingers curled involuntarily around his hand at what she read in his face.

"I love you, Rae," he whispered. "I have loved you so long, my heart. Since one cold, dark night a long time ago in Virginia."

She nodded again, not trusting her control. She leaned against his chest, and his arms encircled her, holding tightly. His cheek rested against the top of her head.

"Come to bed, Rae," he invited softly. "Your mama is apparently working on some kind of deadline." Amusement again enriched the beautiful voice, his teasing as familiar now as the slight accent. And as beloved.

She reached to turn off the light on the table beside the bed and then, her hands on his shoulders for balance, she moved one knee to the other side of his narrow hips. Slowly she lowered her body over his until she rested against the hard chest, his arms enclosing her slender frame.

"*Querida,*" he breathed into the darkness as she began to move above him.

And the word was again only a whisper.

BRIDE'S
BAY RESORT

UNLOCK THE DOOR TO GREAT ROMANCE AT BRIDE'S BAY RESORT

Join Harlequin's new across-the-lines series, set in an exclusive hotel on an island off the coast of South Carolina.

Seven of your favorite authors will bring you exciting stories about fascinating heroes and heroines discovering love at Bride's Bay Resort.

Look for these fabulous stories coming to a store near you beginning in January 1996.

Harlequin American Romance #613 in January
Matchmaking Baby by Cathy Gillen Thacker

Harlequin Presents #1794 in February
Indiscretions by Robyn Donald

Harlequin Intrigue #362 in March
Love and Lies by Dawn Stewardson

Harlequin Romance #3404 in April
Make Believe Engagement by Day Leclaire

Harlequin Temptation #588 in May
Stranger in the Night by Roseanne Williams

Harlequin Superromance #695 in June
Married to a Stranger by Connie Bennett

Harlequin Historicals #324 in July
Dulcie's Gift by Ruth Langan

Visit Bride's Bay Resort each month wherever Harlequin books are sold.

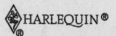

HARLEQUIN ®

BBAYG

Bestselling authors

ELAINE
COFFMAN
RUTH LANGAN
and
MARY McBRIDE

Together in one fabulous collection!

Available in June wherever Harlequin
books are sold.

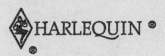 HARLEQUIN ®

OUTB